Juliet Ann Conlin feels lucky to have lots of love and hope in her life. She was born in London and grew up in England and Germany, where she now lives with her wonderful family. She holds an MA in Creative Writing from Lancaster University and a PhD in Psychology from the University of Durham. She works as a writer and translator and lives with her husband and four children in Berlin. Her novels include *The Fractured Man* (Cargo, 2013), *The Uncommon Life of Alfred Warner in Six Days* (Black & White Publishing, 2017), *The Lives Before Us* (Black & White, 2019) and *Sisters of Berlin* (Black & White, 2020).

Subscribe to Juliet's newsletter, NOTES FROM BERLIN (julietconlin.com/notes-from-berlin).

JULIET ANN CONLIN

Love, Hope

HODDER

First published in Great Britain in 2021 by Hodder & Stoughton
An Hachette UK company

1

Copyright © Juliet Ann Conlin 2021

A CIP catalogue record for this title is available from the British Library

Paperback ISBN 978 1 529 35424 9
eBook ISBN 978 1 529 35425 6

Typeset in Plantin Light by Hewer Text UK Ltd, Edinburgh
Printed and bound in Great Britain by Clays Ltd, Elcograf S.p.A.

Hodder & Stoughton policy is to use papers that are natural, renewable
and recyclable products and made from wood grown in sustainable
forests. The logging and manufacturing processes are expected to
conform to the environmental regulations of the country of origin.

Hodder & Stoughton Ltd
Carmelite House
50 Victoria Embankment
London EC4Y 0DZ

www.hodder.co.uk

To my family

Love, Hope

CHAPTER I

FAIRCLEF MUSIC ACADEMY
We Turn Minors into Majors

Dear Mr and Mrs Sullivan,

Further to your application dated 25th May, we are pleased to inform you that Hope has been awarded a place at FairClef Music Academy, beginning next school term, for Early Learning Violin. Thank you for your patience; places at the Academy are much sought-after and the waiting list is always full.

We advise you to refrain from purchasing an instrument until you are certain your child has the interest, aptitude and discipline required for learning the violin; in our experience, this may otherwise prove a costly error. We are happy to provide instruments on loan for a small fee.

We shall provide you with a timetable in due course and look forward to meeting Hope in September.

Kind regards,

George Crow, MA   Pauline Garland ABRSM ATCL
Director   Violin instructor

Dear Hope,

Welcome to fairclef music academy. My name is Janey and I will be your study budy for Theory Lessons. I am 8 and I play the flute here cos my teacher at primary school said I had talent so I should get extra lessons. Mum was worried because it is expensive but I did a audition and they said I could get

lessons for free so Mum is happy about that. I come after school on monday, tuesday and Friday. I don't play the violin so I can't help you with playing the violin. I can show you where the toilets are. I hope you have a nice time at FairClef music academy
    Love Janey
(your new study budy)

Dear Janey,
    My mum read your letter and said I have to write back. Thank you for your letter. I am looking forward to going to FairClef Music Academy to learn violin. I am 8 too and I have a little sister called Autumn but she doesn't go to school yet becos shes too small. What school do you go to? I go to Marchmont Primary.
    Love, Hope

To Hope
Do you want to be my best friend? Tick one box

☐ yes
☐ no

Love Janey

To Hope
Do you want to be my best friend? Tick one box

☑ yes
☐ no

Love Janey

HARRY'S HARMONIES
Strings 'n' Things

One ¾ Cremona SV-175 Premier Student Violin
(spruce wood panel, maple back board and side plate with
inlaid antique varnish)
With Ebony Fingerboard
Incl. Hard Case and Accessories

Total   £ 225.00 (incl. VAT)

Dear Mrs Williams,
Thank you for having me for tea. I think your a very good
cook. Could you please teach my Mum how to cook like that.
Thank you.
Love, Hope

To Janey
Do you want to come round to my house to play? We can play
with the Furby babies I got for christmas or if your aloud to
bring your flute we can practise together because that's fun
too.
I will ask Mum to get us a pizza for tea because she cant cook
very well and neither can my Dad.
Love, Hope

Dear Hope,
You are invited to my 10th birthday party on Saturday
29th April. There will be sandwiches and cake and coke which
I am normally not allowed. The party starts at 3 o'clock and
your parents can pick you up at 6 o'clock.
Love, Janey

Dear Janey,
Thank you for the invitation. Please can I bring my little sister
Autumn because my mum says I was mean to her and I can't
go to your party unless she comes too. She will bring you a
present as well, so you will get two presents from us.
Love, Hope
PS. What do you want for your birthday

Hi Sandra, sorry about that! I was only kidding when I told
Hope she would have to take Autumn along. Thanks for saying
the little one can come too, though – they are both really looking forward to it!
Best, Rachel

No worries, Rachel :) Autumn is a real cutie and she's welcome
any time. Sandra

CHAPTER 2

Knock knock

Who's there?

Shelby

Shelby who?

Shelby comin' round the mountain when she comes

That is the worst joke EVER!

FAIRCLEF MUSIC ACADEMY
We Turn Minors into Majors

Dear Mr and Mrs Sullivan,

Whilst we are pleased that Hope is progressing well with her study of the violin – and she is undeniably talented – it has come to our attention that her behaviour has been less than desirable over the past month or two. She and a fellow student appear to view Theory lessons in particular as an opportunity to engage in gossip, chitchat and even note-passing.

Although we would characterise Hope's conduct as mischievous, rather than malicious, she must learn that talent alone is not enough. Discipline and focus are of equal importance if your daughter is to have a future in the highly competitive world of classical music.

We would appreciate it if you would impress on Hope the importance of concentrating more on her studies and less on cultivating friendships with other students at the Academy.

Whilst we understand that normal twelve-year-olds might find the demands of a classical music education too rigorous and challenging, FairClef Academy seeks to offer instruction to children who can cope with such demands.
Kind regards,

George Crow, MA
Director

Dear Sandra,

Thanks for your letter. While we agree that a sleepover is not the best idea to 'reward' the girls' behaviour, we do feel that they are under quite some pressure to fulfil all their academic and music obligations. As such, we think it would be a little harsh to deny the girls any time together outside the Academy. Perhaps you and Janey would like to come over for dinner one evening this week?

Best wishes,
Rachel and David

Janey, please please please tell your mum that my mum can't cook to save her life and we'll all get food poisoning if she starts experimenting in the kitchen. Hx

Thanks for the invitation, Rachel! How about you all come round to mine, though? I know you work long hours and I don't mind the cooking at all. Best, Sandra

Hi Sandra, thanks for the kind offer! We gladly accept. Hope hasn't been regaling you with stories of my awful cooking, has she?

Best, Rachel

Why didn't the toilet paper cross the road?

I don't know???

Cos it got stuck in the crack

Dear Mr Crow,
I'm very sorry for my behaviour. I will do my best not to talk or tell jokes in theory lessons and I will not be silly any more but please don't sit me away from Janey because she's my best friend and we want to study really hard so we can play in Convent Gardens together when we're grown-ups. I promise that I will be good and I will practise my scales even longer every day.
From,
Hope Sullivan

Hope, have you checked out the
message board?!!!! Jx

ANNOUNCEMENT

The prestigious FairClef Youth Orchestra is delighted to announce that the following students have been selected to join the ensemble, under the musical direction of Maestro Julian Forsythe, from the coming term:

Justin Drummond-Smith (violoncello)
Maximilian Falsworth (clarinet)
Caroline Lee (violin)
Hope Sullivan (violin)
Charles Waters (bassoon)
Janey Williams (flute)
Mark Yang (French horn)

Eeeeeeeeeeeeeeeeeeekkk!!!!

CHAPTER 3

FROM: Hope Sullivan
TO: Janey Williams
SUBJECT: Testing 1 2 3

Hi Janey,

This is my new email address. I'm using my mum's computer, but she says I might get my own for my 14th birthday. Yay! I hope you get to the library soon so you can read this. It'll be so cool writing to each other online! I miss you when we haven't got theory or orchestra together. I wish we went to the same school, but Mum and Dad don't think Parkwood Comprehensive is very good (sorry!!!). *I* don't think Summerfield School for Girls is very good – it doesn't have any boys for a start. The only boys I get to see are the ones at the academy, and their not exactly hot. (Well, I know you've got a crush on that cello player – what's his name, Justin?)

Also, the girls at school think I'm some kind of freak cos I actually *enjoy* violin practice. Lots of them have piano or viola or clarinet lessons, but for them, practising outside of lessons is a drag. Maybe there's something wrong with me, but sometimes I practise for three hours straight and it's like no time has passed at all. I get so lost in the music, everything else falls away. Do you ever feel like that?

I saw a TV programme on BBC2 about the Berlin Philharmonie last night. It's sooooo cool! They said it has the best acoustics in the world! Me and you are gonna play there one day, Janey, I just know it! We're gonna go to lots of places together. Do you actually know how many famous places there are? There's Carnegie Hall, La Scala (that's in Italy), the Sydney Opera House, and lots more places. My grandparents live in Australia, so we could visit them when we go to Sydney. It's weird that you've never even met your grandparents, but maybe we'll also get to go to Jamaica! I don't know if there's any concert halls or opera houses there though.

Right, I have to go now cos Mum wants to use the computer. See you at rehearsals on Wednesday!

Love, Hope

PS. Can you bring the lip gloss?

FROM: Janey Williams
TO: Hope Sullivan
SUBJECT: Re: Testing 1 2 3

Hi Hope,

Finally made it to the library! I got here a bit late so I only have a couple of minutes before they shut down the computers.

I feel you about being the odd one out at school. It's the same at Parkwood, except *everyone* here's a freak one way or another haha. To be honest, though, I haven't really told anyone I play the flute, cos I'd never hear the end of it. At my school, you're either into 50 Cent or James Blunt, no in-between. If I started going on about Reinecke or Kuhlau I'd probably not make it out of the school gates alive. Only kidding, the school's rough but not *that* rough. I'd just end up being the butt of everyone's joke.

Yes, totes agree about getting lost in music. We've got this neighbour, right, who gets really annoyed when I play, hammering on the walls, shouting and swearing etc., so Mum finally built me this little shed down the bottom of the garden where I can sit and practise. It's more of a lean-to than a proper shed; Mum scouted the neighbourhood for reclaimed planks and floorboards, and cobbled it together as best she could. Anyway, the other day I went into my 'studio' (as Mum calls it, haha) and when I came out, it was completely dark outside. I'd been in there for four hours, just me and Vivaldi. We're sisters in spirit, Hope <3 <3 <3

I'm so up for going to Jamaica! And Berlin, and Sydney, and New York. I wouldn't care if I never even made it to second chair (well, I would, but let's cross that bridge when we come to it . . .).

See you on Thursday!

Love, Janey

PS. By the way, I so do not have a crush on Justin! (He *is* cute, though, right?)

Hooooope I'm sooooooo bored.
Zzzzzzzzzzzzzz

> Me too. Forsythe's voice is enough
> to put my violin in a coma.

Haha. Don't let the 'Maestro'
catch you calling him that

> Wanna come round to mine
> for tea after theory?

Can't. I've got xtra tuition with
Grabby Griffin

> ???
> Mr Griffin, my new flute teacher.
> He's a right perv

Eww. Can't you skip it?

No. My mum'll have a fit

OK. Wanna go for a burger after
rehearsal on Fri

I must not write notes in class. I must not write notes in class.
I must not write notes in class. I must not write notes in class.
I must not write notes in class. I must not write notes in class.
I must not write notes in class. I must not write notes in class.
I must not write notes in class. I must not write notes in class.
I must not write notes in class. I must not write notes in class.
I must not write notes in class. I must not write notes in class.
I must not write notes in class. I must not write notes in class.
I must not write notes in class. I must not write notes in class.
I must not write notes in class. I must not write notes in class.
I must not write notes in class. I must not write notes in class.

Hi Justin,
Do you fancy me?
Love, Janey

FROM: Janey Williams
TO: Hope Sullivan
SUBJECT: ~~Friendship~~

Dear Hope Sullivan,

I know you wrote that note to Justin and you are no longer my
best friend.

From Janey Williams

FROM: Hope Sullivan
TO: Janey Williams
SUBJECT: Re: ~~Friendship~~

Dear Janey,

I'm really really really really really really really really really really really sorry. It was a stupid joke. Sorry. Please be my friend again.

Love, Hope

FROM: Janey Williams
TO: Hope Sullivan
SUBJECT: Re: Re: ~~Friendship~~

Dear Hope,

I might consider being your friend again if you get Forsythe to sit on a wet cushion.

Love, Janey

PS. I've gone off Justin anyway cos he keeps staring down Amy Marden's top when she tunes her viola

Hahahahahahaha! I CANNOT believe you did that! Consider yourself my very best friend again.
Love, Janey

Forsythe: Thanks for coming, Mr and Mrs Sullivan.
Rachel Sullivan: No problem. We're— what's that?
Forsythe: What? Oh, that. It's a tape recorder. It's a new Academy policy to record and transcribe meetings. Just to make sure we all have the same takeaway.

David Sullivan:	I'll have a chicken biriyani if you're offering.
Rachel:	[*laughs*]
Forsythe:	No no, not that kind of takeaway. The same key points . . . I mean, we've had problems with parents . . . no, not problems, just, to avoid any misunderstandings, I think it's—
David:	That's fine, Mr Forsythe. Record away.
Forsythe:	It's Maestro.
Rachel:	Sorry?
Forsythe:	My title. It's Maestro. It's what you call the conductor of an orchestra.
Rachel:	[*suppressed laugh*]
David:	The FairClef Youth Orchestra?
Maestro:	[*clears his throat*] Any orchestra. It's the—
[*Muffled noise. Sound of chair legs scraping across the floor.*]	
Maestro:	So pleased you could *finally* join us, Mrs Williams.
Sandra Williams:	That's *Ms* Williams to you. And you can stuff your sarcasm in a sack.
Rachel:	[*suppressed laugh*]
David:	Hi Sandra.
Sandra:	Hello David, Rachel. So, Mr Forsythe, what's so important you called us in? We're busy people.
Rachel:	[*whispers*] It's Maestro.
Sandra:	What?
Maestro:	[*audible huff*] Yes. Enough of that, please. Now. I've asked you in to discuss certain . . . aspects of your daughters' behaviour.
Sandra:	Aspects?
David:	What aspects?
Maestro:	Or should I say, aspects of *mis*behaviour.
Rachel:	Oh.
Maestro:	Oh indeed. Now, I need you to be aware that although Hope and Janey are fortunate enough to be . . . shall we say, gifted—

Sandra:	Listen, Mister, Master, Maestro – whatever you call yourself, I don't know about you, but haven't got time to waste. So please get to the point.
Maestro:	They've been playing pranks, stupid, childish pranks.
Rachel:	But they *are* children, Mr . . . I mean, Maestro.
Maestro:	They're [*rustling of paper*] . . . they're fourteen years old. At that age, Mozart was writing operas and giving concerts to royalty!
David:	Well, that's hardly a fair compari—
Maestro:	[*Raised voice:*] They put a soaked cushion on my chair! It made me look like I'd wet my pants! In front of the entire orchestra!
Sandra:	Hahahaha
Maestro:	[*shouts*] Ms Williams! I must—
Sandra:	HAHAHAHA
Rachel:	[*snort of laughter*]
Maestro:	[*shouts:*] Mrs Sullivan!
David:	[*suppressed laugh*] Mr Forsythe – I mean, Maestro. Please excuse my wife, she's a little [*hisses:*] Rachel, pull yourself together.
Rachel:	Yes, sorry. Sorry, Maestro.
Sandra:	[*wheezing:*] Ye-es, sorry. We'll talk to the gir— HAHAHA

[*Muffled noises, banging, tape cuts out*]

Dear Mr and Mrs Sullivan,

Hope is suspended from the Youth Orchestra for two weeks, effective immediately. I have also written to Ms Williams regarding Janey. It is my expectation that the girls reflect upon their conduct during this time.

Sincerely,

Maestro Forsythe

Hope Sullivan
Janey Williams
Freedom!

Hi Janey,

I'm free again! Sorry I couldn't call you, they took my phone off me and I was banned from using the internet. I wasn't allowed out of my room for a WHOLE WEEK except to go to school. They even brought my tea up and put it outside my room, like I'm some sort of dangerous criminal. I swear if they ever do that again I'm running away. And mum says that for the next month I'm only allowed out if I take Autumn with me. Can you believe that?!! And I know it's only cos mum got a promotion at work and has to work late, and dad's got this new case that keeps him in the office till nighttime. Their just using me as a free babysitter. It wouldn't be so bad if Autumn wasn't so ANNOYING! I mean, she's 8 now but she behaves like a baby. I'm sure that I was able to make myself a slice of toast when I was 8. Sometimes I wish I was an only child, like you. It's so unfair!!!

Anyway, why don't you come round to mine and we can plonk Autumn in front of her favourite cartoon show and lock ourselves in my room? I'm thinking of getting my hair cut and I need you to hold it up in the mirror for me so I know what it looks like.

Love, Hope

deer hope can I play with you
and jani pleeze luv Autumn

No and stay OUT OF MY ROOM!!!

I couldn't hear you properly on the
phone. Don't cry! It'll grow back and
I'm sure it doesn't look that bad!

See?! Your haircut looks fine and all the guys in
the brass section were checking you out . . . Jx

Eeeeeeeeeeeeeeeeekkk!!!!! Mark just
asked me out!!!!!!!!!! We're going to
the pictures on Saturday Hx

You know what, Mark? Casino Royale sucks.
James Bond sucks. Your breath smells and if you
ever make fun of my best friend's hair puffs again
I'll shove your French horn down your throat

To our darling Hope,
    Have the happiest of birthdays!
        Love, Mum and Dad

To Hope,
    Happy 15th birthday
        Love, Autumn
            PS. Mum says I <u>am</u> aloud to come to your party, so
            there

To my BFF
    Happy Birthday! Hope you like the earrings – they're the
    ones you wanted, right?
        Love, Janey xxx

To whom it may Concern:
I am Hope Sullivan's mother and I hearby allow my daughter
Hope to get her ear's pierced even though she is only fifteen.
Signed, Rachel Sullivan (Hope's mother)

They didn't believe me at Claire's :(Can u come
round and do it? I've got a needle and a cork. Hx

It still hurts! I can't believe ur mum could have
done that to you as a baby!!! Seriously tho, I
can't wait to remove the studs so I can wear
those silver clef earrings you got me. Hx

Still keeping it hidden from mum & dad. The left
one is really red and swollen, is that normal? Hx

Now theres a bit of pus coming
out and I feel all hot Hx

Dear Hope,
    Get Well Soon!
        Glad you're feeling better. There's nothing like a good
        dose of septicaemia to teach you that your parents
        (usually) know best.
            Love from Mum and Dad

CHAPTER 4

Hello from the Alps!

I wish you were here and I'm not just saying that! Mum and dad make us get up really early to go hiking even though we're supposed to be on holiday, and I have to share a room with Autumn. But other than that, it's really beautiful here. Mum and Dad want to take us skiing next winter, and I can't wait to see what it looks like with snow on the mountains and tree tops.

But most exciting was that we flew into Vienna and hired a rental car, and we drove past the opera house Statsoper (I think that's how you spell it). It's massive and really, really grand. God, Janey, I can't wait till we play there together!

Right, gotta go, the mountains beckon . . . :(

Love, Hope

Hi Hope,

I wish I was there too, haha! Just in case you're wondering, this is a postcard of the High Street I 'borrowed' from Mr Nowak's shop. Stacking shelves for £3 an hour during my summer holidays entitles me to a little extra, I figured. The Alps sounds great! I went to the library and checked out the Staatsoper on the internet and you're right, it looks gorgeous! You should see the inside, all red & gold! And it seats over 1700 people! I get butterflies just thinking about it.

Obviously you'll be back when you read this, so call me!

Love, Janey

Dear Hope,
    Come celebrate my 16th birthday! On Saturday,
September 8th at 7 pm.
    From Max
    PS. My parents won't be there so BYOB

Did you get the invite too? I think Mark might
be there (*puke*), but it should be a great
night anyway. What r u gonna wear? Hx

                    I'll be there! And I managed to get mum
                        to extend my curfew past midnight!!!
                        I was thinking the gold lamé miniskirt.
                        Meet up an hour before at mine? Jx

FROM: Hope Sullivan
TO: Janey Williams
SUBJECT: Party

Hi Janey,

What a night! My head is throbbing like you wouldn't believe
and if I move too quickly I'm afraid I'll be sick. Dad caught me
coming in at 2 am, 'smelling like a brewery', which means –
yup, you've guessed it – I'm grounded *again*. I don't care
though, cos the way I'm feeling now I don't think I want to get
out of bed for the next five days anyway.

How was your night? We seem to have got separated somewhere between Twister in the living room and spin-the-bottle
in the kitchen. I ended up upstairs, where there was this weird
Strings vs. Woodwind drinking competition going on. Sorry I
didn't say get to say goodbye, but one of the girls at the party
lives near me and she called a taxi and offered me a lift, so I
didn't have time to find you.

You looked fantastic in that outfit, by the way – since when did your legs get that long? If your music career doesn't take off, you can always try modelling . . . No, just kidding, I'm still holding you to our pact of joining the same orchestra and conquering the world. Speaking of, there's no way I'd join an orchestra if Max was in it. I always thought he was pretty cute, you know, those dimples and everything, but it turns out he's a right loser. You know when you were in the living room, showing off your dance moves and putting everyone else to shame? Me and Max found ourselves alone in the kitchen, and I was trying out those flirting techniques you and me practised – you know, tossing my hair and tilting my head etc. Anyway we had a couple of Bacardi Breezers and for some reason we started talking about Venus Williams winning Wimbledon this year, and Max was like, 'Yeah, she might look strong, but I bet any average man would beat her hands down,' which I *definitely* wasn't going to take lying down, and before I knew it, he'd challenged me to an arm-wrestle. Well, you know how competitive I can get, right? Especially if I *know* I'm going to win. So I agreed, thinking it would be a bit of a laugh.

We took up our positions on either side of the counter just as a couple of woodwind guys came into the kitchen. *Wham* – I had his arm down before he knew it. Then Max demanded a rematch cos he'd been 'distracted', so again, *wham*, 2–nil to Hope. He wanted three out of five, which was a big mistake, *naturellement*. Of course the other guys started making fun of him then, which Max didn't take kindly. Anyway, it ended up with him telling me I'd get big beefy arms and no one would ever fancy me and that I'd never get a boyfriend if I insisted on beating people at arm-wrestling. As you can imagine, I told him where he could shove that 1,000-page opera dictionary his parents got him for his birthday (I mean, how lame is that anyway?)

I can't believe he was stupid enough to challenge me in the first place. I mean, I've been playing the violin for nearly ten years now. Didn't he realise I'd have super strong arms from all those hours of practice? I guess that's clarinet players for you, haha.

Anyway, was that Charlie I saw you snogging? I want all the details . . .

Love, Hope

FROM: Janey Williams
TO: Hope Sullivan
SUBJECT: Never again!

Hey there,

Feeling just as rough as you. I'm sitting here at the kitchen table sipping water and hoping my mum doesn't force-feed me more of her 'hangover special' – smushed-up banana with salt-fish flakes and lime juice. I swear it doesn't help; it's more like some recipe from hell she's invented to punish me. She doesn't have to worry, though. I'm never ever EVER drinking again.

Sorry to hear about Max – you were really into him, weren't you? He sounds like a right tosser. I imagine he gets it from his parents, have you met them? His mum looks like she's got a pole up her arse and I swear his dad wears those mirrored sunglasses to secretly ogle the girls. Creepy as hell. FWIW, I think it's really cool that you're so strong, especially because you don't look it at first glance. It's kinda like your secret superhero weapon. *'Violin Girl – Following a shark attack, her biceps were replaced with steel! She makes music during the day and fights creepy dudes at night . . .'*

Thanks for all the compliments, girl! I thought you were rocking it too with that gypsy skirt and the DMs. It's a shame your so skinny, otherwise we could totally swap clothes.

Yup, that was Charlie you spotted. But don't worry, it's not gonna turn into anything serious. Kissing technique: A+, conversation skills: D−. Seriously, the guy's vocabulary consists of grunts of varying degrees of intelligibility. Like, I *think* he was asking if I wanted to go the pictures with him, but he might also have been telling me that he's got a cramp in his big toe. Nah, can't be doing with that kinda thing.

Right, gotta go. Mum's just come into the kitchen and she's headed straight for the spice cupboard. If I'm not at orchestra on Tuesday, call the police! And the poison control centre!

Love, Janey

What do you think?
www.glyndebourne.com/festival/
Hx

> At school right now. Maths
> zzzzzzzzzzzzzzzzzzzzzzzzzz
> Catch u later Jx

FluteyCutey12:	I've just looked it up. Looks excellent! But how do we get there?
ViolinGurl123:	Hitchhiking :)
FluteyCutey12:	U serious?
ViolinGurl123:	Sure. Mum and dad did it all the time when they were students. And I've got a tent. How about Saturday week? We can say we're staying over at each other's
FluteyCutey12:	Yeah, but check out the ticket prices :(
ViolinGurl123:	We don't actually have to go *in*. They have open air performances, so we should be able to hear something. And maybe we'll find a gap in the fence . . .
FluteyCutey12:	I like the way your mind works
ViolinGurl123:	Glyndebourne here we come!

FluteyCutey12: Are we total losers for wanting to go to an
                opera festival?
ViolinGurl123: R u kidding? We're dreaming BIG when others
                are dreaming small

U get home ok?
                                        Yup. Feeling knackered tho
Yeah, sorry, I should've checked the tent.
I never realised it had a hole in it
                            And what was with that guy's car?
                                        Smelled like dead cat
Urgh, I know. I kept thinking what if he's
a serial pet killer or something
                    That's the last time I go hitchhiking, I swear
Me too. Ur mum suspect anything?
                        Nah. She just asked if the shower wasn't
                            working at your house or something
Hey, one day, they'll be paying *us* to go
to Glyndebourne Opera Festival . . . Hx

CHAPTER 5

Hi Sweetie,
Sorry, had to leave early this morning. Could you pick up
Autumn from hockey practice at six? (Please be on time!) Dad
& I won't be home till late. There's cash in the drawer for pizza.
Be good!
Kisses, Mum xxx
PS. Eat the apple, not just the crisps!
PPS. Any idea yet what you want for your birthday? (I can't
believe my baby is turning 18 next week!)

Hey Janey, wanna come round for pizza? Hx

Dear Mum,
I'm sorry me and Janey ate all the pizza, but Autumn said she
was ok with toast. I promise to take her out and treat her on
the weekend.
Love, Hope

Happy birthday, Hope!
From your BFF Janey x

To our darling Hope,
Have a super 18th birthday!
Love, Mum & Dad

Dearest Hope,
    Have a wonderful birthday,
        Love from Nan & Grandpa

Happy Birthday sis!
    Love, Autumn
    PS. Mum told me your treated as an adult by the police
        now so you can get arrested if you break and enter
        into my room
    PPS. So watch it
    PPPS. I *know* you stole my chocolate egg I was saving
        from easter

ROYAL COLLEGE OF MUSIC
Prince Consort Road, South Kensington, London SW7

Dear Ms Sullivan,
    Following your performance at audition, we would like to make you a <u>conditional offer</u> for a place on our Bachelor of Music (BMus) programme. This offer is conditional on your passing the Grade 8 examination for Violin.
    Please see the letter attached for information on tuition fees and funding.
    I look forward to welcoming you in September.
Kind regards,

Jason Larchfield
Director of Admissions

Dearest Hope,
    Congratulations!
        We just spoke to your mum and she told us how well
        you did in your audition! It would be lovely to see you
        and Autumn again (she was only a baby the last time

we saw her!). Perhaps you could all come over at Christmas? We are getting too old for long-haul flights.
Fingers crossed for your exams,
All our love,
Nan & Grandpa

J – what's up? Just spoke to your mum to ask how you were. She said, Fine why do you ask?, so I said, No reason. She said surely we had enough opportunity to talk to each other during Theory lessons (it sounded like she was being sarcastic but I wasn't really sure), so I didn't like to say that I haven't seen you there since MONDAY!!!

Where have you been? We've got grade exams coming up in 3 weeks in case you'd forgotten! I know your good, but even you can't afford to miss a WHOLE WEEK of lessons. This is important, Janey, it's for college, for gods sake. Your not sick, or else your mum would've told me. Your not chickening out on me are you? ARE YOU???

Love, Hope

PS. I'm not performing at Carnegie Hall and Sydney Opera House without you!

PPS. I hope I haven't got you in trouble with your mum

Griffin did it again. But it was way worse this time. He didn't even pretend it was an accident, like all the other times, like he's 'accidentally' brushed his hand off my breast or my bum. He – God, I feel sick just thinking about it – he stood right behind me while I was playing and cupped my right elbow, like he was adjusting my position, and then he let his other hand drop down and – shit it's hard to write this – put it up under my skirt and . . .

I didn't know what to do, Hope. I just carried on playing, *affrettando*, like, even though it was a slow piece, just to get to the fucking end of it. Then I packed my stuff and ran out.

I'm only telling you cos you're my best friend. I haven't even told my mum. She'd go completely ballistic, and not just with Griffin. She'd ask me why I never told her or said anything to him, right when it started months ago. She'd be so disappointed that I didn't stand up for myself. But I never told him to stop the first time or the second time or all the times after that cos I was so embarrassed. So how could I say anything this time?

I'm sorry. I know we had all these plans to travel the world together, but we were stupid little kids back then. I'm sorry. I don't want to go back to the academy. Ever. No one can make me.

Love, Janey

ViolinGurl123:   Janey, u there?
                 Why aren't you answering the phone?
                 I can see ur online . . .
                 I just want to talk, we can sort this out
FluteyCutey12:   I don't wanna talk
ViolinGurl123:   I just spoke to my dad, he wants to help
FluteyCutey12:   U told your DAD??? THIS WAS CONFIDENTIAL
                 HOPE SULLIVAN
ViolinGurl123:   I'm sorry. But he's a lawyer and he says you've
                 got a case. He can help!

FluteyCutey12:	I don't want your charity
ViolinGurl123:	U sound like your mum
FluteyCutey12:	Yeah, and you sound like *your* mum
ViolinGurl123:	If that's supposed to be an insult, try harder Janey?
	Janey, I'm so sorry this happened to you. But if you think I'm letting my best friend give up music cos Grabby fucking Griffin thinks he can grope you whenever he feels like it, think again. I want to help you. This is not charity. This is what friends do for each other. My dad happens to be a lawyer and he says this is sexual harassment. You just have to make a formal complaint. My dad says he can help you do that.
FluteyCutey12:	But what if no one believes me?
ViolinGurl123:	Of course they'll believe u! Why would u make it up?
FluteyCutey12:	It happened to my mum. At her last job. Her line manager kept rubbing himself off her and she couldn't take it no more and told him to go to hell, and she got a written warning and then she made a complaint and then she was sacked for spreading 'malicious rumours'. She got sanctioned by the Jobcentre and it took her FIVE MONTHS to get another job. So don't tell me all I have to do is make a formal complaint.
ViolinGurl123:	Sorry. I didn't know
FluteyCutey12:	Yeah, well, there's lots of things you don't know. Like what it's like to grow up without a dad. What it's like being the only black girl in the orchestra. The only black kid in the whole fucking academy. I mean, how many black classical musicians do you know? How many conductors, opera singers, flautists? Cos I can't think of any.

28

ViolinGurl123:	But we can't just let Griffin get away with it! That's not right!
FluteyCutey12:	Lots of things aren't right in this world
ViolinGurl123:	Janey? You still there? Janey?

FROM: Hope Sullivan
TO: Janey Williams
SUBJECT: Sorry

Janey, I'm sorry. I'm sorry I didn't pay more attention to you, to what your life is like, to what you're going through. It never occurred to me that you might feel different to everyone else at the academy, or in the orchestra. But that's because I take it for granted that I have a mum and a dad and a sister. And that I never have to worry about money. And that I'm white.

But I do know that what Grabby Griffin did was wrong, and it makes me so angry to think he'll get away with it. And breaks my heart that he might stop my best friend, the most talented musician I know, from making music. Do you remember when you told me how you felt playing Debussy's 'Syrinx'? You said you felt free. You felt powerful, you felt like you ruled the world with this beautiful, strange sound that only you could produce. And that's what it felt like, listening to you. You were the QUEEN, everyone was just totally captivated by you.

It might sound selfish, but *I* need you, too. Ever since I picked up a violin, I've dreamt of going to music college, joining an orchestra and travelling the world with you. I don't want to do that on my own! I totally understand you might be scared of not being believed, and if you don't want to make a complaint, I'll still be there for you. Your my best friend remember?

But if you decide you want to stick it to Griffin (as he well and truly deserves), then I'll be behind you all the way (and so will my dad, and he's a really good lawyer). And I know your mum's a bit scary, but I can't for a moment believe she would be disappointed in you. She loves you like crazy!

Love, Hope

PS. Jessye Norman, Chevalier de Saint-Georges, Marian Anderson, James DePreist, Valerie Coleman

FAIRCLEF MUSIC ACADEMY
We Turn Minors into Majors

Dear Mr Griffin,
   Following our recent investigation into allegations of your inappropriate behaviour, I am writing to inform you that your teaching contract has been terminated with immediate effect.
   The student who so bravely stepped forward has decided not to take this any further with the police. Please know, though, that we will not be providing you with a reference and that you are not welcome to enter the premises of the Academy again; any of your remaining belongings will be sent to your home address at your cost.
Sincerely,

George Crow, MA
Director

Thank you for believing me. I will never forget this.
Your best friend forever, Janey x

CHAPTER 6

The Associated Board of the Royal Schools of Music

This is to certify that
HOPE SULLIVAN
was examined and passed

WITH DISTINCTION

GRADE 8 VIOLIN
IN 2009

Presented for examination by
Ms Pauline Garland ABRSM ATCL

ViolinGurl123:	OMG OMG OMFG!!!!!!!
FluteyCutey12:	I know right???
ViolinGurl123:	We're going to college together! I can't believe it!!!!!!!!!!!!!
FluteyCutey12:	There's not enough smileys in the world :) :) :)
ViolinGurl123:	Congrats on the scholarship btw
FluteyCutey12:	I know! Phew, so relieved that came thru
ViolinGurl123:	We're gonna share a room at college, right?
FluteyCutey12:	But what if I meet the flautist of my dreams?
ViolinGurl123:	So?
FluteyCutey12:	And, you know, we wanna a bit of privacy to indulge in some flutter tonguing
ViolinGurl123:	Haha, or should I say, EWWWW . . . seriously, tho, I'm sooooo looking forward to this
FluteyCutey12:	Debussy all the way, baby!

ViolinGurl123:	I vote for Paganini
FluteyCutey12:	So u can show off your solo skills? Yeah, I don't think so
ViolinGurl123:	Shall we talk about that squeaky B# you played the other day at rehearsal?
FluteyCutey12:	It was E3, and it only squeaked cos I can't afford a High E facilitator
	Hope? U still there?
	Helloooooooo???
ViolinGurl123:	I was just rereading our chat . . . we are such pretentious w**kers
FluteyCutey12:	Speak for yourself! Wanna meet up and cele-brate? I'll sneak a bottle of Bailey's from mum's secret stash
ViolinGurl123:	Nah, not tonite. want a clear head for the recital tomorrow
FluteyCutey12:	Spoilsport
ViolinGurl123:	Tomorrow nite though
FluteyCutey12:	Swear? BFF honour?
ViolinGurl123:	BFF honour
FluteyCutey12:	Right. I'm off to get drunk. See ya tomorrow
ViolinGurl123:	Love ya xxx

FAIRCLEF MUSIC ACADEMY
We Turn Minors into Majors

Dear Parents,

It is with great pleasure that we invite you to this year's FairClef Youth Orchestra Annual Concert on Saturday, 27th June, at 6 pm. You will see from the programme attached that I have embarked on one of our boldest and most ambi-tious repertoires to date.

To quote Plato, 'Music gives a soul to the universe, wings to the mind, flight to the imagination, and life to everything.'

May you enjoy listening to the recital as much as we have enjoyed rehearsing for it!
Kind regards,

Julian Forsythe, Maestro

Please note: Photography and/or video recordings will not be permitted during the performance, but there will be ample opportunity to take photographs of the Maestro (and our young musicians) after the event. In the interest of unadulterated listening pleasure, we request that young children (including younger siblings) not attend the recital.

Darling Hope, We are so VERY VERY proud of you! Can't wait to see you knock 'em dead tonight! Love, Mum & Dad xxx

10 minutes to go, J! U nervous?

What, me? Never

Where r u?

In the ladies. U?

Behind the curtain. The hall's really filling up!

Shame we're not charging money, we'd be rich :)

How's the hangover?

I'm dying here. Never again!

Where have I heard that before :)

Ur parents here yet?

Haven't seen them. Your mum?

Probably sat in the 1st row with big cheesy grin on her face

Hang on, I'll take a peek . . .
Awww, she looks so proud!

She's gonna embarrass me, I just know it. Shit, gotta go, maestro's coming at me with a right look on his face

Mum, dad? Where r u? The
recital's about to start!!!!

I can't believe you didn't come! You missed my
solo! I'm going out w Janey now. DON'T WAIT UP

Daily Echo

TWO KILLED IN CAR CRASH

Emergency services were called to Thornberry Road near
Huntingdon, at around 7.10 pm on Saturday, 27th June,
following reports of a car that had come off the road.

The male driver was pronounced dead at the scene; his
female passenger was seriously injured and rushed to hospital, but sadly died forty-five minutes later.

The road was closed for almost four hours; traffic was
diverted at the Central roundabout. The police are appealing
for any witnesses who may have seen the accident.

The victims have subsequently been named as married
couple David and Rachel Sullivan. The Sullivans are
survived by their two daughters, Hope (18) and Autumn
(12).

Oh god, Hope, I just heard.
I don't know what to say.
I'm so sorry. Jx

We are truly sorry for your loss
    Kind regards,
        Ainsworth & Gardener Solicitors

Wishing you find comfort and peace,
Strength to face the days ahead
And loving memories to forever hold in your hearts
   Love, Sandra Williams

With our deepest sympathies
   FairClef Music Academy

Hope darling, Grandpa and I have just
landed at the airport. We'll be there as
soon as we can. Can't wait to hold you
and Autumn in our arms. Love, Nan

ORDER OF SERVICE

~

Entrance Music
Nimrod from Enigma Variations – Elgar

~

Welcome and Opening Words

~

Hymn
Lord of All Hopefulness

~

Tribute to David and Rachel

~

Hope on violin
*Canzonetta: Andante 2nd movement from
Concerto in D, Op. 35*

FROM: Janey Williams
TO: Hope Sullivan
SUBJECT: Thinking of you

Hey there,

I hope you're feeling ok. I didn't want to bug you right after the funeral – just wanted to let you know that everyone understands. You didn't let anyone down, so I don't want you thinking that. And it's ok if you don't want to talk about what happened, but I'm right here for you if you do. Call or txt me whenever.

Love, Janey x

Dear Hope,

I can't remember the last time I wrote a letter old-school style, but seeing as you're not answering emails, texts or calls, I decided to bust out the big guns! (You'd better be grateful, girl! I wouldn't do it for anyone else.)

I understand that you needed some time to yourself. But I'm not gonna lie, I don't think it's good for you to avoid everyone for this long. Talking helps, it really does. And me & you have been best friends for ten years (that's most of our lives, can you believe it?), so if anyone is going to be there for you, it's me. And you might not know this, but I need you too! We start college next month, and there's no one else who can do my braids when my mum's not there. It would be lovely to meet up before we start college. But if you're busy with whatever, I'll see you there. I really, really can't wait!

Right, gotta go, getting cramp in my writing hand.

Love, Janey x

CHAPTER 7

NO WAY I'M MOVING TO
AUSTRALIA WITH THEM!!!

Dearest Hope,

Thank you for you lovely letter. Grandpa has finally managed to shake off that awful cold he picked up on the flight and is feeling much better now. It is also wonderful to hear that you and Autumn are getting back to a normal routine. This situation can't have been easy on you poor girls and you are always in our thoughts.

However, my darling, you cannot possibly expect us to agree with your suggestion. Taking care of Autumn yourself? You're far too young! I do understand how upset you both are at the moment – we are also still overwhelmed with grief. But it just isn't feasible, by any stretch of the imagination. Aside from the emotional responsibility of looking after a child (which, I'm afraid to say, a twelve-year-old is, whatever Autumn may think to the contrary), there are the practicalities: the cooking, cleaning, homework supervision, dealing with teachers and doctors. It is far more work than you might imagine.

In addition, there is also your own life to think about. You're still so young, and due to start college, aren't you? How do you expect to combine your music studies with caring for Autumn? To be frank, I fear that you have an unrealistic notion of what parenting is, and while we understand that you feel protective and responsible for Autumn, it really isn't in the best interest of either of you for her to stay with you.

Hope, dearest, I'm afraid Grandpa and I must veto this suggestion. Besides, Sydney is a wonderful place for a young girl to grow up. Talk to Autumn about this, won't you? Living with us is the only sensible option, and I'm sure she'll come to see it that way soon enough. I trust you are mature enough to come to the right decision.

With all our love,
Nan & Grandpa

Dear Hope,

It was lovely to get your letter. It certainly sounds as though you've made up your mind about keeping Autumn in England. If I'm honest, I still feel a bit apprehensive about it, but perhaps you are right and it would be cruel to tear Autumn away from everything she knows. If Autumn is doing well at school, and if her friends give her the comfort she needs, then that is what's important, I suppose. You know we only want what's best for you and your sister, and we certainly don't want to do anything that will cause you any more sadness.

In light of this, we think it would be a good idea for you to contact Social Services about becoming Autumn's legal guardian. This will make things easier when it comes to all the 'red tape' you will undoubtedly face regarding doctors, teachers etc.

Darling Hope, we will try not to worry about you, but only if you promise to let us know if things ever get too much. We may be on the other side of the world, but we are always only a phone call away.

Look after yourselves,
Nan and Grandpa

Where the hell r u? I been running around
freshers' fair looking for you. CALL ME!!!

HARRIS MUSIC AGENCY
Your Success Is Our Success

Dear Ms Sullivan,

Thank you for your application for the position of Artistic Programming Assistant. I regret to inform you that the position requires *at least* a university degree or five years' relevant work experience. We are, however, also looking for an enthusiastic and dedicated intern (40 hours/week, unpaid position). If this would be of interest to you, please contact me at the number below.

With kind regards,

Francis Craven

OPERA MUSIC CAFE
Musica e caffè

Dear Miss Sullivan,

Thank you for your application. I truly wish that we could accommodate your request for daytime-only shifts. However, flexible working hours, including evening and weekend shifts, are an unfortunate but necessary requirement for this position. We therefore cannot consider your application further.

Sincerely,

Harriet McNeil
Manager

For sale:

Classical music CDs. Beethoven, Sibelius, Mozart, Stravinsky, Schubert, including original recordings of Barbirolli, von Karajan, Kleiber – in very good condition (£100 ONO)

Toby Robertson
Hope Sullivan
Violin for sale

Hi there!

I'm responding to your eBay ad for a used violin. What kind of chin rest does it have? If it's a Dresden, I'm happy to take it off your hands for the asking price.

Regards, Toby

HARRY'S HARMONIES
Strings 'n' Things

Dear Hope,

Thank you for coming in to see me on Thursday. It was lovely to meet you, and I think you will be a great addition to the team (team = me & the missus). It is wonderful that you can start so soon! I think that your passion and knowledge with regard to music more than make up for your lack of retail experience. In fact, we pride ourselves on not 'hard selling' to customers things that they don't really need.

I would like to add that I am glad you were so honest about your personal circumstances. I'm sure we will manage to fit your work schedule around your family responsibilities. Oh, and we were delighted to hear that you bought your first violin here in our shop! It's a small world, isn't it?

I look forward to seeing you on Monday,
Kind regards,

Harry

Dear Hope,

See, you're making me do it again! This is the second time I'm writing you a proper letter, and I expect a proper letter back*. It's lucky Mum told me you'd moved house, otherwise

I would've sent this to the old address. How could you not tell me you'd had to do that? I'm so sorry, Hope. I'm shocked that your parents didn't have life insurance – it's so unlike them.

So you have a new job! Of course I remember Harry's Harmonies. I have vivid memories of Mum trying to barter with the owner over the price of my first flute. Unsuccessfully, of course, but fair play to him – he ended up offering her an interest-free payment plan. I can't really picture you as a sales assistant, to be honest, but I suppose it's as good a job as any in the interim. And it's music-related, so there's that.

College is going well. I'm sharing a room with this girl Amelia – a harpist, so that tells you everything you need to know – and you wouldn't believe what a snob she is (she says 'tiss-ue' and not 'tish-ue'). She hasn't tidied any of her stuff away for days, and when I politely asked yesterday if she'd mind picking her knickers up off the floor, she seriously asked what day the cleaner comes! And she snores like nothing I've ever heard before. You should hear it – it sounds like she's drowning in her own snot.

I lie in bed some nights, listening to her snorting and snuffling, and think: that should be Hope! That should be Hope lying across the room snoring. And it gets me really upset, and then I start feeling guilty. Like this was OUR dream, not just mine, and I'm living it on my own without you. And then I feel really angry that you just didn't turn up. You're my best friend, Hope, and I always thought I was yours. Why didn't you tell me you were dropping out? Was it because you knew I wouldn't let you just give up like that? Because, you're right, I wouldn't have. Do you remember what you wrote to me when I said I wasn't coming back to the Academy? You said that it had always been your dream to join an orchestra and travel the world with me. Well, that was my dream too. I know you've got Autumn to think about, but we would have come up with something. Why didn't you just talk to me about it?

Sorry. I didn't write to get angry with you. I miss you. At least come and visit me.

From your best friend,

Janey x

*Actually, just get in touch, it doesn't matter how

CHAPTER 8

AUTUMN'S ROOM – DO NOT ENTER!

To our favourite granddaughters
  Merry Christmas!
    Love from Nan & Grandad

Dear Hope,

We thought we'd write you a letter separately from our card, as we know how hard this time of year is and we don't want to upset Autumn unduly. They say time heals all wounds, but this is the second Christmas without them, and it feels as raw as ever. Sorry, I don't want to sound morose, but there you are.

We are very pleased that you are settling in to your new role. I must admit, we had our doubts, but it seems like you're up to the task, and that makes us happy. How is your job at the music shop? Your boss sounds very nice. Not everyone gets a Christmas bonus these days, you know!

As for Autumn, please be reassured that her moods will pass. Teenagers are challenging at the best of times. (It's not that long ago that I had similar conversations with your mum about you!). I'm sure you will eventually find compromises that suit you both.

I don't mean to pry, but you sounded awfully tired on the phone. I know you're working hard, but are you getting enough sleep? Young people often think they can get by on the bare minimum, but a good night's sleep is so important.

Now, please give Autumn a big hug from me and Grandpa. I've enclosed a cheque with a little something for Christmas. Please buy yourselves something nice each.

Lots of love,
Nan & Grandpa

TEEN PARADISE

Personalised necklace – *Autumn*	£ 12.99
Makeup set 'Teen Girl'	£ 15.99
Adidas Superstar trainers (size 3 ½)	£ 24.99
Total:	**£ 53.97 (incl. VAT)**

RAY'S APPLIANCES

UniVac X10 Wet and Dry Vacuum Cleaner
Incl. cartridge filter; 5 x F29 paper filter bags

Total: **£ 48.99 (incl. VAT)**

Chores	Responsibility
Daily	
1. Make beds	Autumn
2. Tidy up living room	Hope
3. Cooking	Hope
4. Washing up	Autumn/Hope (alternate days)
5. Bathroom (quick wipe-down)	Hope
Weekly	
1. Hoover carpets	Hope
2. Clean bath & toilet	Hope
3. Big laundry (change bed sheets!)	Hope
4. Mop kitchen floor	Hope
5. Put out rubbish bins	Autumn

Monthly	
1. Check smoke alarms	Hope
2. Clean fridge (check for mouldy food)	Hope
3. Wipe down/hoover furniture	Hope
4. Dust shelves	Autumn

I HATE YOU, HOPE! YOUR NOT MY MUM!

CHAPTER 9

FROM: Janey Williams
TO: Hope Sullivan
SUBJECT: Come back soon!

Hi Hope,

So nice to see you, even if it was only for 5 minutes (that's what it felt like, anyway). Next time, you'll have to take a whole week off and we'll do the clubs. There's this little jazz club on Nevada Street; you'd *love* it. (Me? Jazz? I hear you asking . . . It's this thing called 'personal development' haha.)

So, what do you think of Eric? Pretty gorgeous, right? RIGHT? Aaaaarghh, I can't believe he finally asked me out! And he plays the trombone. Sexy or what?! You shoulda seen Amelia Snotty McSnotface when he came to pick me up the other night. Her tongue was hanging so far out of her mouth it was almost touching the floor. Can't say I blame her, though . . . You and Eric had a nice chat, right? At least that's what he said.

Mum says Autumn's been driving you crazy. Sorry to hear it, Hope. Don't let the girl get you down, you're doing your best. And remember what *we* were like back then? She'll grow out of her moods soon enough. Mum also says to send her round if she gets too much. Says she'd have a 'word' with her . . .

Btw, you are still playing, right?

Speak soon,

Janey x

Hey gorgeous! I was at Harry's Harmonies
last week and you sold me a plectrum
I can't stop thinking about you

Wanna go out some time, gorgeous?

I've got money. I'll see you
right if you see me right

At least send me a photo

Want to see that long dark hair and cute titties

Why you ignoring me? You shuld
learn to take a compliment.

Suit yourself bitch

Message not delivered

You blocked me, bitch?!?

Message not delivered

WILLOWBROOK HIGH SCHOOL

Dear Miss Sullivan,
    We are hereby informing you that your sister Autumn
Sullivan, for whom you have guardianship, has been

suspended from school for one week, following an incident involving superglue and the school trophy cabinet.

At this stage, given your difficult family circumstance, we have decided to suspend Autumn, rather than expelling her. However, we kindly ask you to attend a meeting with myself and the school counsellor Ms Cullen to discuss her behaviour. Aside from the above-mentioned incident, she has recently been displaying conduct that we cannot condone, which includes a rude and hostile attitude towards teaching staff (when she deigns to attend, that is).

Please call the school secretary to schedule a time.
Yours sincerely,

Mr McDonald
Acting Principal

How many times, Hope? UR NOT MY MUM! I'm staying out as long as I want

STOP CALLING ME

No, don't call the police! I'm going to Sandras.

TO: Hope Sullivan
FROM: Sandra Williams
SUBJECT: Autumn

Dear Hope,

Glad to hear Autumn arrived home safely. Please don't be too hard on her. She spent most of the night on my sofa, crying. She's feeling very confused and angry, and I think she just needed someone 'neutral' to talk to. Janey told me you're finding it a bit overwhelming at times, too. Perhaps you and Autumn should have a good chat when things have calmed down?

It must be so hard for the both of you. I realise I could never replace your mum, but please know that my door is always open.

Love, Auntie Sandra

CHAPTER 10

PARTAAAAAY!!!

It's my 21st and I'm celebrating in STYLE! At Oliver's Jazz Bar from 9 pm (first drink's on me). Don't bother with a present – unless you really want to! – as long as you bring yourself!

See you there,
Janey x

PS. 21 is the legal drinking age in most everywhere in the world, which is handy, cos that's where I'm planning to go

Hi Hope, thanks for your message. Of course you can have tomorrow off – you don't need to apologise for asking. You always work so hard, you deserve it. Have fun tonight! Harry

FROM: Janey Williams
TO: Hope Sullivan
SUBJECT: Re: Party

Hi Hope,

I'm so sorry you couldn't make it to the party. Mum called me to tell me what happened. Don't worry about disappointing me – of course it would've been great to see you, but under the circumstances, I totally understand.

Jeez, what's up with Autumn? I mean, supergluing the geography teacher's tie to the trophy cabinet is a *bit* funny, I have to admit – do you not remember all the stuff we got up to at school? And at least the teacher wasn't wearing his tie at the time. But getting picked up by the police for vandalism, that's a whole other level. At least our pranks were mischievous, not malicious. Do you think she might just be craving attention?

Seriously, Hope, I don't really know what to say. You're NOT rubbish at this whole parenting thing, so I never want to hear you say that again. And it's certainly not your fault that your fifteen-year-old sister is running around at night getting drunk and spray-painting the wall behind Tesco's. You're not her mum, and I think you've handled the situation brilliantly for the last few years. Christ, the thought of looking after a moody, stroppy teenager scares the bejesus out of me! Even the normal teenage stuff – bras, braces and boyfriends – would have me at my wits' end.

You need to hang in there, Hope. It will get better, I'm 100% sure of it. In the meantime, I'm always only an email or phone call away. Don't worry about having a good old moan, either. It can do you the world of good sometimes. And Mum says she's happy to take up some of the slack if she can.

Love,

Janey x

THE STAGE

Wanted: Musicians (instrumentalists, not vocalists) for the Festival d'Avignon

We are *The Blazing Buskers*, a group of UK-based freelance musicians planning our annual trip to the 'Off' festival in Avignon, France. Our repertoire ranges from classical through jazz to folk, and we're looking for 1 violin, 1 trumpet and 1 guitar to join us for this year's street music programme. Coach travel and tents provided.

Music, sunshine, freedom, what's not to like?!! If this pushes your buttons, please apply to the address below and we'll contact you for an audition date.

FROM: The Blazing Buskers
TO: Hope Sullivan
SUBJECT: Audition

Dear Hope,

Thanks for getting in touch! We were impressed by your application and would love to have you along for audition. Could you make it next Tuesday evening, around 8.30 pm?

Look forward to meeting you!

Best,
Mike

CHILD WELFARE AGENCY
Family Social Care Services

Dear Ms Sullivan,

We are writing to you following a report made by the local Police Authority regarding the minor Autumn Sullivan, who is in your care.

We request a meeting in order to assess whether Autumn's welfare needs are being met. We will send a Child Protection Officer to your home next Thursday at 6 pm to carry out a welfare check. Please ensure you and Autumn are at home on this date, or contact us on the number below to arrange an alternative appointment.

Sincerely,

Catherine Duncan
Child Welfare Officer

FROM: The Blazing Buskers
TO: Hope Sullivan
SUBJECT: Re: Mix up

Dear Hope,

No worries at all. We understand how difficult it can be to balance work and family commitments. But do let us know if you're interested in joining us next year!

All best,
Mike

Dear Mum and Dad,
I miss you so terribly.
Love, Hope

Hey there, Autumn. Do you want to come round this week for tea and a chat? I'll make that pepperpot stew you like. Auntie Sandra x

TO: Hope Sullivan
FROM: Sandra Williams
SUBJECT: Autumn

Dear Hope,

I had a long talk with Autumn yesterday evening. Now I'm not defending her behaviour, but kids do all sorts of crazy stuff when they're trying to figure out who they are and what their place is in the world. Do you remember when you nearly got thrown out of the orchestra for making the maestro look like he'd peed himself? You and Janey thought it was hilarious at the time (though looking back, he *was* a pretentious idiot and he probably had it coming). And what about that little trip you took to Glyndebourne? Bet you thought we knew nothing

53

about that, didn't you? What I'm saying is that when you're a teenager, you do stupid things and don't for a minute stop to consider the consequences.

Autumn's going through all that stuff you and Janey went through, just without her mum and dad to guide her. But you are doing a spectacular job, Hope, and I know that Autumn is in good hands with you. She's a good girl on the inside, she's just hurting really bad. But the good news is that she confided in me that she's no longer seeing that boy Marc. I met that little fool once, and let me tell you it was all I could do not to grab him by the scruff of his scrawny little neck and toss him to the street. But Autumn's a smart girl; I knew she'd see him for what he was sooner or later.

Listen, Hope, you've both had a rough few years and my heart aches for the two of you young girls growing up without a mum. Autumn would never admit it, but being picked up by the police like that, I think it just might have scared her straight. And if that didn't, my little talking to sure did!

Warm wishes and hugs,
Auntie Sandra

CHILD WELFARE AGENCY
Family Social Care Services

Regarding: Autumn Mary Sullivan

A welfare check was carried out at the above property on Thursday, 15th May to assess the wellbeing of the minor Autumn Sullivan. Autumn (15 years old) is currently in the care of her older sister, Hope Sullivan, following the death of their parents three years ago.

The property was checked with regard to safety and hygiene standards. Both Autumn and her sister Hope were interviewed together and separately.

In my professional opinion as Child Welfare Officer, I can confirm that Autumn's physical, mental and emotional needs are being sufficiently addressed. Autumn is currently going through a typically rebellious phase of adolescence, which includes sullenness, anxiety, but also hopes for the future. On the basis of the lengthy interviews I conducted with both her and her sister Hope, I have no doubts that she is in good hands with her sister and will likely grow into an intelligent and successful young woman.

I would, however, add that the responsibilities of being her younger sister's guardian are taxing for Hope. She appears withdrawn and tired, and I would recommend a follow-up welfare check on the family in around six months' time.
Signed,

Anita Tollman
Child Protection Officer

To my best friend Hope!
   Welcome to the 21-Club :)
      Much love, Janey
         PS. Drinks are on me next time I'm in town!

To Hope,
   Happy birthday,
      From Autumn

Happy 21st Birthday, darling! We hope you like the present.
   Love from Nan & Grandpa

Book gift voucher: *How To Boil An Egg* by Jane Arkless

Hope, dearest, as an extra-special gift, I've had your personalised horoscope created by Madame Zargo here in Sydney. She's a well-known astrologer in certain circles and has given me invaluable advice ever since I met her last year at my Sassy Over-Seventies Ladies Group. A word of caution: Don't mention this to Grandpa; he thinks it's a load of hocus pocus and a waste of money, and wouldn't let me hear the last of it if he found out!

Love, Nan

Personalised Gemini horoscope! Saturn will be seen moving through the ninth position next month. In this period, you shall find peace of mind and restfulness, although Jupiter in conjunction with Pluto on 30 June will bring about radical change. You should avoid making any big financial plans and postpone all the investments that you have wanted to make, but you will be getting some positive vibes related to your financial conditions throughout the year, especially when Venus enters your sign in November. It all depends on how you make use of these opportunities. The progressive Jupiter will directly transit in a fix nature air sign Aquarius, so you will enjoy a great bond with your beloved. However, you are advised to also give space to your partner and not force your feelings onto them. Avoid making drastic changes to your appearance!

TO:	Hope Sullivan
FROM:	A Cut Above
SUBJECT:	Your hair appointment

Dear customer,

We are sorry you've had to cancel your appointment. Please give us a call at the number below if you would like to rebook.

Kind regards,
Sandy
Stylist – A Cut Above

Happy birthday to my longest-serving employee!
May this new year bring everything you 'Hope' for.
Harry
PS. The wife thought you might appreciate a little treat

PureLife Wellness Spa
Rediscover Your Inner Zen At Our Oasis of Tranquillity*

Choose from our range of exceptional massages, including Lomi Lomi Nui, Shiatsu, Abhyanga and Hot Stones to regenerate and revitalise the inner you

*Just off the M40 at Junction 6

So glad to hear you enjoyed your spa day, Hope! No need to keep saying thank you, it was our pleasure. I hope you take more quality time for yourself in future – you deserve it. Love, Harry and Ingrid

CHILD WELFARE AGENCY
Family Social Care Services

Regarding: Hope and Autumn Sullivan
A follow-up welfare check was carried out at the above property on 31st May. I am pleased to write that the minor, Autumn Sullivan, has settled down and seemingly overcome the troubles of adolescence. This impression has been confirmed by Autumn's teachers, who have reported regular attendance and engagement with her schoolwork.
Autumn's guardian, older sister Hope Sullivan, also appears to be coping better than during my last visit, and makes a very mature – if a little introspective – impression for her young age (21 years).

In summary, I have no remaining concerns about either Autumn or Hope's welfare and do not consider any further welfare checks necessary.
Signed,

Anita Tollman
Child Protection Officer

I'm graduating on 10th July! I will not accept any excuses. Jx

To my Best Friend,
Thanks for being there for me and reapplying my mascara. I never thought I'd ever manage to outcry mum! Didn't Eric look fantastic in his suit? I can't believe we're both auditioning for the same orchestra! Sometimes fate gets it right . . .
I'm so sad that you and me didn't get to graduate together, Hope, but if the last three years have taught me anything, it's that music is magic. It lives in your soul, always. It will find you eventually. Put the enclosed up on your fridge – in case you ever forget how special you are.
All my love, Janey x

Hope is the thing with feathers
That perches in the soul,
And sings the tune without the words,
And never stops at all.
                                    Emily Dickinson

CHAPTER 11

FROM: Janey Williams
TO: Hope Sullivan
SUBJECT: Whassup?

Hey sweetie!

I've got a half-hour break between rehearsals so I thought I'd check in with you. I'm sitting in the concert hall cafeteria, where they serve the most disgusting food ever. I'm currently staring down at an unidentifiable something on my plate, wondering: is it a pizza? Is it a burger? Is it a . . . burger pizza? (You know as well as I do that I'm gonna eat it, though!)

How's everything going? Is Autumn still bumming you out? Mum mentioned something about social services – sounds like a nightmare. Chin up, though Hope, I'm sure they'll see how well you're looking after Autumn.

I don't have much news, really. My waking hours revolve around rehearsals, and I have to smother my lips in Vaseline every night cos otherwise they dry out like hell. But I'm not complaining; life is quite exciting. The orchestra is good, and I mean *really* good. I always thought I was pretty talented, if I say so myself :), but playing beside some of the musicians who've been doing this for years is humbling, to put it mildly. But it's a great way to improve, so I'm very grateful for this opportunity.

The conductor's a bit scary, to be honest. He's Icelandic, so I'm not sure if it's a cultural thing, but he kind of sings instead of talking and I only catch half of what he's saying. Like earlier this morning, the strings were rehearsing Brahms' 4th and Álfgrímur (we call him Alfie for short) was waving his hand about in the air and crooning something that came out as 'Eeearrth forrr gdööman'. It sounds like the Swedish national anthem in a mumbly Welsh accent.

I'd record him on my phone to play to you, but he's dead set against phones at rehearsal. He actually confiscated the double bass's mobile the other day and warbled, 'YOU MAAAAY HAVE IT BACK AT ZEEE END OF PRRRRACTICE.' (Alfie is a musical genius, though, so everyone's a little in awe of him. Nothing at all like the maestro at FairClef. Remember him?)

What worries me a bit is I think Alfie's clocked that me and Eric are an item. I don't know if they frown on that sort of thing here, so we're keeping it quiet for now. Well, *I'm* keeping it quiet, or trying to, but Eric thinks we should let the whole world know we're a couple. I mean, I'm still really, really into him, but . . . I don't know how to explain it. After we got together at college, that was it. Everybody saw us as a couple, not as two individuals. Sometimes, just sometimes, I wish people would see only *me*. Does that sound selfish? I feel like there's this whole Brangelina vibe going on and I'm not sure I like it.

But hey, listen to me going on about my love life! What I'd really like to know is how *your* love life is going. I'm going to assume you've been on a date or two (or three), and I want to know EVERYTHING.

OK, that's it for today. Alfie is yelling for the 'Woooodwinds . . .'

I miss you.

Love,
Janey x

FROM: Janey Williams
TO: Hope Sullivan
SUBJECT: Re: Eat your veggies!!!

You sound just like Mum! No, you don't have to worry that I'm living entirely off junk food. Yes, I am getting my five-a-day (appletinis count, right?) and I walk to and from rehearsals, so you can tick off the exercise, too. I'm a grown-up who just happens to like a certain food group more than the others, LOL. So stop worrying!

By the way, if I ever hear you repeat 'Janey + Eric = Jeric' again, I shall cancel our friendship. Seriously though, I didn't want to come across as unhappy or anything. I mean, I love being with Eric, I really do. He's sweet and attentive, we have our music in common and sometimes stay up late talking about augmented sixth chords and harmonic resolution. And I'm really, really attracted to him still. But he's so terribly insecure about us. I've tried to bring it up, gently, but he's incredibly touchy. Hmm, you and me will have to have a proper face-to-face chat about this when I'm back. That's what girlfriends are for, right?

Oh, and another thing we *definitely* have to talk about is your love life, or lack thereof. 'I don't have time' is the lamest excuse ever, and if you think I'm letting you off the hook that easily, you'd better think again. I realise you have a full-time job, but so do millions of other people, and they're still falling in love and having sex and getting married and making babies, right? RIGHT?! Don't make me worry you're turning into some kind of femcel. That is *not* what I want for my clever, beautiful, funny friend.

But – whoop! – great news about Autumn! It must be such a relief that she's finally settling down. And that she wants to study medicine! It boggles the mind, haha. But better wannabe-doctor-Autumn over juvenile-delinquent-Autumn, I reckon. And always handy to have a doctor in the family. Give

her a big cuddle from me and wish her all the best for her
exams.

Love,
Janey x

FROM: Janey Williams
TO: Hope Sullivan
SUBJECT: Sorry

OK, I take it back. You are not going to turn into a femcel and
I'm sorry I suggested it. I guess the sugary snacks I'm living off
are making me a bit overexcited. (Only kidding. I had a banana
for breakfast this morning, so there.) But I promise to stay off
your back about this for a while – only for a while though . . .

In other news, my first concert's in three weeks' time. I'm so
nervous, Hope! What if I mess up? The thing with the flute is
that you can hear every frigging mistake, and I have night-
mares where I'm sitting in front of thousands of people letting
out nothing but high-pitched squeaks. I think I'll have to start
doing some meditation exercises or something. But then I tell
myself that this is what I've always dreamt of, and it does make
me feel better. Actually, this is what we *both* dreamt of, remember? Be honest, Hope, don't you miss it? Just a teeny tiny bit?
The sheer joy of playing, when the music sweeps you up and
makes you forget all the shit – the hangover, the unpaid bills,
the dishes that need washing and the tax return that needs
filing . . . Sorry. I'll stop there. I know this is a sore subject for
you.

Anyway, I'll keep you updated about everything. Maybe I can
call you the night before the concert? It's always good to hear
your voice.

Lots of love,
Janey x

LEEDS SCHOOL OF MEDICINE
University of Leeds, Woodhouse, Leeds, LS2

Dear Ms Sullivan,

<u>Unconditional Offer of Admission</u>

We are pleased to confirm that the School of Medicine, University of Leeds, has made an unconditional offer of admission to Ms Autumn Sullivan for the course shown below

Title of course: MBChB Medicine and Surgery
Department: Faculty of Medicine and Health
Mode of study: 4 years full-time

You may refer to our website for information concerning the academic programme, welcome events and enrolment procedures.

We look forward to welcoming you at the University of Leeds! Kind regards,

Liz Young
Director of Admissions

FROM: Autumn Sullivan
TO: Hope Sullivan
SUBJECT: Cat lady

Hi Hope,

Just wanted to let you know that yes, I did manage to find my way to Leeds without getting lost. The other students are really friendly and I've already signed up for a whole load of clubs & socs (badminton, photography, MedSoc). I'm really excited about the course and can't wait for it to start next week!

It's actually OK living in Halls. My roomie is also studying medicine (2nd year) and she knows *all* the people and *all* the parties! I'm gonna have the greatest time here, I just know it!!!

So, what are you up to? Are you gonna finally get yourself a boyfriend now that your annoying little sister has finally moved out? Or maybe you'll get a cat or two, haha. Seriously though, you should make sure to get out more, or at least get yourself a hobby or something. It's not good to spend so much time on your own. You know all those romcoms you watch are *fiction*, right? If you want to meet someone, you have to get out there . . .

Oh, and can you send me my blue jacket (you know, the water-proof one)? It started raining when I stepped off the train and hasn't stopped since :(

All best, Autumn

PS. Give my love to Sandra if you see her and tell her that I'll miss her pepperpot and her sticky toffee pudding

When I said hobby, I didn't mean knitting. But
thanks for the scarf :) it's really lovely. Don't
worry, the wobbly row gives it character.

Don't suppose you could transfer
£20 to my account? A xxx

CHAPTER 12

FROM: Alexander Forbes-Doyle
TO: Harry's Harmonies
SUBJECT: Complaint

Dear Manager,

I am writing to make a complaint regarding an entirely unsatisfactory encounter with your sales assistant today. Two weeks ago, I purchased an oboe (see attached sales receipt) for my 7-year-old daughter Allegra, who has shown exceptional musical promise since she was very young. It appears, however, that the instrument you sold us is of inferior quality. When Allegra attempts to play, the oboe produces grotesque sounds that can only be described as the noise a strangled duck would make.

Consequently, I went back to your shop to request restitution; specifically, my wife and I are of the opinion that Harry's Harmonies should provide us with a replacement instrument of higher quality. It is, in our view, only right and proper that we should not be made to 'pay the difference', as your assistant put it. Rather, the price difference would reflect recompense for the disappointment caused to our daughter, whose trust in her own musical potential may have been seriously damaged by this experience. Regrettably, and despite my remonstrations, your sales assistant flat-out refused, leading me to write this email.

I await your response and remain,

Sincerely,
Alexander Forbes-Doyle

FROM: Harry's Harmonies
TO: Alexander Forbes-Doyle
CC: Hope Sullivan
SUBJECT: Re: Complaint

Dear Mr Forbes-Doyle,

Thank you for your email. This is quite some coincidence, as I
have already had the pleasure of meeting your daughter
Allegra. She attends Greencross Primary School, doesn't she?
That's where my wife and I run an instrument carousel for the
children. We give the children the opportunity to try out different instruments to see which one, if any, is the best fit. Allegra
recently attended one of our courses, and while she is
undoubtedly enthusiastic and unusually confident in her own
abilities, she is not, in fairness, what one might describe as a
wunderkind. In fact, she displays quite some impatience and
has a tendency to mishandle instruments that fail to do her
'bidding'. Of course, this is quite natural in children of her age,
and I would be loath to dissuade her from enjoying music. The
oboe, however, is one of the more difficult instruments to play,
and in light of this, I would suggest Allegra start with something simpler – a recorder, perhaps? We also have an assort-
ment of triangles in stock.

Best regards,
Harry Clark

FROM: Harry's Harmonies
TO: Hope Sullivan
SUBJECT: Re: Re: Complaint

No need to thank me, Hope. I had great fun writing it!

FROM: Janey Williams
TO: Hope Sullivan
SUBJECT: News!

We're going on tour! Europe first, and if it's a success, then the WORLD. Eeeeeeeeeeeeeeeeeeeeeeeeeeeeeekkkkk!!!

CHAPTER 13

Dear Hope,

Just a quick one to say hi from Vienna! Hardly had a moment to catch my breath between rehearsals and performances and eating all the *Sachertorte* . . .

Sending you love, Janey

Dear Hope Sullivan
You have purchased: *Mozart in the Jungle – Series one*
Click **here** to review

MASALA DELIGHT TAKEAWAY

1 Cabernet Sauvignon (75 cl)	£18.00
1 Chicken biriyani	£9.99
1 Tub Ben & Jerry's Chocolate Fudge Brownie (8 oz)	£6.99
	£34.98

Hey there! Verona is gorgeous – me & Eric (and a thousand other tourists) did the Romeo & Juliet scene. Swoon . . .

Love, Janey

Greetings from Prague! Beautiful city, you must visit when you can, Hope!

Love, Janey & Eric

Dear Hope Sullivan,

Thank you for your enquiry about the Prague City break!!!

With its perfect blend of historic influence and the modern feel of a cosmopolitan city, Prague has everything your heart desires! Wander through the labyrinth of cobbled streets, where you'll find cosy cafes against the backdrop of ancient castles and spectacular cathedrals. Explore the historic Old Town and soak up its medieval splendour. Enjoy shopping and fine dining, or late-night dancing in a trendy nightclub. Perfect for a romantic getaway or a weekend of fun. Book now at dreamtravels.com!

  3 nights incl. flight (London Gatwick – Prague)   £499

Opening balance	**£522.29**
Direct debit MORTGAGE PAYMENT	£450.00
Online transaction SANJI'S DELI	£11.98
Direct debit NETFLIX	£8.99
Online transaction MARCELLO'S PIZZA	£10.99
Standing order AUTUMN SULLIVAN	£50.00
Current balance	**– £9.67**

You have successfully unsubscribed from dreamtravels.com

FROM: Janey Williams
TO: Hope Sullivan
SUBJECT: Never go to Brussels

Dear Hope,

Well, we're on the final leg of the tour and we're all feeling pretty knackered now. I for one will be glad when it's over! I'm currently sitting in the world's skankiest hotel room in Brussels. The room is the size of a closet, the window looks onto a multi-storey carpark, the bedsprings feel like they sprung at least five years ago, and this morning I made the mistake of crossing the carpet barefoot – it was sticky . . . ewww.

The concert hall, Studio 4, has incredible acoustics, but step outside and it is the most booooooring place ever. I guess I've been spoiled by the likes of Prague, Berlin and Barcelona, but unless you've got a good reason to go to Brussels, I'd avoid it. There's a limit to how many waffles, chips and chocolates you can eat – and this is *me* we're talking about! Eric's been great, though. (I take back everything mean I've ever said about him.) Last night he scouted out a sushi bar, so we didn't have to eat in the hotel restaurant that smells suspiciously like boiled nappies. There are little pots with dead flowers on every table. I mean, if you're gonna have flowers, at least have fresh ones! (OMG, I sound like such a diva, haha!!!)

Oh, and you'll never guess who I ran into! Do you remember Max Russell? He used to play clarinet in the youth orchestra, and we went to a party where you arm-wrestled him to tears, remember? Well, I was coming out of the concert hall last night, looking forward (not) to spending the evening in Hotel Skanky, when I was approached by this guy who grinned sheepishly and asked if I recognised him. I did, of course, even though he's grown a bit around the middle and lost quite a bit of hair.

He looked a bit lost and eager at the same time, so I stopped to chat for a little while. He told me that he was working in Brussels as a sound engineer, which surprised me, because he'd been such a gifted clarinet player back in the day (even if he was a tosser). I was sure he'd have his choice of music colleges and go on to have a brilliant career. Do you remember him playing in the Weber Concerto? I swear I saw

Maestro wipe away a tear. So anyway, we got talking and he told me he'd failed to make the cut. Apparently, his parents were seriously ambitious for him, making him practise deep into the night, grounding him if he didn't get all the solo parts. He only just scraped through his A Levels cos his parents made him focus on his music. Then, the night before his audition for music college, he had a breakdown. Panic attack, palpitations, profuse sweating, chest pain – the works. He refused to get out of bed the next morning and just lay there while his mum and dad ranted and raved and yelled at him. The next day, he packed his stuff and moved in with his gran, and after a while met a Belgian girl and moved to Brussels.

So it goes, I guess. But it makes me feel so grateful for the mum I have. I mean, she still can't tell Mendelssohn from Mozart, but she never ever pushed me into doing anything I didn't want for myself. But there is a happy ending: Max says he's happy in his job cos he gets to be around music, which he still loves, but without all the pressure. Plus, he married the Belgian girl and she's pregnant with their first child.

He asked about you, what orchestra you were playing in, whether you and me were still in touch etc. I was at a bit of a loss as to what to tell him, to be honest. I know you don't want to hear it, but I still get upset sometimes that you gave up before you even started. I know you keep saying you're fine with the way things are, but you had so much potential, Hope. Surely there's a tiny part of you that wonders what might have been?

Anyway, 'nuff said. I still love you loads and just want you to be happy. I'll let you know when I arrive back and we'll go out dancing. So get your glad rags ready, ok?!

Janey xx

HARRY'S HARMONIES
Strings 'n' Things

Dear Hope,

As discussed, we are delighted to formally offer you the post of Manager at *Harry's Harmonies*. This new position comes with a pay rise of 5% (sorry it's not more) and use of the company car. We fully trust that you will excel in your new role.

With kind regards,

Harry March

No worries. Would've been nice to have a drink together, but work commitments come first, I guess! I hope you don't have to wait around too long for your supplier. We will DEFINITELY meet up next time I'm in town, though!!! Love, Janey

CHAPTER 14

Dear Hope, can you read this? I've made

Sorry, I don't know what happened there! I think I pressed enter and the message was sent by mistake. Well, your old Nan has made it onto the face book! It's great, isn't it? Write back when you can! I do hope you can read this message. Love, Nan

FINALLY SHE REPLIES!!! I've been waiting for days, Hope. Why are you surprised I'm on the face book? I'm not as rusty as you think. This is great fun though, isn't it? I can see how the young people get such a kick from sitting at the computer all day. We are both well, thank you for asking. Lovely to hear from you, of course, but all you seem to talk about is your work. Not that it isn't important, and congratulations on your promotion to manager, but you need to make sure to have some fun, too. You're still young and you'll have plenty of time for all of that work stuff when you get older.

I was talking to Madame Zargo recently, and your age came up. (And before you start, yes, I am still seeing Madame Zargo. She does Tarot readings and star charts and helps me make important life decisions. When you get to my age, you will realise how even the tiniest decisions can make a huge difference along the line, so you have to make sure you make the right ones.) Anyway, she was thrilled to hear you are 27! Apparently, this number has special energies because it's the 'trinity of trinities'. That is, 3 is the cubed root of 27, and 3 squared is 9, and 9 multiplied by 3 is 27! It all makes perfect sense when you think about it. Long story short, Madame Zargo says it's the perfect age to seize the day! So please, no more messages about work and more about the fun you're having! YOLO (that's what they say, isn't it?)

We haven't heard from Autumn for a while. She's about to head into her final exams, isn't she? Please tell her we're thinking of her, and to let us know how she does.

Right, my love, I'll leave it there. Grandpa is giving me the evil eye from the dining room. Between you and me, he's just irked that he hasn't the first clue about the social media and thinks I'm sitting here gossiping about *him* all day long. Ha! As if he's that interesting . . .

Lots of love, Nan

Dear Hope,
Sorry I missed you! I managed to get an early hairdresser's appointment and needed to head out before you came into the shop. Do you remember I told you about Larry, our neighbours' son? Well, I've spoken to him (and showed him your photo!) and he would love to take you out for dinner! He's very keen on cats, so I'm sure you two would have plenty to talk about. What do you think?
Best, Ingrid

FROM: Janey Williams
TO: Hope Sullivan
SUBJECT: Re: Cat balls

Dear Hope,

I left you a couple of messages, but I suppose you're really busy at work. Congrats on your promotion! Do you wear smart little business suits now, lol?

You have to call me when you've a moment. I need to know more about this date you went on! Was he the one your boss's wife wanted to set you up with? He sounds like a total creep – and what kind of name is Larry, anyway? I suppose it's kind of impressive that he knows so much about cats (though why Ingrid thought *you* were into cats is beyond me. Is there something you haven't been telling me?). You said you were bored out of your mind hearing all the facts about *Felis catus*, but think of it this way: if you're ever in a pub quiz and need to know that the oldest known pet cat existed 9,500 years ago, they can rotate their ears 180 degrees, and that they spend 70% of their lives sleeping, you'll end up thanking Larry :) Besides, he does kind of have a point about a responsible pet owner having a duty to know stuff about their pet, right?

Tbh, I was a *little* surprised to hear you took him home, especially after that story about him mimicking a cat gagging up a hairball over dinner, ewwww. I know you'd had too much wine, but was that really the sensible thing to do? There are so many weirdos out there, Hope. I mean, everyone needs a kiss and a cuddle now and again, but you've really got to set your standards higher, girl! Anyway, glad to hear you won't be going out with him again. A double date with Larry doesn't sound like my idea of fun.

Eric sends his love. Can you believe we've been an item for seven years now? Where has the time gone? If my mum had her way, we'd have been married for the best part of that with me having churned out half a dozen babies by now. Speaking of, she said she bumped into you on the High Street the other day. She's lost loads of weight, hasn't she? I think I'm going to have to ask what diet she's on, cos I must have put on at least a stone when we were on tour.

What's Autumn up to these days? Mum mentioned they'd been out for coffee, but didn't have many details. If you see her, please say hi!

Look after yourself and promise me you won't go on any more dodgy dates!!! I'll try and call again tomorrow, see if we can't come up with a proper plan to meet Mr Perfect.

Lots of love,
Janey

The University of Leeds School of Medicine
has this day awarded the degrees of

BACHELOR OF MEDICINE
and
BACHELOR OF SURGERY
to

Autumn Mary Sullivan

I heard about Autumn! We're ever so proud of her. Do give her our love. I would call her myself, but I can't find her landline number, and my mobile phone operator charges a fortune for overseas calls. Do young people even have landline numbers these days? I'm doing my best to keep up, but things seem to be changing at such a fast pace! Anyway, I see you've changed your profile picture. You look ever so skinny, dear. Still lovely, of course, but I hope you've been eating properly. I know you're not much of a cook – perhaps you might find a boyfriend who's a dab hand in the kitchen? Always a good idea to consider a prospective partner's skill set. Not that I did way back when; if I had, I might have chosen a husband who knows how to unclog a sink or even give a decent foot massage. But at least Grandpa's always up for a bit of fun. We've taken up Zumba! Have you heard of it? I know the sight of Grandpa doing Latin dance moves dressed in Lycra isn't everyone's cup of tea, but he's actually quite the mover. I will post some pictures here so you can take a look. Now listen, love, there's something I've been meaning to ask you. I've been thinking how well Autumn has done, and of course that makes me wonder what your plans are. Don't you think it's time you moved on, too? Career-wise, I mean. Madame Zargo says it's a great year for change for Geminis. I know your opinion on Madame Zargo, but it's just a bit of fun, really. You certainly don't have to start worrying about me 'falling under the spell of some fortune-teller', as you put it so articulately in your last message. But think about it, love. You've been managing that shop for a while now, and as much as you say you enjoy it, is that all you really want from your professional life? Have you thought about getting some proper qualifications? You can learn all sorts of things on an evening course, or even study online. Then you could apply for a proper job. And your work experience at the shop would look great on a CV. Do let me know what you think, I always love to hear from you. Love, Nan & Grandpa

Did you get my message, dear? The little icon at the bottom says that you've read it, but I'm not sure I trust these things entirely. If you have, and you've just been too busy to reply, never mind. I just hope I didn't write anything to offend you in my last message. Please know that you are not and will never be a disappointment to us. We only ever want what's best for you, and if I'm being a silly old goat sticking her nose in where it doesn't belong, it's all right to tell me. All my love, Nan

With their families,

Janey Zora Williams & Eric Matthew Carlson

request the pleasure of your company (+ one)
at their
Wedding Ceremony
On Saturday, 5th July
At the Pavilion, Grove House

Hey there! So happy you can make it, but can't you at least *try* to find a +1??? Jx

FROM: Janey Williams
TO: Hope Sullivan; Autumn Sullivan
SUBJECT: Seriously?

Hi both of you,

Just a quick one, as I'm busy packing for the honeymoon. Eric says I have to limit myself to two suitcases, and I'm not gonna lie – it's a struggle!

Thanks so much for being there yesterday! It was the best, wasn't it? But seriously, Autumn, a whoopee cushion? You're 21 for Christ's sake! (The look on my sister-in-law's face was priceless though, so you're forgiven this once.)

Love to you both, and I'll call when I'm back,

Janey x

Autumn Sullivan
Hope Sullivan
You can't get rid of me that easily!

Dear Hope,

HUGE NEWS!!! That placement at St Michael's I told you about, the one only 10 minutes away from you? I just got a letter of acceptance! Yay!!! We'll be able to see much more of each other. So brush your hair and dig out your makeup, cos I'm gonna be forcing a social life on you! Oh, and don't worry about me and my mess moving back in with you – I'll be house-sharing with two friends from uni till I've saved up enough to afford my own place. Or maybe a place for me and Krish . . .?

See you soon, Autumn x

Greetings from Jamaica! Oh my God, Hope, this is the BEST honeymoon ever! Haven't seen much of the beach, though . . . Kisses, Janey

Dear Hope,
   Congratulations on your 9th anniversary at Harry's Harmonies! We'd just like to express how pleased we are to have you. It's amazing to think that nine years have passed since you first started working here. God knows what state the place would be in without you! Please accept the gift as a small token of our thanks.
   With very best wishes and thanks,
      Ingrid and Harry

The Royal Albert Hall presents
The Royal Philharmonic Orchestra

playing

Paganini – Violin Concerto No. 2 in B Minor

Time: 7.00 pm (doors open 6.30 pm)

Date: 9th September

QWIK BUY MART

Kleenex Extra Large tissues Pack of 6	£ 2.99
Gordon's Premium Pink Gin & Tonic	
Premix 4 x 250 ml	£ 6.00
	£ 8.99

Are you OK? I'm here if you need to talk.
Just knock. Ellie (your upstairs neighbour)

CHAPTER 15

Happy New Year, sis! Got a minute?

Happy New Year to you too. And sure

I met this guy at work today

Another one, Autumn? What happened to Krish?

No, not for me, for you

FFS, Autumn! I've TOLD you about trying
to set me up with guys you meet at work.
That last one was a right weirdo

I thought he was cute

He chewed with his mouth open, all the
better to see the spinach stuck in his teeth

Haha. Yeah, sorry about that. But listen

Please, A. I'm happy as I am. You have
my permission to set me up with s/o
when I've turned into a cat lady and my
house smells of cat litter and Whiskas

Noted. But chill out, Hope, this guy is really
sweet. His name is Arnold, he's about 70 and
he comes in for regular heart checks. He had a
heart attack a year ago and moved into assisted
living. I got the feeling he was a bit lonely

So you thought of me? Thanks

I did, actually. Given that you spend so much
time writing to Janey, I thought you might
like to write to him, too. I've already asked
him if I could give you his address, but fine,
if you don't want to help a lonely old man,
I'll tell him you can't be bothered . . .

I know what ur doing

What?

Ur trying to guilt-trip me

Who, moi?

Ok then. Fine. I don't have the first clue why you
think he might like to hear from me – it's not like
I have all that much to say for myself nowadays –
but I don't suppose I have much choice now, do I?

Not really, sis. But don't worry, I think you and
Arnold are gonna get along just fine . . .

29th January

Dear Arnold,

My sister Autumn gave me your address and suggested it
might be nice to get in touch. I'm not sure that I've got
anything very interesting to say, but I always think it's nice to
get letters in the post. (Well, letters that aren't bills, that
is . . .) I do apologise if you felt pressured by Autumn to give
out your address – she can be pushy sometimes – and I
won't be offended in the slightest if you don't feel like
answering!

How are you? Autumn told me you hadn't been well lately
– I do hope you're feeling better. You're certainly in the best
medical hands with my sister, she was top of her class at uni!
She can be a bit of a busybody (hence her foisting my letters
on you – I can only apologise!) and she's quite headstrong, but
she seems to know what she wants from life, and that's an
admirable quality in anyone. I could certainly do with some of
her motivation at times, but the mundane stuff just seems to
get in the way. I don't know how Autumn does it – the job, the
boyfriend, kitesurfing at the weekends. She's even taking an
online Portuguese course. I mean, where does she get the time
and energy? All I can manage at the weekends is *Strictly* and
an early night.

82

It's been quite a mild winter, hasn't it? I know I should be worried about climate change and all that, but between you and me, I don't miss the freezing cold mornings when I have to get out of bed and go to work. And guaranteed my boiler will cut out whenever the temperature drops below 5 °C, which is a nightmare. Though they do say that cold showers are good for you, don't they? Gosh, listen to me going on about the weather! How English can you get?

Well, that's enough about me. It would be lovely to hear something about you. Do you have any hobbies? A favourite TV programme? If you need any recommendations, I've just about binge-watched every Netflix show available, so I'm happy to share. Drama, true crime, comedy, I've seen 'em all. Or perhaps you like music? Sorry if I'm sounding nosy, it's just that I don't socialise much these days. You'd have thought social skills are like riding a bike – once learned, you never forget – but maybe not. I should probably get out more, like Autumn!

Anyway, it would be lovely to hear from you, but as I said earlier, I wouldn't hold it against you if you didn't write back.

Love, Hope

PS. I hope it's OK to call you by your first name? It feels a little disrespectful without having met you in person, but Autumn said you didn't seem the type to insist on formalities.

15th February

Dear Hope,

Thank you so much for your kind letter. It was lovely to hear from you, and I very much appreciate the time and effort you put into writing to an old man such as myself. I hadn't realised old-fashioned letter-writing was still a thing! It seems to be all emails and text messages these days. Yours is the first hand-written letter I've received in, gosh, I don't know how

many years. And such tidy print! Please forgive my scribbles
– I used to have reasonably legible handwriting, but with age
come the shakes, I'm afraid.

Thanks for offering to recommend TV programmes, but I
don't watch much telly these days. There is a huge flat-screen
TV in the common room here at Sunny Fields (that's the
assisted living facility I'm living in, as you'll know from my
address), which covers most of the back wall. I'd never seen
anything like it before I moved here, but I suppose it's handy
for all the residents here who can't see too well any more. I
don't spend much time in the common room, though. The
other residents are perfectly pleasant, but I'm afraid I find too
much conversation draining these days. I prefer to stay in my
little flat. It faces out onto a park, and it's entertainment
enough for me to sit and watch the dog walkers and couples
and the children playing football. There's a group of local teenagers who meet up in a disused bandstand in the park. Young
people get a pretty bad rap nowadays, but this group is harmless, I think. They just sit and talk and mess around; sometimes
they listen to music that's not to my taste, but it would be a
boring old world if we all liked the same things, wouldn't it?

Sorry for waffling on like this; it's what tends to happen
when you grow old. That and the shaking. 'Waffle & Shake'
– sounds like a dance from the 1950s, doesn't it?

Well, I shall leave it there for now. It was lovely to get your
letter, Hope. And if you wanted to indulge an old fellow with
nothing much left to do but twiddle his thumbs, I'd be
delighted to hear back from you.

With warm regards,
Arnold

PS. Please feel free to call me Arnold. I am a retired schoolteacher, and if I don't hear anyone call me Mr Quince for the
rest of my life, I'll be a happy man.

I'm in town! Let's have a girls' night out! Call me! Jx

Hi Janey, sorry to bail on you – again – but
I've got a really bad headache and think I'll
have an early night. Next time, promise. Hx

3rd March

Dear Arnold,

Thanks so much for writing back, it was lovely to get your letter. It sounds nice at Sunny Fields. I'd love to hear more of what life is like there. Are there lots of activities on offer, or does everyone just do their own thing? I've heard some people say that retirement is the best time of their life, whereas others get totally bored and struggle to pass the time. I suppose it depends on how good you are at keeping yourself busy.

My grandparents, for instance, retired a while ago and they are busier than ever. They've been through more hobbies than I can count: flower arranging (which didn't last long as my grandad has allergies), amateur dramatics (this lasted about two months before they were chucked out for behaving like divas), and most recently, Zumba. Do you know it? It's basically a fitness programme using Latin dance moves, and it's supposed to keep you super fit, although I give my grandparents three months at most before they get involved in some overpriced high-dose vitamin scam. They're incredibly lovely, but very gullible. My nan, for example, has become interested in the 'ancient art' of fortune-telling, and I'm sure my grandad would have a fit if he knew she was paying some charlatan (who goes by the name of 'Madame Zargo') to tell her that it's bad luck to put her left sock on first when Mercury is in retrograde during the second full moon of the year.

I'm joking, really; I'm happy that they seem to be enjoying life so much. They're a very lively couple, but I do worry that something might happen to them before I see them again. My grandpa has had a 'heart issue' for a few years now – they won't tell me exactly what that means, but I doubt it's anything good – and he takes exercise and healthy eating extremely seriously. I only wish I could see them more often. They moved to Australia when I was three, and I can count on one hand the number of times I've actually *seen* them. If I had the time and the money, I'd get on a plane to go and visit them every Christmas. But as I have very little of the former, and even less of the latter, I guess it'll be a while before I see them. Then again, it's only March, and who knows what the rest of the year will bring?

I very much look forward to your next letter.

Love, Hope

10th March

Dear Hope,

Your grandparents sound delightful. How wonderful to be so full of life! I can understand your concern about your grandfather's health, but if he's exercising and eating well, then he seems to be doing the right thing. I have to admit that since my heart attack, I haven't been as disciplined as your grandfather with regard to diet and exercise. One of the nurses keeps trying to coax me into joining the weekly yoga class they put on here, saying it increases bone density and flexibility, but what use is that at my age? I have no ambitions to be able to wrap my leg around my head, and I don't have much inclination for group activities, I'm afraid. A short walk around the grounds is enough for me these days.

How easy it is to take good health for granted when you're young! Your hips, knees, heart – your body just working away as it was meant to do, until you begin to notice the twinges in your joints, or that nagging ache in your lower back that just doesn't seem to want to go away. Before you know it, your weekly schedule revolves around doctor's visits. Though to be honest, I avoided doctors like the plague after my wife passed. Who knows, maybe I would have stayed healthy for longer if I'd gone in for regular check-ups, but my wife was sick for a long time before she died, and afterwards I found that I just couldn't bear the sight of white coats.

And then, out of the blue, I had a heart attack. I was at the post office when it happened. If I had been at home, I don't suppose I would have lived to tell the tale. I remember standing in the queue with this nagging pain in my jaw and thinking that I'd perhaps put my dentures in incorrectly that morning. Then I felt the classic symptoms – the shortness of breath, the cold sweat, the feeling that something was wrapping itself tightly around my chest – and I knew I was having a heart attack. At first I felt incredibly serene; a light, floating feeling that I would finally be going to be with my wife again. I was relieved, grateful almost. If this is death, I thought, then there's really nothing to be frightened of. But then came the pain. A heart attack really hurts, let me tell you, and before I knew it, I was grabbing onto the fellow in front of me and pleading with him to call an ambulance. Then I passed out, woke up in a hospital bed, and the rest, as they say, is history. When I was well enough to be discharged, my GP suggested moving to Sunny Fields.

It's funny, really, how little I minded leaving the house that had been my home for such a long time. I know that many of my fellow residents fought tooth and nail against moving here, and I feel for them. It requires a certain stoicism to just accept your fate. Or perhaps it's surrender, who knows? Personally, I have found it helpful to view life as being made up of individual chapters. If you can close each one with good grace, all the better.

Now, I shall leave this here. The nurse is knocking with my six o'clock pills, and if I don't answer the door within the next five minutes, I fear he'll be charging into my room with the crash trolley.

All very best, and until next time,
Arnold

Hi Nan

Hope! How lovely to hear from you! Is everything all right?
Everything's fine. I just wanted to hear
how you and Grandpa are doing

That's very sweet of you.
Nan, your Facebook relationship
status says 'It's complicated'

Yes, well. You know what your Grandpa can be like.
Leaves his teeth on top of the telly, forgets where
he's put them and then accuses me of hiding them.
And he was out fishing last week and plain forgot my
doctor's appointment so I had to go on the bus, but
then I arrived home to find he'd bought me a huge
bouquet of roses. And I couldn't stay angry at him
after that. But then he complained that the flowers
bring out his allergies! So – it's complicated.
Hahaha! I don't think that's what the
Facebook people had in mind....

I'd like to see one of them married to your Grandpa
for 57 years and not think it's complicated!
Are you still doing Zumba?

Indeed we are! We've added Aqua Zumba to our fitness
schedule – you really should try it, Hope. It's so much fun!
Um, too busy with work stuff right now

That's just an excuse and we both know it.
Don't bully me, Nan!

Take a leaf out of your sister's book. I follow her on
here and she's forever posting pictures of her and
her fella climbing up mountains or windsurfing.
Yeah, I know. It's exhausting to scroll through her feed

88

If Zumba's not your thing, why don't you join
a running group or something? You never
know, you might even meet someone.
How many times, Nan? I'm not looking to meet someone
Of course you are. Everyone needs someone. And
the exercise won't do you any harm, either.
I know, I know . . .
Promise me you'll give it a go?
OK, I promise

RUNNER'S EDGE

One pair running shoes *Lightning Pro*   £89 (incl. VAT)
(red and silver)

FROM: Reluctant Runners
TO: Hope Sullivan
SUBJECT: Newsletter

Dear Hope,

Thank you for signing up for the Reluctant Runners newsletter! Here is a list of running groups in your area:

Road Runners – We hit the road hard! We meet every Monday and Thursday at 6.30 pm. A gentle 2 km warm-up followed by a fun 10 km! Target speed: approx. 5.30/km. And remember: Bring good vibes and leave your ego at the door! Go hard or go home!

Cool Runnings – We like to run and we love to party! We meet Wednesdays at 7.30 pm at the north end of the park and run like hell to the Queen's Head. Last one there buys the first round!

Miles & Miles – looking for a gentle run with like-minded runners? No fixed pace, just run (or walk) as you can. We're a friendly group of silver-haired runners wanting to stay fit past seventy and beyond. Just bring yourself and a bottle of water. We meet Mondays at 7 am.

RUNNER'S EDGE

Goods returned:
One pair running shoes *Lightning Pro*
Refund   −£89 (incl. VAT)

You have successfully unsubscribed from the Reluctant Runners newsletter. We are sorry to see you go!

CHAPTER 16

Are you at work, sis?

Yes, but I'm on a break. What's up, Hope?

Haven't seen you for a while

Been really busy

Do you want to come round for dinner?

Sorry, late shift tonight

Tomorrow?

Sure. Can I bring Krish?

Course. Be nice to meet him

Red wine OK, or would you prefer white?

Red's fine. Chili OK?

Quelle surprise

???

We both know chili is the only
thing you can cook LOL

Thanks for the confidence in my culinary abilities

Ur welcome

See you tomorrow at 8, then?

Sure. Btw, did you ever get round
to writing to Arnold?

4th April

Dear Arnold,

Thanks for your letter. And thank you for being so open. I
for one am glad you survived your heart attack. I'm sure
there's plenty of life in you yet! I would love to talk you into

taking a yoga class or something, but I'm afraid that would be a bit hypocritical. If I'm good, I might go for a twenty-minute run around the neighbourhood once or twice a month. My grandmother recently suggested I join a running group, but I had a quick look at what's out there, and let's just say it looks about as inviting as online dating. Besides, Autumn is the athletic one in our family. If she's not training for a marathon, she's out mountain biking or rock-climbing. It's exhausting just listening to her talk about it!

Speaking of Autumn, she says hello! She came round the other night for dinner and introduced me to her boyfriend, Krish. They've been together for six months now, which is a record, let me tell you! But they seem very happy together, so perhaps she was right not to stick with the others. In fact, I'm very glad she didn't – especially the first. It was this guy called Marc. Autumn must have been about fifteen at the time, and Marc was two years older. He had this banged-up moped, which he thought was super cool (it wasn't) and whenever he came to pick up Autumn, he'd sit outside and rev the engine to call her out. It was pitiful – mopeds are hardly Harleys, and it sounded like a hairdryer! He didn't even have the courtesy to ring the doorbell. It used to drive me mad that she'd jump up and run out like she'd been summoned. And I was always terrified she'd be killed in an accident, because Marc drove like an idiot. He was a real poser who thought he was god's gift. I breathed a huge sigh of relief when she finally dumped him.

Krish is completely different. He's fairly quiet; not in a shy or aloof kind of way, just measured and calm, which is the perfect counterpoint to Autumn's impulsiveness. Opposites attract, as they say. There's something quite sweet about seeing a couple in love, isn't there? You know, when each one tries to anticipate the other's wishes. For example, I'd made chili con carne for dinner, which is about the only dish I can cook, and as per usual, I hadn't stinted with the spices (which is how Autumn and I like it, and the spices cover a multitude of sins).

Autumn must have known that it was too hot for Krish, because he'd only just put a forkful in his mouth when she jumped up and rushed to the kitchen for a glass of water. Then later, she shivered ever so slightly and he couldn't take off his jumper fast enough to put around her shoulders. They were fussing over each other all evening; I felt a little surplus to requirements after a while, if I'm completely honest. But it was lovely to see my sister so happy.

I don't know if she mentioned it, but our parents died ten years ago, and I've always been afraid that it would affect her badly in adulthood. That she might have trouble forming stable relationships or something. It was something I really worried about when she was growing up, so I'm happy for her to have found Krish. I do hope he's 'the one'. Single life can quickly become lonely if you're not careful. I don't mean me, I'm not lonely or anything. I have my grandparents (even though they live in Australia) and a really good friend I've known since I was little, and I get to meet lots of different people at work. Besides, they say that in today's digital world we are all connected all the time, don't they? Although to be honest, I've never really felt that social media can replace real relationships. Do you have any pets? I've been thinking about getting a kitten, but Autumn thinks that would be a slippery slope to me becoming a 'cat lady' . . .

Love, Hope

11th April

Dear Hope,

I don't think there's anything remotely wrong with cat ladies. Pets can make wonderful companions. My wife and I had a dog, a Yorkshire terrier called Chutney, but he sadly died a while ago. He was a cheeky little thing and kept us very active – he needed three long walks a day or he'd end up chasing his tail all night and keep us awake. We probably spent more time outdoors than in, no matter the weather! That's all changed now, though. I'm encouraged to go for gentle walks once a day, but I'm on immunosuppressants due to my heart condition, and as I mentioned before, my exercise is generally restricted to a twenty-minute stroll in the grounds. But never mind all that, I don't want to bore you with tales of an old man's medical condition.

I'm very sorry to hear about your parents. That must have been very difficult for you and Autumn. I also know a thing or two about grief, I'm afraid; enough to know that it never really passes. Some mornings, I wake up and the day seems to stretch out ahead of me, interminably, and I wonder: What's the point? Why put myself through this endless cycle of waking, waiting for the meaningless hours to drag by, go to bed at night and wake up the next morning only to do the same thing all over again? Now I can't even do the things I used to look forward to because of these pills I have to take. They make me susceptible to infection, you see, so even a common cold could be life-threatening. Sometimes, though, I wonder if I shouldn't just take the chance and go out to the pub, and if that means the end of me, then so be it.

Oh, but listen to me moaning! I do apologise, Hope. In fact, I wonder why you're not out with your friends and having fun, rather than writing to a miserable old fool like me. I'm only joking, of course. It's been delightful hearing from you, and there's not much in the way of delight left in my life. So please carry on writing as much as you wish!

If you don't mind me saying so, you write a lot about your sister, and very little about yourself! She is, of course, a very clever and charming young lady, but it would be nice to hear something about you. You are a few years older than Autumn, I believe. Are you also in the medical profession? They say that intelligence runs in families, so I imagine you also have some high-flying job. A lawyer, perhaps? Or a professor? Or maybe something more exotic and unusual. A lion tamer, a golf ball diver (yes, there is such a thing), a private detective? As you

94

can see, I am prone to letting my imagination run away with me, but I am more than happy to stand corrected.

All best for now,
Arnold

Me and Krish are going to the Vibe Tribe tomorrow
night. Wanna join us? I hear the music's great
Sure. Meet you there at 9?

FROM: Dr A. Sullivan
TO: Hope Sullivan
SUBJECT: Last night

Hey sis, where'd you disappear to?

FROM: Hope Sullivan
TO: Dr A. Sullivan
SUBJECT: Final warning!

Don't you ever try to set me up like that again! I mean, it was bad enough that you sprang the guy on me without telling me first, but where the hell did you find him?!!! You might not have noticed because you and Krish only had eyes – and hands – for each other, but Tarquin (what kind of name is that, anyway?) is a total creep, and whoever gave that guy a medical licence needs their head examined. He had so much dirt under his fingernails it looked like he'd been digging a tunnel with his bare hands. And he *reeked* of aftershave. Not that it had any great effect – I had to breathe through my mouth for most of the night to stop me inhaling that heady mix of Axe and oniony sweat. Oh, and when I tell a guy I don't feel like danc-ing, that means I don't feel like dancing. It's not an invitation to try and arm-wrestle me to the dancefloor. For your informa-tion, Tarquin was lying when he said he 'tripped' over a loose cable. I let him get away with it because I think his male pride was dented enough.

Just because I'm single doesn't mean I have no standards. So, please, for the love of god, never ever ever do that again.

Hope

FROM: Dr A. Sullivan
TO: Hope Sullivan
SUBJECT: Re: Final Warning!

Sorry. Won't happen again :(

18th May

Dear Arnold,

Thanks for your letter. I've really enjoyed writing to you, and I don't mind you moaning at all, as long as you don't mind me moaning back! I suppose I write a lot about my sister because her life is interesting. Certainly more interesting than mine! To be honest, I've never had that many friends since I left school and became Autumn's guardian, so please don't think you're keeping me from having fun. On the contrary, it was a genuine pleasure to find your letter waiting for me on the doorstep when I came home from work today.

I had one of those days, you know, the kind that starts off bad and gets gradually worse. I think I mentioned my faulty gas boiler; well, it was on the blink this morning, so I had to make do with a very cold shower. Then I made myself a cup of tea, but the milk had gone off, so I grabbed a coffee-to-go on the way to work and managed to spill it all over my shirt. Then when I got to work, I realised I'd forgotten the keys and had to go all the way home to get them. When I finally got back, there was a queue of rather irate customers at the door. To top it off, my car broke down on the way home (actually, it's the company car, a rather worn-out VW Polo that has seen better days) and I had to wait two hours in the freezing cold for the AA to come and tow me to a garage. It was past nine when I finally got home, and now I'm sitting here with a hot-water bottle on my feet and a well-deserved glass of wine in front of me. It's lovely to have your letter to respond to; it puts broken-down cars and fussy customers and boring paperwork right out of my mind.

Speaking of work, I'm afraid I don't do anything exciting or exotic. Or intellectually challenging, for that matter. I work in a music shop, which probably sounds very boring, but it's fine (except on days like today). It pays the mortgage, and my boss and his wife are two of the loveliest people you'll ever meet. I've been working there for nearly ten years now, straight out of school, so it's become a sort of second home. It's not the route I had planned to take, far from it . . . but life's like that, right? You have to play the hand you're dealt. I took over the shop management two years ago, and ever since then I've thought about ways to inject a little spirit into the place, put my stamp on it, so to speak.

One idea I've had is to incorporate a small cafe into the shop. There is a large room at the back of the premises that serves as a general utility/storage/dumping space, but I've always thought that a bit of a waste. There are two enormous arched windows facing out onto the canal at the back that let in the most beautiful light. The room certainly needs cleaning, and a fresh coat of paint wouldn't go amiss, but nothing major. With a bit of effort, I think I could make it a nice place for people to come and linger; that would be the plan, anyway. Ha – I'm daydreaming out loud now! It's probably a silly idea, but it's always nice to dream, right?

You mentioned that you used to be a teacher; was that primary or secondary school? And which subjects did you teach? I can't say that I was a model pupil – I'm sure my teachers let out a huge sigh of relief when I left!

Sorry for all the questions! Feel free to ignore them – but as always, it would be lovely to hear back from you.

Love, Hope

FROM: Janey Williams
TO: Hope Sullivan
SUBJECT: Auf wiedersehen

Dear Hope,

I'm gutted I have to head off again before we got the chance to go out! But the Bayreuth Festival is a once-in-a-lifetime opportunity, so I'm not complaining, although four straight weeks of Wagner will be a bit grim. I will have to prepare a suitable counter-programme for when I'm back. How does a girly weekend sound? We can drink margaritas and do each other's hair and work our way through an entire boxset of *A Million Little Things* to see who cries first. (I'll tell Eric it's strictly women only, haha.) Seriously though, I'll miss you to bits.

Have you installed that dating app yet? That last guy Autumn tried to set you up with sounds like a walking disaster, and at least with the app you have *some* control over who you're meeting. And don't give me any bloody excuses about being too busy to start dating right now! You know as well as I do that the chances of Mr Perfect walking through the shop door are close to zero.

I'll put it like this, Hope Sullivan: if you haven't been on at least *one* date by the time I get back, I will come over to your house and singlehandedly drag you by your hair to the nearest pub and loudly announce that you're looking for a f**k.

Best, Janey

PS. I'm not kidding

CHAPTER 17

3rd June

Dear Hope,

Thank you for your letter. I'm sorry to hear you had such a rotten day. That must have been the coldest May on record; even the teenagers in the park didn't manage to stay out longer than half an hour. But at least it seems to be getting warmer now.

Please don't worry about asking questions; it's been a long time since anyone took an interest in me and my life, and writing to you is a very pleasant way to pass the time. I used to have a pen pal, years and years ago when I was sixteen or thereabouts. A young lad in New Zealand and I would write to each other every few weeks – in that stilted, awkward way of teenagers who have never met – and report on the daily goings-on in our lives. Our correspondence fizzled out after six months; I suppose we'd run out of things to say to each other. Once we'd settled the (to us) fascinating question of whether our toilets flush in different directions (there's a theory that the water drains clockwise in the northern hemisphere and anti-clockwise in the southern hemisphere, but thanks to Noah I can tell you it's not true) and failed to agree which was better, rugby or Australian football (it's rugby, in case you're wondering), we realised we had too little in common to continue writing.

Then along came email and all that, and while I understand the efficiency of being able to 'fire off' a quick message at the push of a button, that form of communication lacks charm,

don't you think? There's a certain attentiveness, a considera-
tion that goes into putting pen to paper. And because of the
time it takes for a letter to travel from writer to addressee and
back again, it forces you to be patient, but at the same time it
lends you this wonderful feeling of anticipation. Letters arrive
from the past; by the time you receive one, anything could
have happened to the sender: they might have fallen in or out
of love, have lost or gained a fortune, experienced heartache or
tremendous joy. There's a kind of magic to that, I think. I am
so glad to be recapturing that with you.

You ask about hobbies. Well, I've become fairly interested in
etymology recently. I'm no expert, but the previous resident
left behind a collection of books; dictionaries, encyclopaedias,
that sort of thing, including a book called *The Significance of
Names – Origins and Spiritual Meaning*. (Apropos of one of
your questions: I used to teach English and German, so I've
always had an interest in words and language.)

You both have such lovely names, you and your sister. Hope
and Autumn, so evocative. Were your parents poets, I wonder,
or something similarly creative? My name, Arnold, is derived
from an old Germanic name and means 'eagle power'. I think
that's – how would you young people phrase it? – pretty *cool*
(though I can assure you that my own parents had no idea of
the name's origin. They were very loving parents, but not the
most imaginative people you'd ever meet).

My late wife's name was Marion, which comes from the
Hebrew and means 'from the sea'. The name suited her
perfectly. She was a keen swimmer, right until . . . well, let's not
go into all that here. Suffice it to say, we had some wonderful
seaside holidays together – Cornwall, the Isle of Wight, and
even Phuket the year after we retired – but I haven't travelled
much recently. There's something rather sad about travelling
alone, wouldn't you say? And we all get to an age where the
best is behind us, I suppose, and there's little to do but remi-
nisce. But as long as you have good memories, that's something, isn't it? And I have plenty of those.

My main hobby, when Marion and I were still married, was baking – my cakes and pies and pasties were the stuff of village legend, if I say so myself. My late wife always complained that it was my fault she could never stick to a diet. Not that she was ever fat, mind. She had exactly the right proportions and looked ever so lovely in whatever she wore. Her favourite cake was Black Forest Gateau; I used to bake it every year on our wedding anniversary. The secret is to put melted dark chocolate in the batter, rather than cocoa powder, as most recipes suggest. (This is highly confidential information, Hope, so I trust you'll not pass it on!) Yes, Black Forest Gateau and a bunch of lilies-of-the-valley – Marion could count on that for her birthday. To this day I can't smell her favourite flowers without thinking of her.

Your idea for a cafe in the shop sounds wonderful! Marion and I had always toyed with the idea of opening a little tea shop or B&B when we retired, but it was one of the many things we never got around to. Looking back, I think it would have been wonderful, and I've come to the conclusion that there's no such thing as a silly idea. Daydreams are dreams waiting to come true. What's that saying? 'Mostly you regret things you did not do.' What I'm trying to say is that you should give it a go. What's the worst that could happen?

Best wishes,
Arnold

PS. Do let me know if you get a cat, I have lots of ideas for names.

19th June

Dear Arnold,

Thanks for the baking tip! I haven't baked a cake since Autumn left home for university four years ago, which was a very plain and lumpy Victoria sponge for her 18th birthday, so maybe I'll give the Black Forest Gateau a go. It will probably end in disaster and a very messy kitchen, but nothing ventured, nothing gained, right?

I suppose I should apply that motto to my plan of expanding the shop. But isn't that sort of thing always easier said than done? I mean, I do sometimes wonder if I really want to still be working as a shop manager in twenty years' time, and I'm not at all sure that I do. Like I mentioned in my last letter, this isn't the trajectory I thought my life would take, but here I am! And it could be a lot worse. It's hard to explain, but when I picture good things happening in the future (like opening a cafe in the shop) it seems too fantastical, and then I get anxious about failing and think I should be grateful for what I have. (The same can be said about my love life, but let's not go there.) There's so much more to be lost than gained. Does that make any sense?

We're all shaped by experience, aren't we? When Autumn was younger, she went through a difficult period; staying out late without telling me where she was, skipping school, even getting in trouble with the police once. (You wouldn't think it now, would you?) I'll be honest, things were tough at times. Once or twice, I daydreamed about walking out on my life. Just grabbing my violin and hitchhiking to Avignon, or Madrid, or Berlin. But that would've meant walking out on Autumn too, and I owed it to her to stay. At times, though, I was *this close* to chucking it all in. The only thing I could do was try not to acknowledge those thoughts and hope they would go away. Which they did, eventually. What I'm trying to say, in a very roundabout way, is that sometimes you have to stick with what you've got and make the most of that. And I'm not unhappy, not really. So, thank you for your kind words, and be assured that I haven't totally given up on the idea of a cafe, I've just shelved it for later.

I love the meaning of your name! 'Eagle power' sounds amazing. I have no idea how my parents decided on my name. Or Autumn's either, although her birthday is in September, so maybe that's the clue. I suppose I'll never know what was behind my choice of name, though. That's one of those unanticipated things that happens when you lose someone, isn't it? All those unanswered questions, even after you've recovered from the raw pain of grief. But I guess that's something you have to learn to make your peace with. My parents weren't poets, though. Far from it – Dad was a solicitor and Mum was a hotel manager. Looking back, I recall thinking those were the most boring jobs ever, and now look at me!

I know what you mean about travelling alone. I thought about going on a weekend break to Prague a while ago, but I just couldn't get past the 'romantic getaway' description on the website. For some reason, I imagined myself walking through the charming cobbled streets as the only lonely loser amid a throng of love-struck couples. I'm sure there are single people in Prague, but I didn't fancy risking it. Plus, I couldn't really afford the trip. Maybe I'll get round to travelling the world at some point, but now's just not the time.

Besides, I'm quite happy at home. I live in a nice little flat on a quiet road; there's a small park at one end of the street and the shops are within walking distance. I have a smallish bedroom (which used to be Autumn's when she still lived here) and a larger living room. The kitchen's pretty basic, but I'm not much of a cook anyway, and I don't really have the time to entertain. So no loud parties, which I think my neighbours appreciate! Most of my furniture's from IKEA, but there are lots of websites for how to upcycle bookshelves, chests-of-drawers etc., so when I get the time, I like to whip out a paintbrush or some sanding paper. Sounds boring, I know, but it's actually quite therapeutic. There's something satisfying about using my hands to turn a plain template into something beautiful.

Right, that's quite enough about me and my boring life. And it's getting quite late and I've another early start tomorrow. You still haven't told me anything about life at Sunny Fields, so I'm expecting a full report in your next letter!

Love, Hope

FROM: Hope Sullivan
TO: Wilma McDonald
SUBJECT: Name

Hi Nan,

I hope you and Grandpa are well. Just a quick, random question: Do you remember how Mum and Dad came up with my name?

Love, Hope

FROM: Wilma McDonald
TO: Hope Sullivan
SUBJECT: Re: Name

Dear Hope,

Grandpa and I are well. I'm very sorry, but I have no idea where 'Hope' came from. If I remember correctly, they didn't have a name for you at all when you were born! I suggested something unusual, like Lakshmi or Bhagyawati, but apparently, that was too 'hippyish' for your parents. (By the way, did I ever tell you about my trip to that ashram in India in the 60s? It was amazing . . .)

Lots of love, Nan

CHAPTER 18

Greetings from Bavaria!

The festival is FANTASTIC, though so much Wagner's doing my head in a bit. I splashed out and bought myself a boob-boosting dirndl – you should see some of the looks I get, though whether it's my spectacular décolletage or that there aren't many black girls in traditional Bavarian costume I'll never know. Eric is so far flat-out refusing to wear lederhosen . . . Kisses, Janey

Olá de Praia do Guincho!

Having the greatest time – the waves are amazing. Haven't managed a barrel ride yet, but getting really good at tail-sliding. Krish says hi!

Love, Autumn

FROM: Antony French
TO: Harry's Harmonies
SUBJECT: Guitar

Dear Manager, hi!

I was in the shop this morning to see about buying a guitar, but you were busy attending to that group of schoolchildren and I was in a bit of a rush. I was wondering if you had a Gibson ES-355 Premiere in stock? If so, would you please let me know and I'll be back in to have a look?

Thanks and all best, Tony

FROM: Harry's Harmonies
TO: Antony French
SUBJECT: Re: Guitar

Dear Antony,

Thanks for contacting me. You're in luck! We don't stock many electric guitars, as the shop specialises in classical instruments, but I guess the Gibson ES-355 is a classic in its own right. Please come in any time and just ask for Hope – that's me!

Warm regards, Hope

FROM: Antony French
TO: Harry's Harmonies
SUBJECT: Re: Re: Guitar

Dear Hope,

In that case, I'll drop in tomorrow!

Best, Tony

PS. Do please call me Tony? Antony is my dad's name and it makes me feel so old when people call me that :)

18th August

Dear Hope,

It's five in the morning as I write this. Sleep doesn't come easy to me any more, especially during these warm nights. I go to bed at around midnight and if I'm lucky, I manage to sleep for a few hours before I'm awake again. It's one of life's little ironies, isn't it? When you're young and you've got things to do and people to meet and places to go, a third of your day is wasted on sleep, but when you're old and decrepit and have

nothing better to do, you're wide awake most of the night, staring up at the dark ceiling.

In around an hour's time, I'll hear my neighbour Frank
McNaughton start his day. First, it'll be the sound of his
bedsprings creaking as he gets out of bed. He's quite a heavy
fellow – 'big boned', as he calls it. Then the shuffling of his
slippers as he heads for the bathroom, followed by the whoosh
of the toilet flush. Occasionally, I can hear an odd noise that
sounds something like clicking; not a regular ticking, like a
clock. Just a *click . . . click click . . . click*. It drives me mad that I
can't identify the sound! I suppose I could ask Frank what it is,
but I don't want to pry. And he's very talkative; once you get
him started, he won't stop.

As requested, here is a report on Sunny Fields. First off,
I'm not entirely sure where they got the name for it. It isn't
sunny very often, English weather being what it is, and the
closest fields are ten miles away. But I suppose 'Wet 'n'
Windy Former Car Park' doesn't have the same ring to it
and likely wouldn't appeal to many prospective residents.
Joking aside, it's all right here, I suppose. It's not a proper
care home; we all have our own little self-contained flats (or
'apartments', as they are described in the brochure) and
there are on-site carers in case they're needed. Most of the
staff are friendly, barring a few exceptions, though the food
could be better.

My room is quite large, which is nice, and because it
faces west, it gets a lot of light in the afternoons – when the
sun is shining, that is. My bed is at the far wall and has the
most horrible chintz bedspread on it – all pink and purple
swirls – but it was left to me by one of the other residents,
Barbara Tamworth, when she died (she's the one who also
left me the interesting books), so I'd feel guilty throwing it
away. I think I would much prefer something plainer; navy
blue or something. But it wouldn't be worth buying
anything new at this stage, so I suppose I should just try and
get used to it.

To the left of the window is a mahogany sideboard I brought with me from home (the flats at Sunny Fields are furnished for the most part, but we're encouraged to 'personalise' them). Marion and I bought the sideboard at auction. That wasn't normally the sort of thing we did; most of our furniture came from regular furniture stores, or hand-me-downs from family. It was on our honeymoon in Brighton, and we happened upon an auction at a small antiques fair. Marion was a very spontaneous sort of woman, you know, and although we'd agreed not to bid more than £20 (which was a lot of money in those days), when another bidder shouted 'Twenty', up went Marion's paddle. The other bidder followed up with 'Thirty', and Marion: 'Forty'. We finally walked away with the sideboard and £55 less in my pocket. But it was worth it just to see the joy on Marion's face. Goodness, that was a fun day! I hadn't thought about it for years.

But I digress . . . There is a walk-in shower room next to the main door, and a tiny kitchenette opposite that. It isn't much more than two hobs and a microwave, because they're afraid we might burn the place down if we had proper kitchen equipment. More's the pity, because I used to enjoy baking very much – did I already mention that? I apologise if so; my memory isn't what it once was.

Sunny Fields has its own large kitchen, where they prepare meals for the residents, and we can eat in the communal dining room or take the meals back to our rooms. I usually prefer the latter as it can get quite loud with two dozen hard-of-hearing OAPs shouting at each other across the table.

I don't get many visitors, but that's all right. I've learned to make do with my own company. Besides, I must confess that I wasn't the best at keeping in touch with my friends after Marion died. I found it near impossible to put on a pleasant face and talk about the weather, or the latest village gossip. And I was sure everyone was sick and tired of hearing my stories about me and Marion. But I didn't feel like talking about anything else, to be honest. My memories of her were all I had left. So eventually, I stopped answering the door and just turned up the telly whenever someone knocked. I felt awful just ignoring them, but I would've felt a whole lot worse chit-chatting and pretending everything was fine. It's hard to put into words, but I would have felt guilty being happy, like I was betraying Marion somehow. That doesn't stop me seeing everything through her lens, though. I think she would've liked this place, though she would have made it a lot homier than I could ever manage.

Well, I hope I've satisfied your curiosity about Sunny Fields! It's a nice enough place, though I don't imagine I'll be here for that much longer. Like you say, sometimes you have to stick with what you've got and make the most of it.

Well, I think I'll leave it there for now. I can hear the squeaky bedsprings next door. Seems Frank is up and about earlier than usual.

All the best,
Arnold

FROM: Hope Sullivan
TO: Janey Williams
SUBJECT: Mr Perfect

Dear Janey,

Did I or did I not tell you that Mr Perfect was going to walk through the door one day?! Well, he finally did! Actually, it's Mr French, not Mr Perfect, but he might as well be. His name is Tony, he's 30, unbelievably cute, and he plays jazz guitar. Not professionally, but good enough to spend thousands of pounds on an instrument. He mentioned he does something in PR/communications, but he didn't want to bore me with it, and besides, I'd much rather talk Thelonious Monk and Billie Holiday than boilerplates and DMAs.

OK, I realise I'm getting a little ahead of myself. Here's what happened: Tony came into the shop a couple of days ago to look at a Gibson ES-355. It's a beautiful guitar, and quite pricey at around £3,500. He tried it out (his downstrokes were a bit off, but the Gibson does have a high string action that makes it tricky to play) and we got chatting about this and that, really relaxed but with a definite *something* in the air between us, while I tried not to think about the fact that I looked like something the cat had dragged in. (I haven't been to the hairdresser since my nan sent me a dodgy horoscope. Stupid, I know.) Anyhow, Tony said he loved the guitar, but that he'd have to have a think on it – which is fair enough at that price – and that he'd be back soon.

He was just heading out of the door when he turned and said, 'Right, I'd better just say it before I lose my nerve completely. Do you fancy a coffee some time?' and I blurted out, 'Yes please,' which I hadn't meant to say, of course, but it made him laugh. So he picked me up that afternoon after I'd closed the shop and we went for a coffee, which turned into wine, which turned into fish 'n' chips, which turned into him walking me home and asking if I'd have dinner with him tomorrow evening.

We went to that little Italian on the corner of Queen's Street, you know the one. Sadly, he was pretty pushed for time as he had to prepare some kind of presentation for work the next day, but it was just lovely spending any time with him. He has this really sweet way of making compliments without sounding creepy, you know? And we're going out again on Thursday, hopefully for a bit longer this time. He plays in a jazz band, so he's busy with rehearsals a lot of evenings, but he promised to let me know when his next gig is. A musician, Janey, can you believe it? Oh, and he has decided to buy the Gibson, so how's that for a bit of mixing business with pleasure, haha.

Hey, when you get back, we'll go to a jazz club together, the four of us, what do you think? God, Janey, I keep pinching myself – Mr Perfect walking right into the shop! Who would've thought?

Love, Hope

FROM: Wilma McDonald
TO: Hope Sullivan
SUBJECT: Madame Zargo's advice

Dear Hope,

It was lovely speaking on the phone! You definitely sounded chirpier than usual. Is there a special someone in your life, by any chance?

We received Autumn's postcard yesterday. It sounds as though she had a wonderful time in Portugal. She and Krish seem to be getting serious! Back in our day, of course, Grandad and I wouldn't have dreamt of going on holiday together while we were still courting. If we had, I would have known how much he likes to complain about lumpy hotel mattresses, the 'odd' smell of B&B disinfectants, faulty electrics and room service that is either too slow, too dear or simply non-existent. Did you know we spent our entire honeymoon arguing about whether the 'Do not disturb' sign applies to other hotel guests having conversations in the corridor outside? Ah well, you can't turn the clock back and it's too late to change now.

As for you and your question about a cat, I'll just leave this here . . .

'As a Gemini, your best time to get a pet is when you have a transit planet going through the 6th house, aspecting a natal planet in Virgo, aspecting your natal Mercury, or aspecting the ruler of your 12th house. You generally want to see positive aspects (sextiles and trines) so it's an easy transition (through a conjunction by the Sun, Mercury, Venus or Mars). Positive aspects by Jupiter or Neptune to any part of your star chart can be good energy for getting a pet as well.'

Love, Nan

Hey there! I really enjoyed last night. Let's do it again soon? Tony

Yes, let's! Oh, and I've got the Gibson packed up and ready to go. Drop by any time. Hx

FROM: Hope Sullivan
TO: Wilma McDonald
SUBJECT: Re: Madame Zargo's advice

Hello Nan,

Thanks, but there's no need. I'm not buying a cat just yet!

Love, Hope

FROM: Hope Sullivan
TO: Janey Williams
SUBJECT: Mr Perfect

Just a quick one today, Janey! Tony's booked us a room at La Residence Hotel! He surprised me with it yesterday afternoon. He sent me a message telling me to expect a special something. I thought he was finally coming in to buy the Gibson, but instead, a huge bunch of roses arrived at the shop ten minutes later with a card containing the booking for the hotel. I very nearly kissed the courier, who had the good sense to pedal off before I could embarrass myself completely.

We're off on Friday evening, and back on Saturday afternoon. Unfortunately, Tony's got some teleconference thingy with Shanghai first thing Sunday morning, so it's only one night, but hopefully it'll be the first night of many. Check out the hotel, though! I'll put the link at the bottom. A private whirl-pool, a fireplace, his & hers fluffy bathrobes (his & hers, Janey!), rose-scented candles, champagne breakfast, a king-sized bed. Jeez, it's been a while . . . do you think it's possible to forget, how to . . . 'do it'?

I'm so excited, Janey! It's been so long since I actually travelled anywhere, I can't even remember where I put my suitcase. Autumn probably took it when she left for uni. And I can't find my vanity case either. Come to think of it, Autumn probably took that, too. Doesn't matter though, I'll buy a whole new luggage set if I have to! That reminds me, I really need to invest in some new underwear. And should I try and get a hairdress-er's appointment? Only three days to go and so much to do! I can't believe it! It feels like this is going so fast, but then again, I've waited long enough, right? I deserve this, don't I?

I'll keep you informed . . .

Love, Hope

You go girl! Jx

FROM: Hope Sullivan
TO: Janey Williams
SUBJECT: ~~Mr Perfect~~ Shitface

Dear Janey,

I was going to call you, but I probably wouldn't have got through the first sentence without bursting into tears. No, I didn't have the perfect romantic weekend. Instead, I found out on Friday that he's married.

Mr Antony 'I'm-the-opposite-of-perfect-in-fact-I'm-a-complete-shitface' French has a gorgeous wife and two adorable children. Pretty, blond, five-year-old twins. And I probably wouldn't have found out, not for a long time anyway, if I hadn't accidentally bumped into them.

It was around lunchtime, and I'd just popped to the sandwich shop on the corner to grab a bite, although to be honest, I was so twitchy with anticipation about the upcoming weekend I didn't have much of an appetite, but I figured I wouldn't be eating until later that evening. A romantic dinner, at La Residence, with Tony.

The lunchtime rush was on, so the place was pretty crowded. I'd just got to the front of the queue and ordered a tuna salad sandwich when I heard someone say, 'You know, Harry's Harmonies.' I turned and saw a woman – pretty, with perfect blond hair in a perfect ponytail, and two cute blond kids – standing a couple of people behind me in the queue. I couldn't quite see who she was with, because like I said, the place was crowded, but she seemed a bit annoyed with whoever it was. 'But the kids start recorder lessons next week,' she said. 'And you know how I feel about buying stuff from a bloody online giant when there's a music shop just around the corner.'

Then the person beside her spoke and I recognised the voice immediately. It was Tony. I couldn't exactly hear what he was saying, but he was hissing something along the lines of, '. . . other places to shop, you know.' I couldn't believe my ears at first, thought I must be hallucinating his voice because I was so excited about the upcoming weekend, so I paid for my sandwich and made my way through the crowd. And there he was, holding hands with one of the little ones. The look he gave me when he spotted me, it was like he'd been suddenly confronted with all his worst fears. The blood drained out of his face and then he lifted his hand to try to cover it like it wasn't perfectly obvious that I had recognised him!

Janey, it was all I could do not to walk up to him and punch him on his stupid, lying, cheating nose, or at least tell his wife that she was married to a conniving, cheating bastard, but then I looked at those two blond little children and they smiled back up at me, and I thought no, *I'm* not taking responsibility for ruining their lives. I've done nothing wrong, this is not on me. So instead, I forced a smile on my face and said to Tony, 'You found a babysitter for tonight, then?' and he gave me this slack-mouthed, puzzled look that made him look like an idiot, and he blurted out, 'I can explain.' But I ignored him and turned to his wife and told her I was a friend of Tony's and that he'd told me all about the secret romantic weekend he'd planned for her, at a fancy hotel with a whirl-pool and champagne breakfast and rose-scented candles, and the whole time I was crying on the inside, with disappoint-ment, with anger.

Tony's wife turned to him and I could see the excitement – *my* excitement – flashing in her eyes, and she asked if it was true, and he nodded, and she just beamed and hugged him. All I could do was walk out of there, but at least I walked out with my head held high. And if Tony *dares* to set so much as a toe inside my shop again, I will strangle him with my bare hands, I swear.

Oh god, Janey, I feel like such a fool! I was so excited about this guy; finally – *finally* – someone thought I was worth getting romantically involved with. But boy, how wrong could I be? Those short dinners, the 'presentations' and 'Shanghai teleconferences', they were all a lie. Sure, Tony's an arse, but it was *stupid me* who fell for the lies hook, line and sinker because I thought it was only right and proper that a perfect, good-looking, rich, expensive-jazz-guitar-playing man would be interested in me. And to add insult to injury, he didn't even buy the stinking guitar. I bet that 'I'm a jazz musician' was all a fake, too.

I give up. I swear. I'm obviously not meant to be in a relationship.

Love, Hope

RateTheBook.com
Pride and Prejudice by Jane Austen
RATING: 2 stars
The writing is fine, if you like that kind of thing, but the storyline is totally unrealistic. Girl meets boy, stuff happens, boy and girl live happily ever after. Give me a break!

CHAPTER 19

Wow, you went and did it, sis! You bought
a cat! She's totally cute obvs (though you
know I prefer dogs). Just hope this doesn't
mean you've turned into Cat Lady :)

OMG she's soooooo cute!!! Feel free to
send me as many kitten pix as you like. You
haven't given up on men altogether though,
have you? There are plenty of other guys
out there, you know. Kisses, Janey xxx

1st October

Dear Arnold,

It's been a while since I wrote, and this is only a short letter,
do excuse. Just wanted to let you know that I got myself a cat!
I've enclosed a photo – isn't she adorable? I know you offered
to help with names, but I'm afraid I've gone ahead and named
her already. She's called Yuuko, after one of my favourite
violinists, Yuuko Shiokawa. Do let me know if you can find out
anything about what the name means!

My next letter will be longer, promise.

Love, Hope

Harry Clark
Hope Sullivan
All's well that ends well?

Dear Hope,

How are you? Ingrid and I are currently sitting on the balcony of our rented finca, looking out over the beautiful Mediterranean and indulging in a rather nice bottle of rosé. Despite Ingrid's protestations I have been checking my emails, and discovered this piece of lovely news (see below). I just wanted to keep you in the loop.

I hope all is well with the shop! Ingrid and I will pop in when we're back to say hello.
    All best, Harry

---Forwarded message---

FROM: Allegra Forbes-Doyle
TO: Harry Clark
SUBJECT: Triangle

Dear Mr Clark,

I don't think you will remember me, but I took part in your music carousel a few years ago when I was still in primary school. My father really wanted me to learn to play the oboe, which I hated. I'm happy to say he realised that I don't have any talent when it comes to woodwind instruments so then he ended up buying me a triangle. Lots of the other children made fun of me at first, but then I met a lovely music teacher who said that percussionists are the most important players in an orchestra because they help set the tempo, so I talked my father into letting me have percussion lessons. I have been playing the drums for four years now but I don't think I want

118

to play in a classical orchestra after all. I think I'm going to become a rock star instead.

Yours sincerely,
Allegra Forbes-Doyle

FROM: Hope Sullivan
TO: Harry Clark
SUBJECT: Re: All's well that ends well?

This is a beautiful story, Harry. Thanks for passing it on! Now stop checking your emails and enjoy your holiday! Love, Hope

15th October

Dear Hope,

It was lovely to hear from you, as always. Please don't apologise for not responding sooner; I'm well aware that a young person like yourself might have better things to do than write to an old man, and I'm quite happy to hear from you every now and again.

Thank you for the photo. Your kitten is indeed adorable. My clever book tells me that Yuuko (depending on how it's spelled in Japanese, of course) means 'excellence, superiority, gentleness' (Yu) and 'child' (ko). What do you think; is this a good fit for your cat?

Names can be so important, can't they? When Marion and I first got our dog Chutney, it took us ages before we could agree on a name and he spent the first weeks of his life named 'Puppy'. We finally settled on the name Chutney after a day on our allotment. We'd had an excellent harvest of tomatoes that year, and Marion and I were in the kitchen making dozens of glasses of tomato chutney. It was a messy business; the kitchen counter, the floor, the cooker, all covered in bits of tomato and onion and ginger. So then in scrambled the puppy, made a beeline for a large blob of chutney that had splashed onto the floor, and licked it up. Oh, his little face! You should have seen it, Hope, his expression went from quizzical to horrified to disgusted. We'd never seen a dog make so many facial expressions. And then he began to sneeze and sneeze, until he'd managed to eject all the yucky stuff from his mouth and nose. It was absolutely hilarious; Marion and I were in tears laughing. We *almost* went with Sneezy, but decided that Chutney was a kinder choice.

He sadly died of lymphoma two years ago. He made it to the grand old age of sixteen, though his final few weeks were pretty miserable, so when he finally passed, it was a blessing, I suppose. I could tell he also missed Marion terribly; for months after she passed, he'd sit on her favourite chair with such a dejected expression, stirring only when it was time for a walk. In fact, I had Chutney to thank for getting me outdoors at all during the first few months after she died. Eventually, we settled into a routine that suited the both of us: we'd have our breakfast, then go out for a quick walk around the park. Then I'd watch a bit of telly, have a quick lunch, go back out with Chutney to the village pond to feed the ducks. Sometimes I'd drop in at the pub for half a shandy and then go to the shops to get my dinner and a scratchcard. I don't know if scratchcards are something young people do nowadays, but it was a little something to look forward to every day – what a thrill when I won! Then we'd trot off home, have dinner and watch telly until it was time for bed. Gosh, that sounds awfully stale and boring, doesn't it? But it was comforting to have a routine, to not have to think about where to go and what to do.

I have a picture of Chutney somewhere. Perhaps I can get one of the staff to make a copy and I'll send it to you.

Right, that's all for today. It's getting close to dinner time and there's an indeterminable smell wafting into my room that may or may not herald shepherd's pie.

All best,

Arnold

Can I sleep on your couch tonight?
I think me and Eric are over. Jx

CHAPTER 20

3rd November

Dear Arnold,

Sorry it's taken so long to respond – again. And I'd like you to know that I also love to receive *your* letters in the post!

I've spent the past few days playing agony aunt to my best friend, Janey. She got married last year and things have turned a bit sour. Her husband, Eric, is a lovely man, but lately the two of them keep getting their wires crossed and having the worst rows.

So anyway, Janey came round to mine three nights ago and poured her heart out. It was really hard to see my best friend so upset, but after a few glasses of wine and a lengthy chat, I managed to dissuade her from walking out on the marriage completely. Of course, my loyalty is to my friend, and if for a moment I believed she would be better off without Eric, I'd be the first to say. But if you'd ever seen the two of them together, you'd know that there is something special there. And I know it's a bit clichéd, but don't they say that love has to be nurtured?

I'm not an expert in relationships – far from it – but to me, it seems as though she and Eric are probably struggling to find a good balance. They're both classical musicians and play in the same orchestra, so they spend <u>all</u> their time virtually side by side, separated only by the bassoons and French horns. Janey's finding it all a bit suffocating. She eventually went home yesterday, after three days and nights of lamenting and raging and crying (she's the funniest person I know, but she can also be a bit of a drama queen). But eventually, she told me that she misses him like crazy, the fact that he brings her coffee in bed every morning, how he plays with her hair when the two of them watch TV, that he replaces the loo roll and always makes sure they never run out of milk. The little things, you know? So anyway, she's going back to tell him how she feels and see how he responds. If Eric is the right guy for her, he'll know what to do and give her a little space now and again.

I won't lie – it's been nice having her here, someone to share a Chinese takeaway with, someone to watch TV with and giggle at some stupid sitcom, someone to say goodnight to at the end of the day. And we've known each other so long, we sometimes don't even have to speak at all to know what the other is feeling. With Janey here, my flat felt more like a home than a place I only sleep, eat and shower in. It was a bit like when Autumn still lived here, minus the teenage tantrums. But hey, at least I won't have to share the bathroom any more.

Thanks for the photo of Chutney! He's adorable. And I assume that's Marion beside him? She reminds me a little of that French actor, what's her name? Catherine Deneuve – is that the one? Marion's beautiful, anyway, and I love that blue dress she's wearing. It sounds like you were really happy together and I'm so sorry she's no longer with you. May I ask how long ago she died? Please tell me if I'm being too nosy; I'd genuinely love to hear more about her, but I totally understand if you'd rather not. (That's one of the downsides of letter-writing: you can't read the cues in the other person's face or body language telling you to shut up!)

Love, Hope

PS. I've enclosed a scratchcard! I've already done mine and – big surprise – didn't win. If I don't hear from you again, I'll assume you've won the £4,000,000 and are currently enjoying a luxury world cruise . . .

Hey, Thunder Chunk, wanna come home early and lick off this honey I've spread on aaaalllllll my favourite places? Getting all hot 'n' sticky waiting for you . . .

Aaaargh, sent this to you instead of Eric. How embarrassing!!! Plz plz plz delete it and let's never mention it again

HAHAHAHAHAHA
But 'Thunder Chunk'? Really?!!!

9th November

Dear Hope,

Thank you so much for the scratchcard! What a delightful surprise. No world cruise, unfortunately. I could have done with escaping the short days and long, cold nights. My luck seems to be as bad as yours, but it was a lovely thought.

I agree that communicating at a distance can have its drawbacks, though I can assure you that I'm quite happy to talk about Marion. I lost her five years ago. She was the love of my life, and you're right, we were very happy together. We were married for 45 years, can you imagine? And those years literally flew by. One minute, we were this young, vivacious couple, and in the blink of an eye, we'd turned into two pensioners who enjoyed knitting and bowling (Marion would argue that were still vivacious though!).

We met during a very hot summer, one of those sweltering ones – there had been a hosepipe ban for weeks. I had just completed my teacher training and decided to go punting with a couple of friends. There were four of us messing about on the boat, all of us tussling for a go at holding the pole. When it was my turn, I punted round a bend on the river and saw a group of girls coming towards us in a rowing boat. They were all young and pretty, but I was immediately drawn to one of them. She had wilful, sandy-brown curls that she'd tried in vain to tame in a ponytail, and a face splashed with pale freckles, and from the first minute, I couldn't take my eyes off her. (Incidentally, I think she would have been delighted she'd been compared to that grande dame of French cinema, Catherine Deneuve!) She was very pretty, without a doubt, but it was her laugh that drew me in completely. It was one of those infectious full-bellied, carefree laughs that lifts your spirits immediately.

Anyway, there was plenty of good-spirited banter back and forth, then someone suggested we hold a race – punters versus rowers. Of course, I was at pains to show off my punting skills and impress the pretty girl with the outrageous laugh. But just as I dug the punting pole into the riverbed, the rowing boat (with Marion on the oars) inadvertently rammed us and threw me head first into the water. Marion was mortified! The river wasn't deep, but the fall had been so unexpected and I'll admit I wasn't the strongest of swimmers. So there I was, splashing around – and before I knew it, Marion had dived in and was dragging me, quite expertly, towards the riverbank. Along the way, I unfortunately knocked her across the head with one of my flailing arms. We finally got to dry land, and a couple of mutual apologies later we had agreed to go out for a meal.

We courted for one year and saw each other almost every day, and after we got married, we continued to do everything together: knitting, tending our allotment; we even took up learning the piano together! We invested in a lovely cherry-wood upright piano on our tenth wedding anniversary and practised whenever we had a spare moment.

Marion and I only ever played duets, nothing too difficult. There's a lovely little piece called 'The Turkish March' by Mozart (I'm sure you've heard of it) that we used to play all the time. It was our party piece, so to speak, and we entertained at more parties than I can remember. If we'd ever had an argument (which didn't happen very often, but remember, we were married for nearly half a century), one of us would go and sit at the piano and play our half of whatever tune we were practising. Soon enough, the other would join in and the argument would dissolve into nothingness. I suppose it was our way of showing that we were two halves of a whole; that one cannot function without the other.

There's a piano here at Sunny Fields, in the common room, but without Marion by my side I haven't much had the inclination to play. I don't mean to sound self-pitying, but when you've shared most of your life with someone, when everything you did was as one half of a whole, then it's not that simple to pick up where you left off and just carry on. We had a very busy social life, Marion and I, organising the village summer fete, singing in the choir, chairing the local rambling society. So when I lost her, that all ended too.

The most frightening thing about her stroke was its unexpectedness. One minute she was kneeling beside the sweet peas on the allotment, the next minute she had suddenly keeled over. I can't remember much of the days that followed; I think I was in shock. She was put on life support and for the longest time, I'd tell myself she was just sleeping and she'd wake up having fully recovered and make some joke that would have us creased up with laughter. I just couldn't imagine losing her, and truly believed that by the sheer force of willing her recovery, everything would turn out all right. She lost so much weight towards the end as she lay in that hospital bed; it was like she was wasting away before my eyes. Eventually, I understood what the doctors had been saying from the start: there would be no 'all right', no happily ever after. This was it. I agreed to switch off her life support, and it was the most difficult decision I had ever made.

For ages afterwards – to this day, in fact – I was never entirely sure I did the right thing. I mean, she hadn't been conscious for a long, long time, so she wouldn't have had any idea what was going on. That's a small blessing, I suppose. I remember sitting at her bedside, trying to block out the sight and sounds of those awful machines she was hooked up to, and telling myself that I would have wanted her to do the same for me. It was the last thing I'd ever imagined doing, but after so many months of sitting there holding her hand, I knew somewhere deep inside me – just as I knew when I first set eyes on her that I loved her – that she was gone. My final thought, just before I finally agreed with the doctors that it was time, was something Marion had told me years earlier, when we talked about what we would do if either of us ever ended up in such a position. She'd said, 'Don't hold on to me, live your life.' At that moment, I didn't stop to consider the consequences, I just knew I had to let her go.

Goodness, this is sounding more morose than I intended! Yet right now, I'm not feeling morose in the slightest, to be perfectly honest. In fact, writing to you about Marion, about our marriage, about that magical day we met, has made me feel better than I have in ages. So, thank you for that.

I do hope your friend and her husband reconcile. There's nothing more fulfilling – or more valuable – than a happy relationship. Who's your special person, Hope? I have to assume such a lovely young lady has a suitor (or two?).

All best wishes,
Arnold

Call me? Jx

28th November

Dear Arnold,

Thanks for you lovely letter. I'm so sorry about Marion. I can't imagine what it must be like to lose someone you've been married to for so long. It certainly puts things in perspective. But what a lovely first-time-meeting story. We call that a 'meet cute' – and yours was a proper only-in-the-movies one!

Nowadays, all you hear about is couples getting together at work, or in a club, or – horror of horrors – via the internet. Makes me sound really old-fashioned, I know, but I always loved the idea of fate bringing people together. Do you believe there is someone out there for everyone? I used to think so, but now I'm not so sure. Maybe some people just get really lucky – like you and Marion, or Autumn and Krish – and the rest of us have to make do with whoever we happen to end up with. I just realised I'm the same age now my parents were when they got married. That's a very odd thought. I've always assumed they were happily married, but I'll never really know, will I? Just one more of those unanswered questions.

So, no suitors here, I'm afraid. Janey and Autumn keep calling me out on my 'singledom'; they seem to think if I don't get on the dating market (as they call it) soon, I'll end up as an old maid and with more cats than you can count. But going by the kind of guys out there right now, I'm quite happy as I am, thank you very much! Also, relationships aren't exactly effort-free, are they? Take Janey and Eric, for example. Well, as you know, they sorted things out and were happier than ever and then, out of the blue, Eric's been offered a four-month contract with the Tokyo Symphony Orchestra as a guest player. Janey called me last night, in tears. Sure, she understands that this is a once-in-a-lifetime opportunity for Eric (they're *huge* on Western classical music in Japan), so she doesn't want to stand in his way and has insisted that he go. But at the same time, she's going to miss him terribly. I reminded her that Tokyo isn't on the moon, and that she could always fly out and visit him. Four months will be over before she knows it and it will give her that space she's been craving. Besides, I told her, she still has me. Now I only have to come up with ways to keep her busy and distract her for the next few months . . .

You can play the piano – how lovely! I've never heard of someone only playing duets – what a beautiful idea. It's such a shame you don't feel like playing any more, though. Having said that, I'm guilty of the same offence, except in my case, it's the violin. I started when I was young and was on course to become a professional musician, but I haven't picked up a violin for ten years. Although, that's not strictly true: I did *sort of* play today. A little girl came into the shop this afternoon. She was about eight, the same age I was when I first started playing. She came in on her own; she said she lives on the estate opposite and told me her parents could never afford any of the instruments, but that she just wanted to come in and have a look.

We chatted for a while – she asked all sorts of interested questions – and I ended up telling her that I used to play the violin. Then she asked if she could touch one. She was so sweet, very solemn, but I could see the excitement bubbling beneath the surface. So I got one down from the shelf, a 3/4 Stentor, and showed her how to place it on her shoulder. Then I gave her a bow and guided it across the strings for her (I always help first-timers; you'll know as well as I do that a badly-played violin is the worst sound in the world!).

Arnold, I can't describe her expression. She closed her eyes and submitted completely to the sound. It was glorious to watch. Unfortunately, at that moment another customer came into the shop and we had to stop. But I told Maisie (that's her name) to come back whenever she felt like it and I'd show her some of the other instruments. I'm not exactly sure why I'm telling you this; it's just that I felt like I was doing something really meaningful when I was guiding the bow across the strings. There was such an energy coming off Maisie, like I knew she wanted to shake me off and produce this beautiful sound all by herself. Hmm, I don't know. Perhaps I'm imagining things, but I do hope she comes back in.

Anyway, it got me thinking about music, about how classical music is the purest expression of our humanity. It's what differentiates us from other animals, our ability to produce highly sophisticated art. Paganini, Mozart, Britten – they show that music is uniquely human and humane, don't they? It makes me sad to think that so many people don't think they'd ever 'get' classical music, so they don't even try listening to it (*really* listening), let alone play it. But learning to appreciate music is no different to appreciating literature: if nobody teaches you how to read, how will you ever be able to enjoy a book? These people just don't know what they're missing out on!

Something about the sound of the bow on the strings – the trills, the different types of vibrato, the glissando – it just makes my soul soar. I would challenge anyone to listen to Vivaldi's *Four Seasons* and not feel moved. When I used to play, it was the most glorious feeling. I often played in orchestras, which gives you this incredible feeling of power, like you're part of something indescribably amazing where the whole is so much more than the sum of its parts. And the feeling of drawing the bow across the strings, it was so meditative, tranquilising almost.

Have you ever heard of Anne-Sophie Mutter? She's a world-famous violinist who always wears strapless dresses when she plays. Not because she wants to look sexy, but because she needs to feel the wood of the instrument against her bare skin. I totally understand that. When you play, there's a vibration that travels through the instrument right into your very core. It's difficult to describe in words. I somehow got the feeling that Maisie understood, even at such a young age. In fact, I think I'll make her a playlist of my favourite violin concertos, just in case she does come back in.

Sorry for the length of this letter! I'll leave it here for now. My stomach just let out the most alarming grumble and I think it's time to pop the mac & cheese in the microwave. Tastes a bit like cardboard, but that's about as good as it gets with my cooking skills, I'm afraid.

Love, Hope

CHAPTER 21

FROM: Janey Williams
TO: Hope Sullivan
SUBJECT: YOLO

Hi Hope,

I found this online. Give it a go!

Jx
www.perfectlovematch.com

Perfect Love Match™

RESULTS FOR: Hope Sullivan
According to your score, your Perfect Love Match™ is an
INFJ – Introverted, Intuitive, Feeling, Judging

THE PROS: He's a great listener, gentle and warm. An idealist at
heart, the INFJ is looking to build the perfect relationship and
will never pass up an opportunity to show you how special you
are to him.

THE CONS: The INFJ has high expectations for himself and of
others. His aversion to conflict means that he is tempted to
sweep difficult relationship issues under the carpet.

The INFJ is a rare type, but if you manage to grab one, don't
let him go!

FROM: Hope Sullivan
TO: Janey Williams
SUBJECT: Re:YOLO

OK, J, you and Autumn have twisted my arm long enough. I'm going in. Wish me luck. Hx

FROM: Hope Sullivan
TO: Janey Williams
SUBJECT: Re: Re:YOLO

What do you think? Hx

DATE MATE
Making The Match That Matters

About me: Uncomplicated, creative, calm, hardworking.
I love: Reading, binge-watching Netflix, my cat Yuuko, nice
    meals, writing letters.
Looking to meet: Someone new who doesn't hate cats and/or
    have allergies

                                        No. Just . . . no. Jx

DATE MATE
Making The Match That Matters

Two truths and a lie: I can touch my nose with my tongue /
    My cat is named after a Japanese violin virtuoso / I have
    never lost an arm wrestle
                Swipe right if you want to know more

Much better. Fingers crossed and let me know. Jx

YOU MATCHED WITH LIAM

Hey there!

Hi!

So you've never lost an arm wrestle, eh?

Are you challenging me? Be warned,
my biceps may look ladylike, but
they're deceptively strong

You're funny. I like that in a girl

That's good, cos I like funny guys!

Then you're not like my ex. Whenever
I told a joke, she'd give me a look like
she'd just eaten something disgusting

Sorry to hear that :/

Well, she used to think I was
funny when we first met

Right

We were together for five years

That's a long time

It is, right? And I don't want to put her down or
anything. She's actually really sweet, it's just . . .

What?

I dunno. We'd both been really busy at work
and I guess we stopped talking to each
other. One thing led to another and we'd
have these almighty rows. And she'd end
up crying and that made me feel awful

Listen, Liam, I don't really know you, but
it sounds like you're not quite over her

Really?

It does, I'm afraid

Maybe you're right

Why don't you write her a letter
and tell her how you feel?

133

You know what, I'll give it a try

You do that :)

Thanks, Hope. And sorry for wasting your time

No worries. Good luck!

END OF MESSAGE

YOU MATCHED WITH FELIX

Hello

Hi!

Your profile says you have a cat

Two truths and a lie, Felix ;)

So do you or don't you have a cat?

I have a cat

Did you know the record for the loudest purr is 67.8 decibels?

Err, no. I didn't know that

And did you know cats are actually lactose intolerant? So don't feed your cat milk

You seem to know a lot about cats

I take my responsibility as a cat owner seriously. As should you

Larry, is that you???

Umm, wrong number, sorry

END OF MESSAGE

YOU MATCHED WITH DAVE

Hi. I like your profile pic

Thanks!

Wanna send me a pussy pic?

You want a picture of my cat?!!

What? No – I mean a *pussy* pic. I'll send you a dick pic in return ;)

Urgh, no thanks

134

> Why are you on here if your so uptight?
I'm starting to wonder that myself

END OF MESSAGE

Merry Christmas, BFF!
 Janey xxx

Seasons Greetings!
 Love from Nan & Grandpa

Wishing You a Bright and Beautiful Christmas and
New Year
 Best wishes,
  Ingrid and Harry

                                    4th January

Dear Hope,

Thank you so much for the Christmas card. I'm sorry I didn't
think of sending you one, but I stopped sending cards years ago.
Next year, I promise; or perhaps you can tell me when it's your
birthday? That would give me a chance to make up for it.

I hope you had a good start to the New Year. Mine started
with a bit of a bang, unfortunately. There was a leak in the
celling of my flat, just above the bed, and I've had to move out
temporarily while they fix it. A burst water pipe can do quite
some damage, apparently – huge chunks of plaster came down.
I wasn't in bed when it happened, or else I might not be writing to you at all. That's good fortune or bad luck, depending
on how you look at it. What old person doesn't dream of going
to bed one night and just not waking up in the morning?

135

Anyway, I'm currently bunking with my neighbour Frank, who was kind enough to let me sleep on his pull-out sofa. He's perfectly pleasant, but he snores like a bear. Oh, and I finally discovered the source of that strange clicking noise I told you about. It's Frank cutting his toenails! He has these thick, talon-like nails – god knows how and why they grow so quickly, because he's cut them twice since I've been here. It's not a sight for a weak stomach, let me tell you. I shall be glad when I get my flat back!

Like I say, there was quite a bit of damage, though most of my things aren't valuable and have become, quite frankly, unnecessary. What does an old man like me need with an ornamental candle holder? Or a set of novelty placemats? And besides, I'm finally rid of that awful bedspread – all with a clear conscience. Frank, the cheeky devil, says I should put in an insurance claim for a valuable heirloom or two, but even if I did have any valuables, I probably wouldn't bother. Maybe it's an age thing, but I've found possessions increasingly burdensome. I am the opposite of what you would call a hoarder, I suppose. I carry all my memories in my heart; goodness, if I'd kept every item that has meant anything to me across my lifetime, I'd need a warehouse to store them all. No, I don't need to accumulate belongings to retain memories of what matters to me. On the contrary, all these things – all this *stuff* – you accrue over a lifetime only serves to highlight what is missing.

I recall on the day Marion died, I came straight home and immediately began packing up her things. I worked late into the night, just wanting to be free of her clothes, her favourite books and records. I knew it would break my heart every day I saw them, or used them, or even just thought about them. I boxed them up, ready to give to charity the next day. Eventually, it must have been past midnight, a neighbour from across the street knocked on the door and asked if I was all right. She said she'd been on her way to bed when she saw me through the living room window (I'd been too busy to draw the curtains), rushing in and out of the room 'like a berserker'. She

136

knew about Marion being in hospital, so she was concerned it had all got too much for me. I told her Marion had passed and that I needed to pack away her things for charity.

'Are you sure you want to give everything away?' she asked. 'What if you regret it later? You should wait a while and see how you feel in a month or two.'

I tried to explain what I've told you just now, but she didn't understand. How would two months make any difference to my pain? Or three months, or four? She went on to say something about 'moving on', and 'that's what Marion would have wanted', and I knew she was just trying to be kind, but I suddenly couldn't bear her gibbering on any longer and more or less pushed her out of the door. I'm still ashamed to think about how I behaved, like a bitter and cantankerous old man. I still had Chutney, though, and my memories of Marion. But this was a very painful episode of my life, so I'll change the subject if you don't mind.

I very much enjoyed your last letter, especially the part when you described playing the violin. May I ask why you gave up? It seems odd to me that you haven't played for so long. When you write about it, you sound so full of passion and *joie de vivre*. I would have thought that someone with so much enthusiasm, and – I assume – talent, would take every opportunity to play, especially as you are around musical instruments all day.

Incidentally, I do believe there is someone out there for everyone. Call me a hopeless romantic, but I firmly believe in True Love. Yes, perhaps not everyone is as lucky as Marion and I were, perhaps not everyone hits the jackpot the first time around, but it would make me sad to think you'd given up at such a young age. I hope you don't think I'm being forward, and I'm quite sure some people can lead perfectly happy and fulfilled lives as singles, but could it be that this is something else you're 'shelving for later'?

Wishing you a wonderful and happy New Year,
Best wishes,
Arnold

CHAPTER 22

U awake?

Just about. What's up, Janey?

Sorry, I know it's late, but I needed to talk to you

Hang on, let me switch on the light

Right, got it. Everything ok?

Not sure

Now I'm getting worried. Is it Thunder Chunk?

If ur gonna be like that . . .

Sorry :) I mean, Eric?

No

Well what then, r u sick?

Yeah, but only in the mornings

OMG does this mean what I think it means?

Um, I guess so

OMG OMG OMG!!!!!!!

OK, sod my beauty sleep, I'm ringing u now

15th January

Dear Arnold,

Happy New Year to you too! Sorry to hear about the leak. I for one am very glad you weren't in bed when the ceiling came down! I've grown accustomed to receiving your letters and hope to receive many more. Besides, having chunks of the ceiling fall on top of you when you're sleeping doesn't sound like the nicest way to go.

I hope you've settled back into your own flat by now. Your

neighbour Frank does sound a little peculiar! But then again, I suppose we all have our little quirks that we're probably not aware of most of the time. Like when Janey stayed at mine for a few days? She has this really annoying habit of leaving soap suds on the dishes when she does the washing up. It was driving me up the wall! I mean, what's so hard about giving the plates a quick rinse? Then again, she claims I do this clicking thing with my jaw when I'm deep in thought. I'm not at all sure she's right, but it goes to show how little things can quickly become annoying.

Speaking of Janey, I was up for hours on the phone to her last night. But it wasn't about Eric this time. Or rather, it was *kind of* about Eric. Janey's pregnant! She's due in October. Actually, she's a bit worried (hence the late-night phone call) because Eric's still in Tokyo and they're not sure if he should come back here, or if she should fly out there. They hadn't planned on starting a family just yet, so they've got lots of stuff to consider. But they seem closer than ever (relationship-wise I mean, obviously not geographically), and whatever happens, I know Janey's going to be a great mum.

We talked for hours, and eventually got into stories from our childhood and all the silly stuff we got up to back then. We were so wicked sometimes! Most of it was fairly harmless stuff. Like once, we snuck into a cinema through the back to watch a horror film – I can't remember the title, something to do with an exorcism – and were terrified for weeks. I remember us texting back and forth at 3 in the morning because we were too frightened to sleep. On occasion it was a bit more serious, though. We must have been fourteen or so and got our hands on a pack of cigarettes. (I can't remember where, but it seems like everyone smoked in those days.) So then we had a competition to see who could smoke the most cigarettes before being sick. I didn't win, but it put me off smoking for life.

Janey said she's worried about what she would do if her own child ever did that sort of thing. I can't say I had an answer for that. I didn't say as much to Janey because she's anxious enough as it is, but I think I'd like to take younger me by the scruff of the neck and shout 'SMOKING TILL YOU PUKE? WHAT WERE YOU THINKING?!!' I guess Janey will have to play it by ear and hope things turn out for the best. But she's such a loving person, I know she'll be the best mum a kid can have.

Actually, I've just realised that I've never asked you about your own family. Do you have any children or grandchildren? (Apologies if I'm making you out to be older than you are!) I guess you would've mentioned if you and Marion had children, but then again, the topic hasn't come up yet and we've had plenty of other things to talk about.

On the subject of children, Maisie came back to the shop today. I showed her some of the other instruments, but she was only really interested in the violin, so we had another little playing session like last time, except today, I let her hold the bow on her own and showed her how to move it across the strings. She grasped it immediately, intuitively almost. It's quite amazing the sound some people can produce without effort! Then I showed her the basic finger placement and had her practise some scales. Arnold, she was in the shop for three whole hours! When it was time to lock up, I almost had to prise the violin from her hands. It's such a shame she can't afford tuition, although I said I could talk to her parents about buying an instrument on instalments. She gets so much joy from it, I'd really like her to be able to continue.

Now that I don't play any more, it would be nice to pass the baton on, as it were. I won't go into why I gave up, if you don't mind. It's . . . complicated, and I don't want to bore you with it. Besides, my left fingertips have grown far too soft now. Back when I used to practise for hours every day, I had these hard, calloused fingertips from holding down the strings. Autumn used to tease me about them all the time, which was rich, coming from her. When she was little, she h*ad* *the* smelliest *fee*t y**ou** can i*M*agine------------------------------------

Sorry if that last sentence is illegible; Yuuko just jumped up and sat on the letter. I've been ignoring her for the last half an hour and I think she's jealous I'm spending so much time writing. She can be a real nuisance sometimes, like she sleeps everywhere she shouldn't – on my laptop, in the sink, in my clothes drawers. And she's scratched my curtains to shreds; they look like they've been in a fight with a chainsaw.

Having said that, I wouldn't miss her for the world. It's amazing how pets grow on you, right? Speaking of, have you never thought about getting another dog? I don't know if they allow pets at Sunny Fields, but if they do, perhaps it would be nice for you to have a companion? And I'm sure I've read somewhere that pet owners live longer.

OK, got to go now, before Yuuko knocks the pen out of my hand again. Till next time.

Love, Hope

P.S. My birthday is on the 7th June, but you'll have to tell me yours now, too

Hello my dear. Just checking in.

Hi Nan, how are things?

Fine. Same old. How about you?

Also fine. Also same old. Ah, in fact, I do
have some news. Remember me
telling you about Janey? My best friend?

Yes! Well, I remember your mum telling me about
all the stuff you two got up to when you were
younger. You were a right pair, apparently.

Least said, Nan :) Anyway, she's pregnant!
My best friend Janey Williams is having a baby!!!

How lovely! Please pass on my congratulations when you
see her. When's the baby due? I'll get Madame Zargo to
do a horoscope. Get the little one off to a flying start.

The due date is in October, but I really
don't think that'll be necessary

When in October? Before or after the 23rd?
Not sure. Does it matter?

Does it matter whether the baby is a Libra or a Scorpio?
I should think so!!! I'm not too keen on Scorpios, if
I'm honest. Secretive and jealous. And uptight to
boot. No, give me a peace-loving Libra any day.
Nan, I think you're taking this all far too seriously.
Is this Madame Zargo charging you money?

Well, you have to cross her palm with
silver, otherwise you'll have bad luck.
Hmm. Sounds a bit dodgy to me. Does
Grandpa know what you're up to?

No, and you'd better not tell him. He started playing
golf a couple of months ago, and when I found out
what the club membership costs, I was fuming. Two
hundred dollars a month! Can you believe it? So
I marched down there and told the club secretary
he'd made a mistake and that I was terminating his
contract. They refused at first, so I had to pretend your
Grandpa isn't quite right in the head any more and
could no longer make legally binding agreements.
So, after all that, he'd go mad if he knew I was paying
even a single *cent* for Madame Zargo's services.
OK, I promise not to tell. Anyway, Janey's
coming round next week before
she's off to join her husband in Tokyo (of all places!)
and plans to stay there until the baby arrives. Eric, her
husband, has extended his contract with the orchestra
for another twelve months – there's a whole other
level of appreciation for classical music in Japan,
apparently – so Janey's going to have the baby there.
Jeez, Nan, I'm going to miss her so much! I'll have
to see if I can fit in a week away from the shop.

Well, if you're planning on travelling all that
way, you should get a fligHT TO SYDNEY
WITH A STOPOVER IN TOKYO

142

No need to shout, Nan! I promise to try
and visit if I go and see Janey

         I'M NOT SHOUTING. I TURNED THE CAPS LOCK
         ON AND THE BLOODY THING IS STUCK NOW.
         BLOODY COMPUTERS!!! BUT NEVER MIND

Maybe you've got some crumbs or something stuck in the
keyboard? Turn it upside down and give it a little shake

         ADJFAHL%UBEKBLU§BAFLYLKJSW=J OIER
         LIJLXKKKKKKKKKKKKKKKKKKKKKK

Well, any luck?

         OBVIOUSLY NOT. HOW ANNOYING! I ONLY BOUGHT
         IT FIVE MONTHS AGO; AND IT'S NOT AS IF GRANDPA
         IS A WHIZZ AT FIXING THESE THINGS. OH WELL;
         I'LL JUST HAVE TO TAKE IT TO THE REPAIR SHOP

Ok, Nan. I think we should leave it there. Love you!

         LOVE YOU TOO

         10th February

Dear Arnold,

Here's a little something to cheer you up. Hope you like it!
Love, Hope

         18th February

Dear Hope,

Thank you so much for the bedspread! It looks absolutely terrific and brightens up the room no end. I particularly like the little silver quavers embroidered on the
corners. I am no expert in home furnishings (that was
always Marion's forte – if you'll pardon the pun!), but they
are most unusual and set off the navy blue very elegantly. A
one thousand percent improvement on Barbara's chintzy
quilt (may she rest in peace). I am very touched by your

generosity and I only wish I had something to offer you in return.

I've made a note of your birthday – you've just missed mine by a few weeks (3rd February), which is probably for the best. Some of my fellow residents still celebrate with banners and balloons and party games, but I can't help but feel that birthdays only signify that I'm getting past my sell-by date.

My days of being a pet owner are over, I'm afraid. I suppose it would be nice to have company on my daily walks, but I wouldn't dream of inflicting my dreary old self on a defenceless animal. No, I'll just cherish the memories and leave it at that. I am glad you derive so much pleasure from Yuuko, though. By the way, you may want to consider getting her a cat tree. That might stop her climbing up and scratching your curtains. Of course, they say that dogs are much easier to train than cats, though I don't remember Chutney being the most obedient of pets.

Maisie sounds like a tremendous girl. (For what it's worth, her name comes from the Greek and means 'Pearl'.) Such enthusiasm and focus; that's unusual in a child that age. I can remember only a handful of such pupils throughout my teaching career, but I remember them very well. They were the children who reminded me why I became a teacher in the first place. Of course, that doesn't mean I disliked my other pupils (though there's a bad apple in every bunch, it seems), but it's the really special one, the keen, dedicated pupils, that are every teacher's *raison d'être*.

In this vein, may I ask you a question? Have you ever considered becoming a teacher yourself? I don't mean a schoolteacher, but the way you speak about Maisie, the joy you seem to get from showing her how to play the violin reminds me of how I used to feel when I connected with pupils. I know people who subscribe to the 'Those who can, do. Those who can't, teach' view, but I find that a pretty ignorant and small-minded stance, to be honest. Teaching never needs to get boring, as long as you keep your own mind fresh and sharp. I can't describe how amazing it was when a pupil showed an insight I never expected to see; when they suddenly 'got it'. Or when the class clown – you know, the one who'll do anything to get a laugh – secretly stayed behind in class to share his remarkable poetry with me. And teaching others helps *you* learn, too. More than you might think. When you've taught the same thing over a lengthy period of time, you realise you understand it differently than the first time you taught it.

Goodness, I think I should leave it at that. I sound like I'm trying to recruit you to join some kind of teacher cult!

All very best wishes,
Arnold

FROM: Hope Sullivan
TO: Janey Williams
SUBJECT: Re: Kiwi fruit

Dear Janey,

Thanks for the copy of the sonogram! It's pretty grainy, but I can definitely see the family resemblance, haha. I'm not saying you're big-headed or anything . . . But seriously, he or she* is so perfectly formed, it's amazing! And to think you're carrying that little kiwi-sized being inside you. I'm so happy for you, Janey, and I know you're going to be an amazing mum.

How does next Thursday sound? I'll close the shop early (one of the few benefits of being the manager) and we can say goodbye properly. Since you're not drinking, shall we have a go at making some mocktails?

Love, Hope

*You have to swear to tell me as soon as you find out!

Dear Arnold,

I'm so glad you like the bedspread. I was a little worried you might hate it, or think I was being forward. Actually, I embroidered the quavers myself; I thought I'd add a little something special to personalise it. Please consider it a belated birthday present :) I'm quite a few years younger than you, but I think I understand your feelings towards birthdays. I mean, I'm only 27, but every birthday reminds me of opportunities missed and gone forever. Does that make sense? Thinking back ten years ago – the things I had planned for my life! And with each birthday, they seem more and more out of reach. Ha, listen to the two of us. We sound like birthday equivalents of the Christmas Grinch! How about we make a pact to force each other to celebrate our birthdays? I for one am glad that you're alive, and I look forward to sending you a birthday card next year. In return, I will graciously accept birthday greetings in June. What do you think?

You describe teaching with such genuine enthusiasm; you must have been wonderful at it. Although I had to laugh out loud at your idea of me becoming a teacher, sorry! It's very sweet of you to say, but I really don't think I'd have any talent for that. If I were a teacher, though, I wouldn't think twice of becoming Maisie's. She comes into the shop regularly now. I've been showing her the basics, and though I still think she needs proper tuition, because she's undoubtedly talented, I know that if it's meant to be, the music will find her. That sounds a bit airy-fairy, I know, but I really believe it.

And it can happen the other way around, too. What I mean is, you can play music as much as you like, but if you're only doing it out of a sense of duty, and not because it sings to your heart, then it's not going to stick. There was this boy in my youth orchestra, Max, who was a brilliant musician (he played the clarinet) and who everyone thought had this starry career ahead of him. He was *driven*. I mean, he practised for hours every day until his lips were cracked and swollen. Anyhow, a while back, my friend Janey ran into him while she was on tour, and it turns out he *hated* playing. He loved the music, but the only reason he practised so hard was to fulfil his parents' expectations. They'd had plans for him to become this famous classical musician from when he was four years of age. Every family holiday they went on was music-related – Salzburg, Bergen, Prague, Leipzig. The poor guy even had to dress up as Mozart at Hallowe'en. Eventually, shortly before he was due to go to music college, he had some sort of breakdown and so he just stopped playing. From one day to the next, just like that. He went out and got a regular job and a regular girlfriend, and never touched his clarinet again. The funny thing is, Janey said he seemed really happy.

I don't know why I'm mentioning this story here, but something about it resonated with my own life, about whether I could ever be happy without music. It was, in a way, my choice to stop playing, but I suppose you hit the nail on the head about 'shelving things for later', and to some extent, I agree. It's just . . . oh, I don't know. It's like there's this internal battle going on inside me, and it can get so exhausting that I just want to crawl into bed and pull the covers over my head and wait for everything to pass over me. And before you say anything, I'm well aware that this isn't a solution to anything.

But it has got me thinking about shaking things up. Writing to you, and receiving your lovely letters, has tipped the balance, I suppose. I'm not talking about giving up my job, or reinventing myself, but perhaps the idea of a shop cafe isn't that stupid after all. I know some bookshops that offer coffee and cake, and that seems to work well. It would be nice to make something happen for a change, rather than waiting for change to befall me. Does that make sense?

Oh, and on the subject of cakes, I don't suppose you have a good recipe for *Sachertorte*? Janey adores it (she was on tour in Vienna a couple of years ago) and I would love to bake her one as a goodbye present. She's off to Tokyo next week and I'd like to send her off with a bang. She's pregnant and can't drink, so I thought I'd treat her to the next best thing: chocolate cake. I am going to miss her so much; we've been best friends for as long as I can remember, and even if we don't see each other as often as we used to, the thought of her going to live on the other side of the world makes me feel like I'm losing something precious. Does that make sense? I'd love to fly over and visit her, but if I move forward with the cafe, I guess I'll be pretty much tied up with that. Decisions, decisions . . . Maybe I should consult Madame Zargo, haha.

Love, Hope

11th March

Dear Hope,

I'm so happy to hear that my letters have helped motivate you to consider moving forward with the cafe idea. And I agree, there is something very powerful about making change happen. I think you should absolutely go for it! It seems to me that you have a huge amount of creativity and enthusiasm, and it would be a shame to let that go to waste. Perhaps I could even come and pay you a visit once the cafe is up and running! As regards a trip to Japan, why not do both? The cafe and Tokyo? A word of advice from an old man (who is no Madame Zargo, but who has over 70 years' life experience): You're only young once, so live your life. Besides, life would be pretty boring if we knew the answers to everything.

Regarding a cake for your friend, personally I think *Sachertorte* is overrated unless you can get your hands on the real thing (i.e. in Vienna). The original recipe is famously secret, so I'd be doing you a disservice to encourage you to bake one. However, the Hotel Sacher isn't the only one with a secret recipe for the most delicious chocolate cake. In fact, I have one of my very own, which I am happy to share with you. I borrowed Frank's typewriter to copy it out, and I've added a few scribbled tips to help you along the way. A few of the ingredients might sound odd, but trust me, they work.

This cake regularly won the annual village fete baking competition and it's delicious, if I say so myself. I've kept the recipe very close to my chest for all these years (which is why I didn't get a member of staff to make a photocopy), but I'd like to share it with you as a small thank-you in return for the bedspread!

Warm wishes (and all the best to your friend),
Arnold

CONFIDENTIAL

Ingredients
- 4 oz cooked sauerkraut (rinsed thoroughly and rubbed dry)
- 4 oz melted dark chocolate
- 2 tbsp cocoa powder
- ¼ cup boiling water
- 4 oz butter, room temperature
- 5 oz caster sugar
- 2 eggs
- 4 oz apple sauce
- 8 oz self-raising flour
- pinch of salt

(I used old-fashioned imperial measurements, so you might have to convert these to grams)

For the ganache
- 4 oz melted dark chocolate
- 4 oz melted milk chocolate
- 8 oz double cream

This brings out the full flavour of the cocoa: it's called 'blooming'

170° C (for modern ovens)

Preheat the oven to 335 °F. Chop the sauerkraut very finely. Melt the chocolate slowly in a bain-marie and set aside. Mix the cocoa powder with ¼ cup of boiling water. In a separate bowl, cream the butter and sugar together in a bowl until fluffy. Beat in the eggs.

Stir in the melted chocolate, the cocoa, the sauerkraut and the apple sauce, then sift in the flour and salt and fold in carefully.

Divide the mixture equally between two 8-inch lined cake tins. Bake on the middle shelf of the oven for approx. 25 minutes, or until the top feels spongey when touched lightly.

Set aside to cool for 15 minutes, then tip out onto a *The cake should feel sticky* wire rack and cool completely.

For the ganache, break the chocolate into pieces and put in a heavy-bottomed pan with the cream. Heat gently *Do not boil!* and stir together until the chocolate has melted and the mixture starts to thicken. Leave to cool slightly. Use half to fill the cake, spreading the rest on top.

Happy baking, Hope!

Dear Mr Quince,
    We've never met, but I'm Hope's best friend, Janey. I'm writing to say THANK YOU for the most delicious cake I've ever tasted!!! If I weren't already married, I would seriously consider getting down on one knee and proposing to you.
    Kind regards,
    Janey Williams

    Bon Voyage!
        Have a wonderful time out there, Janey, and look after yourself and the kiwi fruit (although probably more of an avocado now, right?). I promise to come and visit you in Japan.
        Love, Hope

10 Things To Do Before I Turn Thirty

- Visit another continent
- Learn French
- Run a half marathon
- Finish reading ~~War and Peace~~ *Lord of the Rings Trilogy*
- Pay off all credit card debt
- Have savings
- Learn to cook a five-course meal (with wine accompaniment)
- ~~Play violin solo *Méditation (from Thaïs)*~~ Learn to meditate
- Fall in love
- Be brave

CHAPTER 23

Dear Arnold,

I have BIG news!!! Drumroll please . . .

I've spoken to Harry and Ingrid (the shop owners) about the cafe, and they love the idea! They will have to talk to their bank first about taking out a small loan, because they don't have so much ready cash to hand. But I've assured them that I'll try and keep the costs as low as possible and put in all the hours I can to get the place ready, and I'm 100% sure the investment will pay off quickly. I'm just brimming with ideas, Arnold! I haven't felt this excited about anything for a long time. We could have music-themed cakes (feel free to offer suggestions!) and musical elevenses and afternoon tea. And perhaps regularly showcase an instrument – an 'instrument-of-the-month' sort of thing, and perhaps a voucher for tea and cake when customers make a purchase in the shop etc. etc. etc . . . I'd better stop here before I bore you to death! Thanks so much for your encouragement, I know I wouldn't have dared to try this if not for your support.

Love, Hope

21st March

Dear Hope,

That's wonderful news about the shop! I am so happy to hear you're taking some positive steps forward. You must keep me posted – I want to know all the details. I'll also have a look through my recipe collection to see if there's anything suitable I can recommend. Cake and music – what a delightful combination!

All very best wishes,
Arnold

FROM: Dr Autumn Sullivan
TO: Hope Sullivan
SUBJECT: Brilliant news!

Hey there sis!

I've just put down the phone to Nan and she told me the news. Wow, that sounds exciting! Let me know if there's anything I can do to help. Krish and I are working mad hours, of course, but I'll let you know if we get a minute or two to drop by and get out the paintbrushes. Well done, Hope, I'm so glad this is working out for you!

Love, Autumn

FROM: Harry Clark
TO: Hope Sullivan
SUBJECT: Chat?

Hello Hope,

I know it's your day off tomorrow, but do you think you could drop by for a little chat?

Best, Harry

FROM: Hope Sullivan
TO: Harry Clark
SUBJECT: Re: Chat?

Sure, Harry, 2 pm ok?

ASHENDEN PETROL STATION

Smirnoff Red Label 70 CL	£13.00
Häagen-Dazs Salted Caramel Ice Cream 460 ML	£4.50
	£17.50

MIDNIGHT MEDICINES PHARMACY

Boots Ibuprofen 400mg Tablets Max Strength – 16 Tablets	£2.59
	£2.59

TO: Hope Sullivan
FROM: Jobs4U
SUBJECT: Job alerts

Dear Hope Sullivan,

Thank you for signing up to job alerts! Here are the results for your area:

Retail Assistant
Posted 6 days ago
£8.21 per hour, temporary (maternity cover)
Our company believes in investing in our workforce and making a difference. We are now recruiting for a
Retail Assistant to join our supportive corporate family on a temporary basis. As a Retail Assistant . . .

See more

<u>Sales and Marketing Assistant</u>
Posted 8 days ago
£16K–£18K (depending on experience) per annum, permanent, full-time
An exciting position within a growing and ambitious company. This varied role will involve both sales support and marketing duties across the business. An excellent opportunity . . .

See more

<u>Retail Assistant</u>
Posted 9 days ago
Competitive salary, temporary, part-time
As a result of our expansion plans and our continued ongoing success we are looking to appoint a part time Retail Assistant. In this role you will be responsible for our flagship store delivering great service and promoting our store as a unique one-stop shopping experience . . .

See more

FROM: Janey Williams
TO: Hope Sullivan
SUBJECT: Everything ok?

Hi Hope,

You've been awfully quiet and you haven't been answering your phone. Is everything ok? Have you changed your number and forgotten to tell me??? Autumn says you're probably just busy at the shop, but I'm starting to get a bit worried. Please please please call me, or I'll be forced to hop on a plane and come and see you. And I'm getting absolutely HUGE now, so I'd have to book two seats (if they even let me on the plane) and that will bankrupt me. Or you, cos I'll make you pay me back.

Love, Janey

Dear Arnold,

I know it's been a while since I last wrote – many apologies. Things have been crazy around here, and I've only just now managed to catch my breath and put pen to paper.

Where to start? Well, as you know, I discussed my idea of the shop cafe with Harry and Ingrid, and they thought it was a great idea. I was on cloud nine, Arnold – this was the first good thing that had happened to me for years and I was all pumped up and ready to take on the world! And it all went downhill from there . . .

First, the Food Standards Agency informed us that there was no way we'd get permission to run a cafe on the premises. They gave us a long list of things we'd have to change or install: handwashing facilities and additional toilets, equipment storage, food preparation areas. The ceilings would have to be re-rendered, and the windows and doors replaced to comply with fire safety and food hygiene standards etc., etc. Just reading the list gave me a headache. All I wanted was to offer good coffee and a few cupcakes. Who would've thought there would be so many hoops to jump through?

My first thought was, 'That's disappointing, but hey-ho, *c'est la vie* etc.' And then it went from bad to worse. For some reason, the local authority environmental health department got wind of it, maybe the Food Standards Agency copied them in or something, but the next thing I knew was there was an inspector in the shop asking all about fire hazards and emergency exits and insulation retardants. It turns out the place needs a complete overhaul to comply with regulations. New doors, new insulation, everything. We've been given six weeks to complete the work or they'll shut us down. But there's no way Harry and Ingrid can afford it. I know, because I've been doing the accounts for the past few years. We just about manage to stay out of the red, but there's absolutely no wiggle-room. And a bank loan to cover the costs would keep them in debt for their whole retirement.

I feel so guilty, Arnold. If I hadn't had this stupid idea, if I'd been happy with what I've got rather than wanting more, this would never have happened. Now Harry and Ingrid have no other choice but to sell the shop. I've gone through the sums a thousand times, but even if I re-mortgaged my flat, it doesn't come close to what I'd need to buy it off them. And I can't get a loan from a bank, I've already enquired. That means I'm out of a job and back to square one.

I hope you are doing well.

Love, Hope

FROM: Janey Williams
TO: Hope Sullivan
SUBJECT: Re: Life Sucks

Oh babe! What a nightmare. Hang on in there, everything will turn out right, I just know it. Just wish I was there to give you a big hug. Jx

CHAPTER 24

23rd April

Dear Hope,

I am so sorry to hear about your troubles. Please don't feel guilty about it, though. It wasn't a stupid idea, far from it, and there was no way you could have anticipated a visit from the health department. I don't know Harry and Ingrid, but from what you've told me about them, I very much doubt they blame you either.

I've been thinking a lot about your predicament since I received your letter. I would dearly like to help you, but sadly I have neither the financial means nor the expertise. However, there is a chap here, Hugh Warner, who is a retired bank manager. He's getting on a bit – over eighty, I think – but from what I gather, he's still full of life and is bound to know a thing or two about financing and investment and that sort of thing. If you give me a day or two, I'll see if I can pick his brains. To my shame, I haven't made much of an effort getting to know my fellow residents, so I'm not at all sure he'll want to talk to me. But I will give it my best shot and let you know if he has any helpful advice.

Chin up, Hope!
All my best,
Arnold

29th April

Dear Arnold,

Thank you for your kind words. It's lovely to get your support, but I didn't mean to burden you with my problems. Please don't feel you have to do anything on my behalf, and certainly not anything that would make you uncomfortable. I got myself into this mess, and I have to try and get myself out of it. I will try and write as often as I can, but I might be busy sorting out my life for the next month or two.

Love, Hope

4th May

Dear Hope,

If you'll forgive me for completely ignoring your instruction, I went ahead and spoke with Hugh. He is a bit hard of hearing, and my voice is now somewhat hoarse from shouting at him, but he is actually a very pleasant fellow, and is as bright and sparky as a 30-year-old. We had a nice (if somewhat loud) chat over a pot of tea and garibaldi biscuits in the common room. It turns out that Hugh was born only a mile away from the village I grew up in! It might sound silly to a young person like you, but there is something very comforting about finding someone whose roots have a connection to yours.

Anyway, to cut a long story about two old men reminiscing short, I laid out your predicament to him, and he considered it with a lot of care and attention. He asked a few questions about you and the business, and then suggested applying for funding from something called an 'angel investor'. Do you know what that is? I had never heard of it, but Hugh tells me it's an investor who gives financial backing to small businesses in return for ownership equity. He says there is a plethora of information to be found on the internet, though I'm afraid I couldn't quite follow all the details. Hugh is miles ahead of me in that regard. But I'm sure a smart young woman like you will be able to find out more.

Again, please forgive me if I've been too forward by consulting Hugh, but I so want to help if I can. After all, what are friends for?

Best wishes,
Arnold

11th May

Dear Arnold,

No, you haven't been too forward at all. At this stage, I need all the help I can get, though I'm not so sure about me being 'smart', considering the situation I now find myself in. But I've researched angel investors and I'm definitely going to give it a go. I'll keep you posted.

By the way, Hugh sounds lovely! I'm so glad you've found someone nice to talk to. Please pass on my regards and thanks.

Love, Hope

UNDER OUR WING Inc.
Seed Investments

Dear Ms Sullivan,

Thank you for your recent application, which we reviewed with interest. However, based on our team's evaluations, we will not be able to partner with your venture at this stage. Our biggest concerns included:

- Failure to provide a bottom-up analysis
- Not connecting your final model to the narrative
- No indication of your TAM and SAM
- Underestimating your variable expenses
- Not knowing your comparable market metrics

In general, we do not consider a business that has shown consistently average performance to be an attractive proposition for investment.

We wish you all the best for the future.

Sincerely,

Under Our Wing Inc.

Business Glossary Online™ Search Result:

TAM -> total addressable market
SAM -> serviceable addressable market

Hello! Any news?
Best, Harry

Hi. No luck yet, but I'm working on it. Hx

FROM: Kingsfield Library
TO: Hope Sullivan
SUBJECT: Your borrowing request

Dear Ms Sullivan,

We can confirm that we have the following books in stock:
How To Secure Investment 101
Flying With Angels – A Comprehensive Guide to Angel Investment
Writing Persuasive Business Proposals
Holistic Retail Interior Design – Creating Successful Retail Spaces

To click & collect, please follow the link below.

Kind regards,
Kinjal Singh, Librarian

YWAIT INVESTORS
Why Indeed?

Dear Hope,

Thank you for applying to YWait. While we consider your application thoughtful and comprehensive, we are sorry to say we are not in a position to accept your proposal for funding.

Due to the large number of proposals we receive, we are not able to provide individual feedback on your application. (This link explains why.)

Please don't be discouraged by this rejection. In today's uncertain market, we are obliged to focus on ventures that we consider to have the most certain chances of success.

We wish you the best of luck in securing funding elsewhere.

YWait

BARTON & HANLEY BUILDING SOCIETY

Dear Ms Sullivan,

Our records indicate that your mortgage payment is now 60 days overdue. If you have already submitted payment, please disregard this notice. If you have not yet paid this account, we would appreciate your remittance or being advised of your payment plans as soon as possible.

In the event that you are struggling to make payments, please contact a member of staff at the number below. (Please do not respond directly to this email.)
Sincerely,

Customer Service
Barton & Hanley Building Society

To my very best friend
  Happy Birthday!
    This will be a great year for you, Hope, I just know it!
    Love, Janey x

Happy 28th birthday!
  All best,
    Autumn & Krish

To our dear granddaughter
  Have the best of birthdays!
    Love, Nan & Grandpa

To Hope
  With all our best wishes for your birthday.
    Fingers and toes still firmly crossed!
      Best,
        Harry and Ingrid

To my fellow Birthday Grinch
  Many Happy Returns of the Day
    Warmest wishes,
      Arnold

                                                    10th June

Dear Arnold,

It was lovely to receive the birthday card. I've been feeling quite miserable lately, and the card brought a smile to my face, so thank you. I promised to keep you posted about the shop, but I don't have much news other than to tell you about the latest round of rejections I've received.

It's beyond frustrating. I lie awake at night, unable to stop my brain from generating yet more ideas – sponsoring local music competitions, creating a website for online sales, partnering with instrument makers – while at the same time knowing it's probably all futile. I know I have to be patient and that it would be a miracle if I found an investor overnight, but I feel like I'm treading water and I'm slowly running out of energy. It's all I can do not to drown.

I've now begun sending out job applications to be a retail assistant. It's a far cry from what I'd like to be doing, but unless some fairy godmother out there waves her magic wand and deposits a wad of money in my bank account, it's my only realistic option.

Sorry for sounding so glum. I'd much rather write something cheerful but I'm afraid I haven't got the energy for that, either.

Love, Hope

17th June

Dear Hope,

Thank you for taking the time to write to me. Your letters also truly brighten up my days. I'm glad you appreciated the card, though I'm sorry to hear you're feeling so miserable. The rainy weather isn't helping, is it? But I don't want you worrying about sounding glum. I know how hard it can be to feign cheerfulness when you feel close to despair on the inside, and I'd much rather you were honest with me about how you're feeling.

It seems you've given the changes to the shop a lot of thought. Your ideas sound wonderful and I would invest in you without hesitation if I were able. I'm not sure how much comfort it is for you to know that I am cheering you on, but it means you are not alone, if nothing else. Motivational quotes are ten-a-penny these days, but I genuinely believe that cream always rises to the top. Please don't give up, my dear.

Best wishes as always,
Arnold

FROM: Harry Clark
TO: Hope Sullivan
SUBJECT: Offer

Dear Hope,

I trust you are well. You're probably very busy, but I needed to let you know that Ingrid and I have been approached by a large retail chain with a view to purchasing the property. As I hope you know, Ingrid and I would be loath to sell the business, which has been our life's work and which we are very much attached to, to one of these faceless global companies. However, the deadline to implement the necessary health department renovations is coming up fast and we are running out of options.

With no children of our own, it had been our hope for some time to come to an arrangement to pass the shop on to you. We are aware of how much Harry's Harmonies means to you and are truly grateful for all the time and effort you have put into the shop over the years. But as our only old-age provision, we sadly cannot afford to lose out on it and will be forced to accept the offer if you are unsuccessful in securing alternative funding.

I am truly sorry to put this added pressure on you, Hope. If there were any other option, I would happily take it, believe me. If there is anything I can do to help in the meantime, please let me know.

All best wishes,
Harry

Janey, I give up. Hx

Stay strong, sweetie! I believe in you. Jx

Lighthouse Investments
TO: Hope Sullivan
SUBJECT: Your request for funding!

Hi!

Thanks for reaching out to Lighthouse! Building a business is hard work, so we truly appreciate your passion and commend you on all your progress so far!

Here at Lighthouse, we are looking to invest in young, dynamic entrepreneurs who are looking to rock the market!

From your request we understand that the business in question was established some 30 years ago and therefore does not fall within our scope of interest.

Enjoy the rest of your week!

The Lighthouse Team

FROM: Janey Williams
TO: Hope Sullivan
SUBJECT: Harry's

Hi babe! I've had an idea. (If it's rubbish, just ignore it.) You remember Eric's sister Denise from the wedding? The pompous one in the ridiculous feather-trimmed hat who complained the champagne wasn't the proper vintage? Yeah, what a fun gal she was! Except for when Autumn put a whoopee cushion on her seat, remember? She didn't think that was fun at all. Ah, happy days . . .

Anyway, Denise happens to be an investment banker (who is absolutely *loaded* btw) and Eric's spoken with her and explained your circumstances. At first, she was a bit 'Um, yeah why should I care?', but Eric explained that the shop was situated in a prime location with booming passing trade (OK, I might have made him exaggerate a little), and that due to an unforeseen and unfortunate series of events you've got a slight cashflow problem, and she'd be crazy not to get in there before some big-shot property developer snapped it up and turned it into a huge profit.

To get to the point, she *might* be willing to put up the money for you as an angel investor to buy the shop from Harry and Ingrid. (Personally, I find the terms 'angel' and 'Denise' a bit hard to reconcile in a single sentence, but maybe that's just me.) Long story short, she said she'd need more information before she committed to anything – a proper application with business plans and all that sort of stuff (sorry, I have no idea what I'm talking about, but hey, I'm a musician, not a business-woman). I hope you don't mind, but I've forwarded your details to her and she'll be in touch.

Darling Hope, I'll sign off here. Tokyo is great – even though I'm not allowed any sushi or sake while I'm pregnant :(

Do let me know what Denise says – fingers firmly crossed!!!

Sayonara, Janey x

PS. Baby is now the size of a grapefruit, which might not sound very big, but when it sits on your bladder all day, you know about it!

FROM: Denise Carlson MBA
TO: Hope Sullivan
SUBJECT: Investment proposal

Dear Ms Sullivan,

Following a thorough review of your application and our meeting on Monday, I would like to formally submit a proposal regarding the business under discussion. I was particularly impressed by your range of ideas regarding the scalability and defensibility of the business and look forward to working with you on furthering those ideas to exploit their full potential.

Please find attached the Term Sheet for Angel Investment in Harry's Harmonies. The Term Sheet summarises the principal terms with regard to the private placement of equity securities. I would kindly request that you sign and return the document. If you have any further questions or need for clarification, please contact my office.

Yours sincerely,
Denise Carlson MBA

FROM: Hope Sullivan
TO: Janey Williams
SUBJECT: Fairy Godmother

You're the best mate ever, Janey Williams. I love you!!! Hx

FROM: Janey Williams
TO: Hope Sullivan
SUBJECT: Re: Fairy Godmother

Nothing to do with me, hun – it was all your hard work! X

FROM: Harry Clark
TO: Hope Sullivan
SUBJECT: Congratulations

Dear Hope,

We are so very, very pleased for you! It is, of course, with a heavy heart that we say goodbye to our shop, but we couldn't be happier to have you to pass it on to. We have every confidence that you will be successful with whatever changes you plan to make. It's your shop now!

We wish you all the very best for the future. Do stay in touch and let us know how everything goes.

With our warmest wishes,
Harry and Ingrid

FROM: Hope Sullivan
TO: Harry Clark
SUBJECT: Re: Congratulations

Dear Ingrid and Harry,

Many thanks for your words of encouragement. I will always be grateful that you hired me all those years ago, and for your love and support along the way. It means so much. I'm glad you're happy about all the changes I have planned, but rest assured that I will be keeping the name 'Harry's Harmonies' :)

Have a wonderful retirement.

Love, Hope

10 Things To Do Before I Turn Thirty
- Visit another continent
- Learn French
- Run a half marathon
- Finish reading ~~War and Peace~~ *Lord of the Rings Trilogy*
- Pay off all credit card debt
- Have savings
- Learn to cook a five-course meal (with wine accompaniment)
- ~~Play violin solo *Méditation (from Thaïs)*~~ Learn to meditate
- Fall in love
- ✓ Be brave

CHAPTER 25

15th July

Dear Arnold,

Again, sorry to be so slow in responding to your lovely letters. But my news will hopefully make up for the delay: it turns out that angels really do exist. I am now the proud owner (well, co-owner) of Harry's Harmonies!!! It has been an incredible, nerve-racking, rollercoaster of a process, but I've finally managed to find an investor. My fairy godmother in this case was my best friend Janey, who put me in touch with a woman who loves my ideas for the shop and is willing to finance them. It means A LOT of work, of course, but then again, it's not like I have anything else to do, right?

Thank you for your support during this difficult time, Arnold. I can't describe how much I've appreciated your letters. Some evenings, I've returned home dreading the pile of mail in my letterbox. But then spotting those cream-coloured envelopes with your beautiful handwriting among the funding rejections and payment reminders has meant more to me than you will ever know.

You were right; knowing I am not alone is the best feeling in the world.

Love, Hope

Dear Hope,

I was very pleased to receive your letter. For a while, I thought you had had enough of writing to this boring old man and, although I wouldn't have blamed you for moving on to pastures new, I realised how much I look forward to hearing from you. But your letter was definitely worth the wait – what wonderful news, Hope! I am so pleased for you. You thoroughly deserve this bit of good fortune.

Actually, you've inspired me to 'shake things up' a little myself. Nothing major (like owning and running your own business!), just something to help while away the hours. I'll admit that seeing how open-minded Hugh is with regard to new technology shamed me into overcoming my fear of these new-fangled, blinking machines. It's taken a little getting used to, but I'm 'online' now, as they say, and I've joined the International Etymological Society! Everything seems to be about the internet these days (the IES is based in Houston, Texas, of all places), so I had to ask one of the staff to help me set up an account. Membership is not at all dear, and they send out a monthly magazine, so that'll be something to look forward to – other than your lovely letters, of course. I do hope you'll continue writing to me, even if your work days will presumably be busier than ever.

Kind wishes,
Arnold

FROM: Janey Williams
TO: Hope Sullivan
SUBJECT: Congratulations!

Hey there,

Missed your call again! You've got to get a grip on the time difference, girl! We are <u>eight hours ahead</u> of you here in Tokyo.

So when you tried to call last night (at 7 pm in the UK), it was 3 am here. And there's no way in hell I'm dragging this whale of a body out of bed in the middle of the night cos you can't do simple maths!

I'm so happy things worked out with the shop! It just goes to show that you have to have a little faith sometimes. And Denise really came through, didn't she? I promise never to say anything nasty about her ever again – well, not until the next time she complains that Waitrose has run out of goji berries and – what a nightmare! – she has to make do with cranberries instead.

Oh, and Mum's finally coming to visit! She's flying out Tuesday after next and she's already started packing. I told her there's a 22 kg maximum on her baggage allowance, but she swears she'll be able to charm the airport staff into letting her take a second suitcase. Good luck charming airport staff, I told her. She hasn't flown since she was a young woman, and boy have things changed since! I have this recurring nightmare of her getting into a fist fight with airport security over the 7-inch steel nail file she just *has* to have in her hand luggage because you never know when you might break a fingernail. Hm, maybe I should keep a criminal defence lawyer on standby . . .

I must remember to ask her to bring loads of the shea moisture conditioner I use at home. It's horrendously expensive to buy here. My hair is so dry and kinky, I can't do anything with it. You straight-haired people have no idea! It doesn't help that these bloody pregnancy hormones increase hair growth. Like I really need any more of the stuff! My nails and skin are looking gorgeous though, so I'm not complaining haha.

It's true what they say about the second term. I've finally shaken off this terrible exhaustion and am able to stay awake past 8 pm, and according to Eric, I'm 'glowing'. I'm not sure this is true (I *am* sweating a lot, but the rainy season is upon us and it's humid as hell) but I think he read that somewhere and he says it to be nice. No stretch marks yet, but maybe that's because Eric rubs my belly with cocoa butter every night – or is that TMI?

I miss the orchestra sometimes, but it's also nice having a bit of time to myself. I've read loads of novels and I tend to stay in bed until eleven or so, until the baby starts doing a tap dance on my bladder. And I'm going to savour every last minute of it. Mum's already warned me that I can forget about having a weekend lie-in for the next ten years . . .

It's also the first time in my life that I can pick up the flute for the sheer joy of it. I only play the pieces I like, how I like, without some conductor telling me to speed up or slow down or cut out the embellishments. Funnily enough, being pregnant really helps my breathing when I play. It's the way the bump supports my diaphragm, I guess. I've even mastered that Ibert concerto! When the baby's here and I can finally come to visit, we should have a session together, what do you think? Just the two of us – a Mozart duet maybe?

I'm soooooooooooo happy things worked out with the shop, though I guess that means you won't be travelling any time soon? I miss you loads,

All best, Janey

PS. Oh, and by the way, I had another scan today . . . It's a girl!!!

FROM: Hope Sullivan
TO: Janey Williams
SUBJECT: Re: Congratulations!

Hi Janey,

Sorry if I woke you with my phone call the other night. I spend so much time staring at numbers, Excel spreadsheets and cash flow statements, I'm all mathed-out when I get home. I will set my alarm for 8 am and call you then. That should make it 4 pm in Japan, right?

A little girl! Oh my god, Janey, that is fantastic news! And far too important to be a mere PS – what were you thinking?! OK, a boy would've been just as wonderful, but to think you're carrying around a mini version of yourself! I really, really can't wait to meet her. Have you got a name for her yet? (By the way, in answer to your question: Yes, Thunder Chunk rubbing *any* kind of butter on you is *definitely* TMI. Keep this up and I will be forced to cancel our friendship.)

I've been really busy, but the shop is shaping up nicely. I promise to send you some photos once I'm happy with it. I'm on a pretty tight budget (Denise watches my spending like a hawk), but I've been binge-watching upcycling videos on YouTube. It's amazing what you can do with wood pallets and a nail gun! It feels like I've been in training for this: all that DIY I've been doing at home for the past few years is finally paying off. Everything has to be done in bits and pieces, because otherwise the shop would be a permanent building site, so I have to get to the shop really early to sand down a shelving unit or whatever, then pack up the tools and stuff to put in the back room (which is now earning its keep, albeit not as a cafe) before giving the shop a quick once-over before opening up to customers. It really has become a 12-hour-a-day job, but it'll be worth it, I hope. I really can't wait for you to come over and see it!

I'll make sure to call your mum and talk her through the ins and outs of 21st-century airport security. She doesn't still carry that pepper spray with her everywhere she goes, does she?

Love, Hope

FROM: Janey Williams
TO: Hope Sullivan
SUBJECT: Note to self – call criminal defence lawyer

Oh god, totally forgot about the pepper spray . . .

CHAPTER 26

Hi Hope, can you call? Autumn's in hospital. Krish

Autumn? Krish texted me and I tried
to call both him and you but neither or
you picked up. What happened?

I broke my ankle

You broke it? How?

Stupid accident involving inline
skates and a tree root

Are you ok?

Fine. Waiting to go into surgery

Surgery?

Needs a screw, apparently

Shit, Autumn. Are you in a lot of pain?

Not so much since they gave me the morphine :)

Why didn't you call me?

I'm fine, Hope, really. Didn't want to bother you

It's not a bother if my sister is about
to go into emergency surgery!

And Krish is here, he's being really sweet

I'll be there asap. Gotta close up the shop first

No! I'll be under by the time you get here anyway

I don't care. I'm on my way

Getting a bit woozy now, gotta
ggggggggggggggggggggg

Thanks for the chocolates! Sorry I was so out of
it when you were here – that general anaesthetic
was a doozy! Don't worry about coming to visit;
I know how busy you are and they're letting
me out on Thursday anyway. Hugs, Autumn

3rd August

Dear Arnold,

Quick warning: This isn't going to be a particularly cheerful
letter, so you're welcome to stop reading here.

I had a row with Autumn yesterday. Or rather, I'm not sure
if it was a row. There was no shouting or yelling, just this
undercurrent of annoyance and frustration with each other. It's
difficult to describe. What happened was this: Autumn was
rushed to hospital on Tuesday with a broken ankle and had to
have emergency surgery. But did she call me? No. I only found
out about it because her boyfriend Krish sent me a text
message. Apparently, Autumn didn't want to bother me. (Oh,
just so you know, she's fine now.)

So anyway, I went in to see her, straight after closing up the
shop, even though she'd told me not to bother. She'd just come
out of surgery and was pretty out of it from the anaesthetic, so
there wasn't much in the way of conversation. I left the chocolates I'd brought and went home and the next day she texted
me to say she doesn't want me to visit. Well, of course I visited
her – she's my sister for crying out loud! I know I'm up to my
eyeballs with work and fixing up the shop, and then with
paperwork most evenings, but how could she possibly think I'd
be too busy to see her at hospital? The expression on her face
when I walked in, though, it was like she'd just bitten into a
lemon.

I got straight to the point and asked her why she didn't
call me as soon as she was admitted to A&E. 'It's fine,' she
said, 'I know you're busy. And it's not like I'm on my own,

Krish's here.' And when I insisted that I'm never too busy for my sister, she went all silent and avoided eye-contact. Krish must have noticed it too, because he absented himself after a few minutes and rushed out mumbling something about coffee.

This is what it's been like lately. She rarely calls me, and when she does, it's to bully me into going out or finding a boyfriend. Or making fun of me for watching romcoms. I *know* they're fiction, duh! But what's wrong with a little distraction? Allowing myself to wallow in some shallow sentiment. I'm not harming anyone, am I?

I'm still so angry with Autumn. It's like she's flaunting all her success in my face, what with her great career and her lovely boyfriend and her super-exciting travels. Hold on . . .

. . . sorry, I just had to go and get a paracetamol. Stress headache, I guess. I don't know why this thing with Autumn bothers me so much. Her not wanting me to visit brought it all to the fore, I suppose, though it probably sounds a lot worse than it is. I'm not saying she's parading her brilliant life in front of me – she's not that mean – just that she gives me the constant feeling that I'm being judged. And it's not like I can talk to her about it. Sisters are supposed to be really close, right? I don't understand why she didn't want me at the hospital. Almost like I'm an acquaintance and not the closest family she has. She's not really the passive aggressive type though, so I'm at a total loss as to what her problem is. In the end, I just said my goodbyes and left. I can't help feel she's somehow accusing me of never making time for her. And that's what gets me so angry, I guess. I gave up so much so that she wouldn't have to move to Australia to live with our grandparents. My music, my career, a large chunk of my twenties. And I won't get any of that back. The least Autumn could do is appreciate what I've done for her.

I'm sorry if I'm using you as a sounding board, but there isn't really anyone else I can tell. My best friend Janey is on the other side of the world, and she's pregnant, so I don't want to burden her with my stuff. Now I'm stuck with not knowing whether to call Autumn, or to just let things lie. She'd probably deny it all, anyway. And maybe I'm just being over-sensitive. But wouldn't *you* call your closest family if you'd been admitted to hospital?

Well, that's all I have for you this time, my apologies. Now – I'm off to find Yuuko. Stroking a pet is supposed to help reduce stress.

Love, Hope

10th August

Dear Hope,

First of all, I hope Autumn is recovering well! I have an appointment for a check-up soon and Autumn is one of the few doctors who bothers to warm up the stethoscope before placing it on my skin. Small things can make a big difference, you know.

Secondly, don't worry about using me as your sounding board, if in return, you don't mind listening to an old man's advice. On this note, I don't want to interfere, but I think you should talk to Autumn about how you feel, even if it takes a little coaxing. Perhaps she was feeling tired or 'off' (pain, medication etc.), as is often the case after surgery. Believe me, when I had my appendix out ten years ago, I was as grumpy as a bear for days.

What I'm trying to say is, too often, things are said – or not said – and before you know it, a small misunderstanding will have grown into an insurmountable barrier. If there is anything I have learned, it's that over a lifetime, there will be many things you do or say that you will regret. Some of these you might come to regret instantly, other mistakes may only become apparent over the years. If I had my time back, I would certainly do some things very differently. But my life is drawing to an end now and it has become near impossible to put certain things right again.

Please promise me that you and Autumn will talk to each other and sort it out before it's too late. Like I said, it's probably just a silly misunderstanding.

All the very best,
Arnold

CHAPTER 27

FROM: Janey Williams
TO: Hope Sullivan
SUBJECT: Probably a coconut but feels like a watermelon

Hey there,

I am getting absolutely huge. I can no longer tie my own shoe-laces, let alone paint my toenails. There's something infantilising about having to ask your husband to do up your shoes for you. And I look like a bloody whale. My ankles are puffy and my lower back is killing me and I need the loo every five minutes. And I've got another 10 weeks to go and this baby's not getting any smaller!!! Christ knows why I thought this was a good idea. Only kidding, I really can't wait for that first special cuddle.

It was great having Mum come to visit, although she's not looking well, if I'm honest. She assured me it was only jetlag, but I've never seen her looking so skinny. She must have lost at least two stone since I last saw her, and her skin has this worrying greyish hue. I hope I'm just imagining things, but being so far away I'm worried about her, you know? We both know that she's been dieting (unsuccessfully!) for years, and I'm concerned she might not be eating properly. Maybe she should start taking some vitamin supplements or something.

It's great that she and Autumn are in regular touch, though. Did you know they meet for coffee at Chez Philippe every Saturday? Mum says it's high time that Krish proposed to her, but jeez, Autumn's only 23! I told her to stop her old-woman interfering, because she does seem to hold some sway with Autumn. Apparently though, Autumn gives as good as she gets, because she got Mum to promise to cut down on those god-awful menthol cigarettes. She says Autumn keeps fussing about her health and trying to get her to go for a check-up. She obviously doesn't know how Mum feels about doctors (I'm not sure she's fully realised that Autumn is an actual doctor – she probably still sees her as that scrappy ten-year-old she used to be). Seriously though, it's good to know that someone's looking out for Mum. You know how proud she is; she'd never admit needing help from anyone. I sit here sometimes thinking I should be back there, doing her shopping for her, cleaning her flat, making sure she's looking after herself. Bloody hell, I think being pregnant has triggered all sorts of mothering hormones!

Are you still writing to that old guy? The one with the out-of-this-world cake recipes? I'd give my right arm for a slice of that chocolate cake right now! And don't think I haven't been trying to copy it: Eric wants to ban me from the kitchen cos he's tired of cleaning up after me haha. I don't know what you did to get Arnold to share his secret with you (on second thoughts, I'm not sure I *want* to know), but I don't suppose you could cheat and share it with your very very very best friend?

Okay, so now I just had to wipe away some drool from the side of my mouth. You know what, I've put on so much weight, I'm convinced it can't all be the baby. I mean, they only weigh seven pounds or so when they're born, so where have the remaining twenty pounds come from? Will I be carrying that weight all around with me for the rest of my life? Will I have to wear leggings from now on in? Will I have to choose between endless dieting and liposuction? So many questions . . .

Gotta go, all this talk of food is making me hungry.

Love and miss you,
Janey

Hope Sullivan
Janey Williams
What are you pregnant with? A fruit salad?

Dear Janey,

Please send me a picture of you and the bump! I swear I won't post it on Facebook haha. But I'm sure you look gorgeous. If it's any consolation, I woke up this morning with the most horrendous spot on my face, right on the tip of my nose, argh! I guess that's it for my hot date tonight with the hunky cello player from the Hallé Orchestra who asked me out last week . . . only kidding (about the cello player, not the spot, unfortunately). I bet I had you there for a minute though, right?

It's lovely to hear that your mum enjoyed the visit, and I promise to call her first thing tomorrow. I had noticed that she's lost weight, but maybe she's finally stumbled across a diet that works? Please don't worry about her too much; Sandra is the most resilient person I've ever met. She would frighten the living daylights out of any illness that dared to even come near her! By the way, I had no idea she and Autumn met up for coffee every week. But then again, Autumn and I haven't been speaking much recently. A stupid sister thing, I guess, and I'm sure it'll blow over soon enough.

In completely other news, you'll never guess who came into the shop the other day. It was this guy in his early fifties, with a very young woman on his arm. Apparently, she was his 'student' and was looking to buy a flute. I thought he looked familiar – just the way he had his old-man-hands around her waist – but I couldn't put a name to the face. So anyway, I asked her the usual questions, how long she'd been playing, what her budget was, if she was looking for a silver or nickel-silver head joint etc. She was quite lovely, and knew what she was talking about, but the guy kept telling her to try this one, then that one, and to me: 'Is this all you've got? Not the biggest selection, is it?' The woman finally settled on one (a Yamaha 677H, so she obviously knew her stuff) and when she went to pay, the guy ran his hand up and down her back in a way that was obviously creeping her out, and I suddenly *knew* I had recognised him. It was Grabby Griffin – I kid you not!

Well, before I blurted anything out, I politely suggested to the woman (I say woman, but she was a girl, really) to come through to the back just to 'test the acoustics' in a different room. Grabby Griffin wanted to come with us, but I told him it was strictly two people only for fire safety reasons. When we got to the back room, I told the girl – Melissa – a thing or two about Griffin, and she confirmed more or less everything, but said she'd been too embarrassed to speak up, poor thing. So I marched back out and told Griffin that I knew what he was up to, and I'd make sure to tell everyone I knew what his game was, and that he was barred from the shop from here on in. He started bleating about libel and slander, but I pointed out that it was the easiest thing in the world to set up fake social media accounts and good luck with tracing me there. He opened and closed his mouth a couple of times, like a dying fish, and stalked out. God, it felt bloody fantastic! I was on a real high for hours afterwards.

I guess I'm lucky being my own manager. Even before I became my own boss, I only ever had Harry and Ingrid telling me what to do, and they were always lovely and supportive. I don't suppose many people can say that.

I'm sorry, but I won't be revealing Arnold's secret cake recipe – I've been sworn to secrecy. I'm happy to bake you another one when you come to visit, though! Arnold is really sweet. I don't know what it is about him, but I've really enjoyed this whole letter-writing malarkey. He's so genuine, you know? And witty and charming with it. It's just so sad how very lonely he's become since his wife died. I don't know if he has any other family – I've asked him, but he just clams up. I guess his parents are long gone, and I've no idea if he has any brothers or sisters. Or maybe there's a whole 'dysfunctional family' story he doesn't want to share. It's a shame he's so reclusive though. Maybe he just needs someone to give him a nudge. Actually, that gives me an idea . . .

Look after yourself and speak soon.

Love, Hope

CHAPTER 28

Mayfield Baking Competition

Dear Mr Quince,

Thank you for your interest in this year's Bake-Off! We hereby acknowledge receipt of your entry fee of £20. As you will be aware, the competition will take place at Mayfield Community Hall on Tuesday, 29th January. We look forward to seeing you there and wish you the best of luck!

With best wishes,

Minette Stewart

1st September

Dear Hope,

I've thought long and hard about whether to write to you at all, but on balance, I think it is best to be upfront. I can only assume that it was you who entered my name in the baking competition, without my knowledge or permission, and I'm not happy about it. I'm not sure what drove you to do this, or what you thought it might achieve, but suffice it to say I will not be competing. Please let me know your bank details so I can refund you the entry fee.

With kind regards,

Arnold

Dear Arnold,

I'm writing back as soon as I can. I'm very sorry if I've offended you in any way, but I feel we've become quite close over the past months, and quite honestly, I thought this would be good for you. Your sauerkraut cake was absolutely divine, and when I read about the competition, I thought it might be just the kind of push you needed to get back out into the world!

You see, Arnold, I don't for a moment believe that you are the hermit you make yourself out to be. When I hear about your life with Marion, about how much you enjoyed being around people and socialising – not to mention baking! – I wonder whether you might just have given up on yourself a little. Do you really think this is what Marion would have wanted? I never met her of course, but I doubt she would have liked to see you sitting in your room, listening out for your neighbour's morning routine, staring out of the window, content to merely watch life go by. I'm sure she would have wanted you to be happy, meet new people, take an interest in life. I've checked out the Sunny Fields website, and it says they have all sorts of social activities. They have line dancing and a chess club, and of course, bingo nights. You should join in, Arnold; I'm sure it would do you the world of good. There's plenty of life left in you!

I realise you might worry that your baking skills have become a bit rusty, but there's no need to. I'm sure you'll beat your competitors hands down. Do please tell me you'll reconsider.

Love, Hope

Dear Hope,

How can you for one moment think this has anything to do with my baking skills being rusty? In fact, I'm not sure whether to be angry or merely disappointed that you have so profoundly misunderstood me. Have you any idea what the last five years have been like for me? From the moment I allowed the doctors to switch off Marion's life support, I have felt like I'm missing a limb. It takes every ounce of strength I have just to get out of bed in the morning. Perhaps if you knew how I was feeling, *really* feeling, you might understand how trivial the act of baking a cake is to me.

And who are you to assume to know what Marion would have wanted? You're right, you didn't meet her, because if you had, you would know she was the sweetest, kindest, most non-judgemental person there ever was, and that she would never lecture other people on how to live their lives.

And on that note – you have a cheek, young lady. Aren't <u>you</u> the one who put her life on hold? Ever since your parents' death you have used it as an excuse not to live your life. Yes, I know you had a younger sister to take care of, and you have my utmost respect for that, especially as she turned out so well-adjusted. You even gave up the violin, which must have been a terribly difficult thing to do. But Autumn is an adult now, living her own life.

I have so far avoided addressing the topic of your friendship with young Maisie – but do you not see that you are trying to get her to live the life you wish you had? I still think you would make a wonderful teacher, but it saddens me beyond belief that you have given up on your dreams. You are young and full of potential. Unlike me, you have no excuses not to use it, none at all.

Best wishes,
Arnold

13th September

Dear Arnold,

I am literally shaking as I write this. With anger, with disappointment, with sorrow. You have no _idea_ what I've been through. My parents died on the way to _my_ recital. Do you want to know the last time I picked up a violin – to play, and not to sell? It was at my parents' funeral. I was supposed to play their favourite piece in front of the congregation. A solo from Tchaikovsky's Violin Concerto in D major. Have you ever heard it? It's the most exquisite piece – filled with light and shade, darkness and hope. It pulses through your veins and touches your heart and makes you understand why music is a universal language.

But when I was standing there in front of everyone, my bow poised on the strings to perform this spectacular piece of music, I froze. Not because of nerves, or because I couldn't remember the notes, but because I realised I wasn't worthy of it. I wasn't worthy of the music, the profound feeling of joy it gave me to play, the way it connected me to everything that matters. It is painful even now, ten years later, to describe my feelings at that moment. My lungs were so tight, I couldn't breathe properly and thought I might pass out. All I could think of was that if I hadn't ever started playing in the first place, my parents would never have been driving that night so never would have died – so how could I even think of playing at their funeral? I didn't play then, and I haven't played since.

Over the last ten years, I've had to watch year after year of children like Maisie buying their first instruments, progressing with them just as I did, but then going off to realise their musical dreams while I continued to work in a dead-end job so that my sister could go to university and have the life she deserved – a life as close as possible to the one she would have had if I hadn't robbed her of her parents. You have no idea how it felt to watch Autumn suffer the loss of a mum and dad at an age when every child needs their parents to love and support them.

189

I tried my best, I really did, but I could never replace them. Or let me rephrase that: Autumn has made a success of her life in spite of me, not because of me.

THAT'S why I haven't touched my violin ever since: because I don't deserve the soul-soaring happiness it gave me to play. I don't deserve anything close to happiness. Because it's my fault my parents died.

You spent 45 years with Marion; I only had 18 years with my parents. So don't you try to talk to me about grief.

I'm sorry, but I think it's best if we stopped writing.

Hope

CHAPTER 29

FROM: Hope Sullivan
TO: Janey Williams
SUBJECT: Fuming

Hi Janey,

Well, I've just had my first ever 'letter fight'. Arnold had the nerve to lecture me about my life. I am absolutely furious!!! I really opened up to him, Janey, I told him things in confidence, thinking he was my friend. And all that time he was sitting there, judging me, thinking what a sad loser I am. Can you believe it? All I did was give him a little nudge to help him come out of his shell. I could've pointed out that he was disrespecting his wife's memory by wallowing in self-pity (which of course I didn't, even though it's true). And he responds by telling me I'm using my parents' death as an excuse not to live my life. What does <u>he</u> know about me and my life? <u>Nothing</u>! We've never even met in real life, for crying out loud. Me not living my life? What is that supposed to mean, anyway? I own my own business! Just because I choose not to play the stupid violin doesn't mean I've put my life on hold. Oh yeah, and he also accused me of living my dreams through this little girl who comes into the shop. He has NO IDEA what he's talking about. She's just some kid who wants to learn to play the violin and all I've done is be nice to her.

Right, rant over. I promise to write about nice things next time.

Love, Hope

FROM: Janey Williams
TO: Hope Sullivan
SUBJECT: Re: Fuming

Hope, I hate to say it, but perhaps Arnold has a point? I'm not saying he's right about everything, or that it was even his place to say it, but to be honest, I'm glad someone's finally said something. You know, for all these years, I've had to watch this bright, vivacious, funny girl, who had bags of musical talent, turn into a quiet, withdrawn shop worker who spends her evenings doing accounts and watching cheesy TV series. And before you start, of course there's nothing wrong with being a shop worker, and I'm hugely proud of what you've achieved with Harry's Harmonies since taking it over, but is this really what 18-year-old Hope Sullivan was dreaming of? The same Hope Sullivan who had men, women and children in the audience crying when she performed her Shostakovich solo?

Darling Hope, I think it's time you took a long, hard look in the mirror and asked yourself if Arnold may be right. If not, that's fine. But if you see even a *glimmer* of the old/young Hope looking back at you, you need to ask yourself some tough questions.

Love you always,
Janey

FROM: Janey Williams
TO: Hope Sullivan
SUBJECT: Friends?

Dear Hope,

Please don't ignore me. You're my very best friend and I love you dearly. It breaks my heart to think you might be angry at me. I told you the truth because I genuinely believe you needed to hear it, and because I only want the best for you.

Also, I have a little person growing inside me that will need a godmother very soon. And if it's not you, then I'll have no choice but to ask my sister-in-law Denise to be her godmother and that wouldn't be fair on little one, would it? Besides, I'm starting to freak out at the thought of giving birth in a country where I only speak the very basics of the language (how do you say 'Give me all the drugs and give them me NOW' in Japanese?). And Eric's sick of me moaning about haemorrhoids and puffy ankles and heartburn. But I need to talk to someone about it, and that's what best friends are for, no?

Maybe you should let the dust settle a while and write back to Arnold. From what you've told me, he's a really special man, and I think writing to him has done you the world of good. Genuine friendships are not worth losing over a little hurt pride.

Hugs and kisses,
Janey

FROM: Hope Sullivan
TO: Janey Williams
SUBJECT: Re: Friends?

Hi Janey,

Sorry I haven't got back to you sooner, but I've been busy. Denise has asked me to send her monthly business reports, to 'ensure alignment and create a shared perspective'. (So basically, I do the work and she gets to tell me how to run the shop.) It's a bore, and a complete waste of my time, but I've got her to thank that the shop is still up and running, so I don't want to seem ungrateful. Business is going well, actually; since we had to renovate the whole place anyway to comply with health & safety regs, I took the opportunity to tackle the shabbier parts of the shop, so it's looking brand new and shiny. We have quite a few more customers coming in, though I still think it's a shame the cafe didn't work out.

I've had a whole new website commissioned that lets me sell stuff online – musical scores and accessories like strings and plectrums – and although I prefer to interact with customers face-to-face, it's a good side-earner. I'm also looking into opportunities to sponsor local music competitions to drum up more business.

I've had a while to think about what you wrote in your emails. I know you're my best friend, Janey, and that you want the best for me, but I'm a bit tired of everyone and their dog thinking they know what's best for me. I realise this sounds hypocritical, given that I've spent months trying to dissuade Arnold from giving up on life, but Mum and Dad's death left a huge tear in my soul – bigger and deeper than you could imagine – and it's just not that easy to put that behind me and move on. You don't know how much pressure I feel under to live my life in a way that other people approve of. Yes, I do sometimes think that I should be out there, having fun, dating, getting drunk, enjoying my twenties. But that's not my life right now. I've got plenty of time for all that stuff in the future. And maybe it's OK *not* to be what I said I'd be when I was eight years old.

I still think Arnold was completely out of place to write what he did. I'm not sure I'm ready to just forgive and forget, and go back to what was (admittedly) a warm and friendly relationship. Besides, I was pretty angry in my last letter to him and if I'm honest, I don't think he'd want to hear from me again. Maybe some friendships have a sell-by date, and mine and Arnold's just expired.

That's not true for our friendship, of course. You are and always will be my very BFF. Thanks for caring.

Love, Hope

CHAPTER 30

Autumn, what's wrong? You weren't
making sense on the phone. Call me!

Hi Hope, Krish here. Have you heard about
Sandra? I had to give Autumn a sedative
to calm her down. She's devastated.
Best if you call again tomorrow

What's going on, Janey? Krish told me
that something's happened to Sandra.
What's the time now in Tokyo, 3 am? I'll
call you first thing tomorrow. Hx

Dear Janey,
   Words can't even begin to describe how sad I am for your
loss. I loved Sandra like a mum and she was there for me
whenever I needed her. I'm going to miss her so much.
   With love, Autumn

Dear Janey,
   I hope you're feeling a bit better. It's really hard to know
what to say – I'd like nothing more than to give you a big hug
right now. I know what it's like to lose a parent, yet I'm finding
it hard to find the right words. But I share in your sadness, and
I want you to know that it will pass. Or at least, it will lessen

over time. What's important now is that you be good to yourself, cry when you need to, take comfort in the fact that your mum was one of the loveliest people ever and that she will remain our hearts forever.

Don't worry about the formalities; Autumn and I will sort everything out on this side and keep your mum's ashes safe until you can travel again. And when you do, we'll have a memorial to remember – with food and drink and singing and dancing – like Sandra would have wanted.

Make sure Eric looks after you, and get him to give you as many back rubs and foot rubs as you need.

Love, Hope

CHAPTER 31

FROM: Julie Welsh
TO: Harry's Harmonies
SUBJECT: My daughter

Dear Manager,

I am Julie Welsh, Maisie's mother. I found out yesterday that Maisie failed to hand in her homework assignments at school for the second week running, and she admitted she'd been spending her afternoons at your shop instead. I don't know if you are aware of the fact that she's falling behind on her school work, or whether you've ever asked yourself why a nine-year-old has so much spare time on her hands. But before I start throwing accusations around, I was wondering if it would be possible for us to meet and discuss this?

Yours sincerely,
Julie Welsh

FROM: Harry's Harmonies
TO: Julie Welsh
SUBJECT: Re: My daughter

Dear Mrs Welsh,

My name is Hope Sullivan, and I am the manager of Harry's Harmonies. I'm so sorry to hear Maisie's been falling behind on her schoolwork. I honestly had no idea and it is certainly not something I would encourage! Please drop by at the shop any time. I think it would be good to chat as well.

Regards, Hope

FROM: Maisie Welsh
TO: Harry's Harmonies
SUBJECT: THANK YOU!!!

Dear Hope,

Thank you very much for talking to my mum. She's grounded me for a month for not doing my homework but I don't care because she says you think I should get violin lessons and that makes me sooooooooooooooooo happy!!!!!!!!!

Love, Maisie

FROM: Harry's Harmonies
TO: Maisie Welsh
SUBJECT: YOU'RE WELCOME!!!

Dear Maisie,

It's great to hear you want to learn the violin! But your mum is absolutely right – school comes first. How about we make a deal: you go to school every day, do <u>all your homework</u> and your chores, and then you can come round to the shop and I'll show you a few basics before you get lessons from a proper teacher. But just so you know – learning the violin isn't all fun and games. There's a lot of theory involved, too!

Love, Hope

☺

Hope, it's time! Dhes hoinh inzo lsnouz

What?

Sorry, my hands are shaking & my fingers slipped. Janey's gone into labour!

How? When? What? Where?

She's in the delivery room. Contractions every 10 mins

OMG! How's she doing?

Fine, I think. She's shouting a lot

She's in bloody labour! Of course she's shouting

She's shouting at *me*

Haha

Thanks for the support :/

Sorry, but what did you expect?
Anyway, why r u texting me? GET IN THERE!!!

Yes, ok, yes. See you on the other side!

Be strong for her, Eric. Give her a
big cuddle from me and tell her to
call me as soon as she can!

Dearest Janey,

Congratulations, sweetie! Thank you for the photo. That is the most adorable baby I've ever seen! Didn't I tell you years ago that you and Eric would make gorgeous little babies? And I was right.

You two are going to make such amazing parents. I only wish I were there right now. I'm sorry to hear how tough labour was; I can't imagine going through 18 hours of agony like that. But you got through it, and one day, little Aika will get to know how strong and tough her mother is.

Love always, Hope

Dear Aika,

Welcome to the world! I am Hope, your mum's best friend. She and I have known each other for most of our lives, and I'm so happy she's become a mama. She and your dad will be the most wonderful parents, I'm sure. They already love you to bits and you're only two weeks old!

I used to have a friend who was interested in the meanings of names. I looked up your name and it means 'love song' in Japanese. Isn't that beautiful? And your middle name is Sandra, after your Grandma. She was the loveliest, funniest, warmest person you can imagine and she met you even before you were born. When your mum was carrying you inside her tummy, your Grandma would sing to you for hours (until your mum got tired and told her to stop!). So I think the name 'love song' suits you perfectly.

Now, your parents have asked me to be your Godmother. What this basically means is that I'm the person who loves you most (other than your mum and dad of course), and that I'll always be there to protect you. So, for example, if anyone ever bullies you at school, or takes away your toys, or makes you cry, you can come to me for help. If you ever get in any kind of trouble and don't want to tell your mum and dad, I'll be there for you. If you're ever in a situation that makes you uncomfortable, I'll be there for you. You will have my number on speed dial and you can call me any time. I mean that, Aika. I don't care if it's three o'clock in the morning, or if you're a hundred miles away – you can call me and I'll be there to get you.

But I'm jumping ahead of myself! For now, I'll be the one to buy you the toys you want and take you to the zoo and let you have two whole scoops of ice-cream. I'm really looking forward to being a part of your life as you grow. You're halfway across the world at the moment, and I'm sure you have lots of travelling ahead of you, but whenever you're here, I'm here for you.

Anyway, I hope you're good at keeping surprises: I've decided I don't want to wait to see that beautiful smile your mum and dad keep telling me about, so I'm going to come and visit you! But shhhh – I haven't told your mum yet.

I'm so looking forward to holding you in my arms, darling Aika! See you very soon,

Love, Hope (your soon-to-be Godmother)

Hi Autumn

Hey

Um, I need someone to do me a favour
There's no one else I can ask, really

Sure, what is it?

Can you look after Yuuko for a couple of days?

Oh. Of course. When?

Next week?

No problem

Thanks. She just needs food and fresh litter
I'm off to see Janey in Tokyo

Wow, great! Tell her congratulations

Will do

Listen, sis

Yeah?

Are we OK?

Sure. How's the ankle?

I'm still hobbling, but no pain

Good to hear

Have a great time in Tokyo

Thanks. Speak soon

Harry Clark
Hope Sullivan
Bon voyage!

Dear Hope,

Of course I'll mind the shop while you're away! Retirement is all well and good, and I wouldn't want you to think I was complaining, but between you and me, it can get a little boring at times. Ingrid has caught the hiking bug since we gave up the shop, and I've seen enough of the Lake District and the Yorkshire Dales to last a lifetime. Next up is the Pennine Way, so a week off to give my bunions a rest is just what the doctor ordered. Have a great trip!

All best, Harry

Hi Autumn!

Greetings from Tokyo! Not seen much of the city, tbh, cos I can't take my eyes off Aika :) She's the cutest little thing you've ever seen! Gutted that I have to leave tomorrow . . .

Thanks for looking after Yuuko, and please DO NOT let her sleep in my undies drawer!

Love, Hope

27th November

Dear Arnold,

I've had a couple of glasses of wine, plus I'm still jetlagged from my flight home, so forgive my ramblings and don't take anything I say too literally. But writing you a letter seemed the right thing to do just now, so the hell with it!

I've just returned from a trip to Japan. Japan, can you believe it?! That's one more item to tick off my '10 Things To Do Before I Turn Thirty' list. Did I ever tell you about that? It's basically a list of things I thought would be good to do to 'grow' as a person (learn French, pay off my credit card debt etc.), so I decided to start with 'Visit another continent'. Actually, that's not strictly true. I did start with 'Be brave' – one of the few things in my life that actually turned out well. But I only have a little under two years left to work my way through the rest of the list and time is running out fast.

I flew to Tokyo to visit Janey and her beautiful little baby, Aika. I only stayed for a short week because I can't afford to be away from the shop for too long, but I wish I could've stayed for much, much longer. Aika is gorgeous. She has perfect little fingernails, like those tiny mother-of-pearl shells you find on the beach. And she has the cutest little dimple in her chin! Just like Eric, although her eyes and mouth are Janey's.

It's amazing what a woman's body can do, right? Growing a whole, perfect human being right inside her. I held Aika for hours. I couldn't get enough of the softness of her skin, or that honeyed newborn scent. And the first time I held her I cried. I just couldn't stop the tears. I told Janey it was because her baby's so perfect and I was so happy for her and Eric, which wasn't really a lie, but the real reason for my tears was that I was so deeply, deeply jealous. I'm not saying I want a baby, at least not right now, and besides, me getting pregnant would be a miracle, or an immaculate conception if you will, seeing as no man wants anything to do with me. So, no, I'm not feeling broody or anything. It's just . . . just seeing Janey with Aika, it's like, she has something to give her life meaning, somebody to live for and, if necessary, to die for.

And Janey's looking fantastic. I'll be honest now, because this is just between you and me, but a small, nasty part of me had hoped the pregnancy would've left her with flabby thighs and sagging breasts. But no – she's got curves in exactly the right places and looks more stunning than ever. So as you can see, I'm also a rubbish friend when it comes down to it. Shit. I'm happy for Janey, really and truly I am, but I can't help feeling this acute resentment that she has it all.

God, this sounds melodramatic! But it's true. I look at my own life and see . . . nothing. It's so fucking empty. Sorry for swearing, but that's just how I feel right now. Janey's got her music and now the baby; Autumn's got her career and Krish. All I've got is a job I never really wanted and a maxed-out credit card. And I'm lonely. There, I've said it.

But I so urgently want something to give *my* life meaning. Is that selfish? I guess it is. I had that once, I had something to give my life meaning, and I was so wrapped up in my own wants and needs that I ended up causing unimaginable pain. It's my own fault that Autumn doesn't want much to do with me. She deserves a better sister.

So now I'm back here, in my one-bedroom flat, with Yuuko purring at my feet and a nearly empty bottle of cabernet sauvignon beside me, feeling utterly sorry for myself. I really should eat something, but I can't be bothered to even shove a frozen chicken curry in the microwave. Pathetic really, isn't it?

I miss your letters terribly. I also miss writing to you. A few times, I nearly started writing a diary, but it's not the same thing. Knowing you were there, on the receiving end, helped me feel like I wasn't just screaming into the void. But like I said, I'm a rubbish friend, so you're probably better off without me.

Well, you and me both know that I'm not going to send this letter. I'm feeling quite drunk now, and not a little maudlin. As much as I'm mourning our friendship, if there's anything that life has taught me, it's to leave the past in the past.

Goodnight, Arnold. I hope you're doing well.

Love, Hope

CHAPTER 32

FROM: Wilma McDonald
TO: Hope Sullivan
SUBJECT: If the mountain won't come to Muhammad

Dear Hope,

You know I'm not a moaning Minnie, so I won't give you a lecture about how disappointing it was that you flew to Tokyo without coming to see us. But I'm not really cross you didn't come; in fact, it's rather spurred us into action, your Grandpa and me. It made me realise that we have spent far too long waiting for things to happen, rather than making them happen ourselves. And lately, we've been feeling so full of energy – I'm not sure if it's the Zumba, or the superfood smoothies Grandpa makes us for breakfast every morning (between you and me and the lamppost, they taste a lot like liquefied lettuce, but I suppose it's the effect that counts), or because the older you get, the more acute the realisation that life is too short! To top it off, I had an upright Judgement Card in my last Tarot reading (although there was also a reversed Ace of Pentacles, but that's another story . . .).

So – we're coming to see you!!! We arrive at Heathrow on 19th December and will be staying for two weeks, so we can spend Christmas and New Year together. We're even flying Business Class, can you believe! We had a surprise windfall from an investment we made yonks ago; it isn't much, but enough to take us halfway across the world in style. Would it be too much trouble to pick us up from the airport?

I gather from your posts on Facebook that you had a lovely time in Tokyo. Your friend's baby is delightful – any chance at all she made you feel broody? I see your Facebook relationship status still says 'single'. Honestly, Hope, there must be *someone* out there who meets your exacting standards. Perhaps you're just being too fussy?

Well, I'll leave it there for now. We'll have plenty of opportunity to talk *all* about it when we're there.

Lots of love,
Nan & Grandpa

FROM: Hope Sullivan
TO: Wilma McDonald
SUBJECT: Re: If the mountain won't come to Muhammad

Dear Nan,

This is the best Christmas present ever! What a lovely surprise! I know Autumn will be thrilled to see you and Grandpa (as will I, of course). Any chance Grandpa feels like cooking Christmas dinner?

Love, Hope

PS. Of course I'll pick you up from the airport! And I'll hold a sign up, just in case you've forgotten what I look like :)

    Dear Janey, Eric and Aika,
       Merry Christmas!
          Have the loveliest of family Christmases
             Love, Hope

    ~~Dear Arnold,~~
    ~~Have a very Merry Christmas and a Happy New Year!~~
    ~~Love, Hope~~

Dear Hope,
    Merry Christmas and a Happy New Year
        I hope Santa brings you lots of presents and I also hope
        Christmas is over soon so you can open the shop again.
        Love, Maisie

Is this an OK time?
                Sure, although I'm so tired, I've lost all sense of time. Is it
                Monday, or Thursday, or maybe even Easter, who knows?
It's Tuesday, 7.31 am GMT. I set my alarm so we
can chat before I go to the shop. And it's Christmas
in three days, so not too far off Easter, haha
                    Thanks. Sorry we have to chat on Facebook. I can't talk
                    on the phone, cos Aika's only just gone down for a nap
                        after hours of crying and I don't want to risk waking
                        her up. I think she's teething, or maybe it's colic.
She's so cute, Janey. Without a doubt the
most adorable child I've ever seen.
                                    Well you're not at all biased . . .
Not in the slightest. I know perfection when I see it.
U still there?
Janey???
                            Yeah, sorry, I had to sneeze. Silently.
Oh. Bless you.
                            whispers I peed myself a little.
Haha
                    Don't laugh, Hope. It's awful. That and the leaking
                        nipples – fluids coming out every which way. I
                            feel like a freakish human water feature.
Hahaha
                                        Just you wait . . .
Not you as well! My grandparents are here
over Christmas and it's all my nan
goes on about.
                            A family Christmas! Sounds lovely.

207

It is. It's a bit of a squeeze, though; they're sleeping in my bedroom and I'm on the couch. But it's wonderful seeing them after all these years. I haven't seen them since Mum and Dad died, so it's great to catch up. Plus, my grandpa is an excellent cook, so I'm eating proper meals for a change.

Must be strange seeing them again after all this time. It was at first, especially as they look so old!

What did you expect? Australia doesn't exist in some kind of black time hole, you know. I know. It just makes me realise how quickly time passes without you noticing. But it's not just me, my nan can't seem to understand how Autumn and I have become grown-up women. Autumn was only 12 when they last saw her, and whenever she comes into the room, Nan says, 'Goodness, how you've grown!', like she's surprised every time. It's become a running joke.

Your nan sounds lovely :) How long are they staying? They fly back on 2nd January. I'll really miss them. Except for . . .

Except for what? Well, judging by the noises that come out of the bedroom at night, they're still 'doing it'.

LOL!!! Easy for you to say, you don't have to listen to it.

But that's so sweet though, right? Being married that long and still fancying your partner. It is, I suppose. Speaking of, how's Eric?

Well, we're both still sleep-deprived, so not 'doing it' much. But other than that, everything's fine. Eric performs in the evenings, so he's here during the day, which is a great help. He does everything except for the breastfeeding :) I love the fact that he can't get enough of me and the baby. I can't believe I used to complain about him being clingy! That seems like a lifetime ago.

It does. Hey, is Krish still in the picture?
Very much so. Nan's been chasing him around
with her Tarot cards and dropping not-so-subtle
hints about him popping the question.

She must be channelling my mum!
Ha! You know what, that's a really
lovely way to think about it.

I still miss her loads, Hope. Especially now, since
I became a mum myself. And I can't help but
feel guilty that I didn't know she was so ill.
She didn't want to burden you with it. An
act of love, right? And there wouldn't have
been anything you could do, anyway.

I know, it's just . . . shit, I'm getting all weepy now. What
was I saying about being a human water feature?
It's OK to cry, sweetie.

Yeah, I know. It Just would've been so nice for her
to meet Aika, and for Aika to meet her Gramma.
Stop it. You're making *me* tear up now.

Sorry. No, I'm fine really. Focus on the
positives, that's my motto.
It's the best.

Speaking of, I'm not going to ask about your love life . . .
Good. Seriously though, I'll have enough going on with
the shop in the New Year as it is. Denise has a whole
schedule written up for things to do in January.

Sorry about that.
Oh, no need to apologise! Once you get to
know her, she's actually not that uptight. She
has a surprising wealth of dirty jokes.

Denise? Really? Talk about dark horses . . .
Yeah, I think she has a dirty horse joke, too.

Ewwww
Well, I'll tell her you said hi, anyway.

You do that. Now, tell me if it's none of my
business, but have you written to Arnold?

Um, no. I was *this close* to sending him a
Christmas card, but I chickened out.
It's weird though, how much I miss his letters.

                           I think you should write to him.
And say what? No, I think that boat's sailed.
I should have written to him the day after I
sent the nasty letter and apologised.

                    Just tell him you bumped your head
                          and had temporary amnesia.
No. That would sound stupid.

                    That's never stopped you before ;)
Thanks, BFF.

               Hey, I think we'll have to call it a day. Aika's making
               little mewing noises, which means she's just about
                  to wake up and demand to be attached to my
                 nipple for the next hour. But thanks for the chat,
                    lovely. You've made me feel 100% better.
You're welcome. And same here. Speak soon.

          Oh, before you go, has my x-mas present arrived yet?
No. And now you're making me feel guilty
for not sending you anything.

                 Don't be. It was only a silly fridge magnet.
Jeez, that Royal Mail really needs to get its act together.

Hope smiles from the threshold of the year to come,
whispering, 'it will be happier'.
                    Alfred, Lord Tennyson

CHAPTER 33

Arnold James Quince
has been awarded
First Prize
in the Mayfield Annual Bake-Off Competition

5th February

Dear Hope,

I hope you had a wonderful Christmas and a good start to the New Year. I'm never sure where the cut off is for wishing a Happy New Year, so I'm hoping it isn't too late now.

I am not at all sure you wish to hear from me, but as you can see from the enclosed, I did enter the baking competition – and won! You never did send me your bank details and I thought it would be a shame to let the entry fee go to waste. Actually, that's not strictly true. When I copied out the recipe for my sauerkraut cake to send to you, I got what I can only describe as an itch to bake again. I disregarded it at first, but after a while I found myself mentally going through the motions of measuring out the ingredients, mixing them together in just the right order with just the right amount of wrist-action, inhaling the delicious aroma as the cake gently bakes in the oven. Finally, I couldn't ignore the longing any more and decided to bake one last cake; to make it the best cake I've ever baked. As it turned out, your prediction was right – my baking skills had become a bit rusty and it took quite a few efforts to achieve perfection. But I finally got there! Please excuse my bragging, but I knew the cake would win, even before the judges had tasted it.

So this led me to think about what you wrote. Not just in your last letter, but in all the letters you've sent to me. You have been nothing but kind and understanding, and I gradually began to understand that for these past several years, I have wilfully chosen to disregard the second part of my dear Marion's instructions to me: Live your life. I felt so lost and broken after her death that I was almost fixated on the fact that I had had to let her go.

As I say, I don't know if you want to hear from me, but I would like to thank you for caring enough to remind me of what you wanted for me. If it weren't for you, I'd still be leading that same miserable, self-centred existence.

But I'm pleased to tell you that I have been making more of an effort with my life. I've even made some friends here at Sunny Fields. My neighbour Frank (with the claw-like toenails, remember?) and I have lunch together now and again, and Hugh (the bank manager) has finally had a hearing aid fitted, so we can have conversations at a normal volume. But the biggest change since we last wrote to one another is that I followed your advice and got a new dog! He's a rescue dog I have named Marmalade. I'm not entirely sure of the breed; he's somewhere between a Dachshund and a Jack Russell with a little Yorkie thrown in. He has reddish fur (hence the name) and short stubby legs, which is perfect for me as I'm not too quick on my feet any more, and so we have little problem keeping up with each other. The weather has been pretty grim lately, but with Marmalade as company for my walks, I've hardly noticed. He has a wonderful personality; not as cheeky as Chutney, but he's loyal and needs plenty of cuddles. And I'm happy to give him those!

My life, as they say, has taken a turn for the better, and it is because of you. I can only hope that yours has, too. On rereading your final letter, I realised the hurt I had caused with my words. I am so sorry, Hope. I never meant to hurt you and hope you can forgive me. Thanks to you, I am now 'living my life', and although I miss Marion desperately, and will continue to do so until we meet again, there is plenty of potential for happiness until then.

Dearest Hope, it may be too late to wish you a Happy New Year, but I sincerely hope it isn't too late to rekindle our friendship. It would mean so much to me.

Warm wishes,
Arnold

12th February

Dear Arnold,

I was so happy to receive your letter. No, more than happy, I was absolutely delighted! I can't tell you how sorry I am for the way I left things; it was unkind and cowardly and I can only apologise for what I said and how I said it. My only excuse is that the letter was written in anger.

I'm so pleased to hear that you decided to get a dog, and even more so that you've made some friends. We all feel lonely from time to time, but it did concern me how much you seemed to be withdrawing from the world. I know I'm one to talk; I ignored all your efforts at getting me to stay positive and I'm truly sorry for that. I guess it's easier to give advice than to take it. But it sounds like you've finally given yourself permission to make positive changes, and that genuinely makes me very happy.

Congratulations on winning the competition! It was presumptuous of me to enter you without asking, I realise that now, but I'm glad something good came of it. And it would have been a crime to withhold that cake from the world, right?!

I don't have much news here; I went to visit my friend Janey in Tokyo to see her new baby. I was only there for a week and didn't see much of the place, because I was so enraptured with the little one, Aika. Janey seems very happy and settled, which was great to see, but I'm pleased that she will be returning to the UK later this year when her husband's contract ends.

Christmas was unusually lively: My grandparents flew over from Australia and my grandpa cooked our Christmas dinner, which meant that for once, Autumn and I enjoyed a succulent turkey and perfectly crisp roast potatoes (neither of us is an expert in the kitchen, I'm afraid!). I'd been a bit anxious that being around Autumn would be awkward, but having our grandparents there seemed to defuse the situation. There were no uneasy silences or silly quarrels; in fact, I felt like I had some rare happy time with my sister.

Oh, and that little girl I told you about, Maisie? She now comes in almost every day and plays on one of our practice instruments. Whenever I have a moment, I show her what I can, although I still think she'd do better with a proper teacher. She's currently practising Bach's Minuet in G, which is a fairly advanced beginner piece. Unfortunately, her mum is out of work and her dad isn't very well, so they can't afford professional tuition, and scholarships are fiercely competitive these days. But in the meantime, I'll do what I can. It would be a real shame to let such talent go to waste.

The shop is going really well. Denise (she's the investor) has taken a lively interest in the business side of things. At first, I wasn't too happy at the thought of her interfering, but recently we've become quite friendly. She can be difficult to warm to, but once you get past the prim-and-proper facade, she's actually quite funny. And she's a very astute businesswoman. We've finally got a qualified accountant who knows all the ins and out when it comes to taxes and accelerated depreciation and rollover relief etc. (god knows what I've been doing all these years!), and I'm currently in contact with a luthier in Aberdeen about establishing a partnership whereby we become his preferred sales outlet. He makes string instruments for players all over the world, so this is a big deal. I've even been considering booking a stand at this year's trade fair in Frankfurt, the Musikmesse. So, lots to do!

Goodness, that's more news than I thought! Do please write and tell me more about your friends. And I'd love to hear all about Marmalade. Thanks again for writing to me, Arnold. I've missed you.

Love, Hope

PS. A very happy belated birthday!

19th February

Dear Hope

I've missed you too. I don't think I've upheld such a lengthy 'long-distance relationship' with anyone before, and it's become clear to me that I was writing to you because there are things I need to say, just as much as things I need to know.

It certainly sounds like you're busy! That's great news about the shop. It's always useful to have a professional accountant, but you shouldn't be so modest about your own efforts. You kept the place running for years, remember.

Regarding my new social life: Frank and I have established the Sunny Fields Four O'Clock Club, and we meet every afternoon with several of the residents in the common room to chat and play cards. As it turns out, Frank's a dab hand on the piano. He used to earn a few bob in pubs as a sing-along pianist back in his youth, and we've had quite a few sing-alongs in recent weeks. He keeps trying to get me to play along with him, but that is something I'm not comfortable with yet. Perhaps I never will be, but I don't dwell on that for now.

As I told you in my last letter, I had to refresh my baking skills for the competition. While the quality of my practice cakes was nowhere close to the cakes I baked years ago, they quickly found admirers at Sunny Fields, among residents and staff alike. Then just before Christmas, one of the nurses asked if I might bake something for her grandson's christening; she had tasted my lemon cake with lavender Swiss meringue buttercream and had apparently enthused to her daughter about it. As I had nothing better to do that week, I agreed and set to work. (Credit here to the kitchen staff, who have given me free rein in their kitchen, as long as I clean up after myself!) The nurse – Krystyna – asked me how much I wanted for the cake and I told her it was a gift, but she wouldn't have it, and twisted my arm into accepting the cost of the ingredients.

Well, then it all took off: The guests at the christening loved the cake, and soon I had orders for five more! Apparently, Krystyna had told them I charge £25 per cake, which they were all happy to pay. Believe me, Hope, I was more than a little uncomfortable with taking the money to begin with, but Krystyna said that no one should work for free and that giving the cakes away for free devalues them in people's opinions.

I thought, she's right, even though I don't need the money. So I reluctantly accepted payment for the cakes, and decided to put it aside for my favourite charity. The latest news in my cake-baking saga (the orders continue to flood in; I have no idea where people are hearing about me) is that the local newspaper wants to run a small feature on me. Marion would have thought it a right hoot! Anyway, I'm so busy, I hardly have time to sit and watch the teenagers in the park. I do make sure to take Marmalade out, though. Thankfully, he's not as active as Chutney was, so he's content with two walks a day.

But I will never be too busy to write to you. It does me good, I think, to get everything off my chest, and also to hear what's going on in your life. Believe it or not, I became quite invested in your story. When you are old and alone, it can be very easy to become self-absorbed, and so I am grateful for your friendship and the opportunity to view the world through someone else's eyes.

Which leads me to my next point: I have been thinking a lot about the last letter you wrote before we, shall we say, squabbled. First of all, thank you for trusting me enough to tell me everything you feel – even if it was in anger, I'm glad you finally gave voice to something I suspect you've been hiding all these years. I was very moved by your letter, and hugely saddened to hear that you think your parents' death was your fault. Now, I'm not a psychologist, so I can't offer you any counselling. But what I can offer is comfort, from the perspective of someone with a great deal of life experience. I think you have been living with this burden for so long, it has become a part of you. But your parents' death wasn't your fault at all. How could you have possibly known your parents would die on that night? The fact that they were in the car, at that particular time, on that particular stretch of road, is due to a random sequence of events that led to an unbelievably tragic outcome. You are not to blame for anything that happened, and it saddens me beyond belief that you have carried this guilt around for your entire adult life.

I appreciate that after what you've been through, you have felt unable to play the violin. You know how I felt after losing Marion – it would have been unthinkable to play a piano duet with someone else. I realise our situations may not be comparable, but what I'm trying to say is that I understand. I have a feeling that if it's meant to be, the music will call you when you're least expecting it. You wrote in your letter about me giving myself permission to make positive changes. I hope I'm not being facetious by throwing that advice right back at you!

My final piece of advice (if you can stomach any more of it!) is perhaps the most important one: talk to Autumn. Tell her everything you wrote to me. We often think we know what is going on in another person's mind, and it can be quite surprising to find out that they view things very differently. Perhaps I'm wrong, but I have a feeling that might be the case here.

All very best wishes,
Arnold

Hey sis, sorry I missed your call, work
is crazy. Is everything OK?

Yes, all fine thanks. You busy this weekend?
I'd like to talk to you about something.
Dinner on Saturday? Just you, if that's OK

Sounds ominous, but I'm free. I'll
bring plenty of wine . . .

28th February

Dear Arnold,

I had dinner with Autumn on Saturday. Arnold, you were
right about everything! We had the most glorious, heart-
wrenching, emotionally exhausting weekend. Autumn was a bit
nervous when she arrived, because I'd asked her to come
round for a 'talk'. God knows what she was expecting! So I
poured us a generous glass of wine each (I was nervous, too)
and got straight to the point. I know you said that I was not to
blame for what happened to my parents, and I appreciate that,
I really do, but up until the moment I started talking to
Autumn, I still believed it. How could I not? It's the first thing I
think about when I wake up in the mornings, and the last thing
I think about before I go to sleep. I'd prepared a kind of script
before Autumn came round, because I was worried I'd get all
muddled up and upset, and I wanted to get things across in
some coherent order. I needn't have worried though. I just
opened my mouth and it all came pouring out. I told her
everything I'd been bottling up and the guilt I'd had at being
the reason she didn't have parents any more. I said how sorry I
was that she'd grown up without having a mum to confide in,
or a dad to give her a huge cuddle when she was feeling lost or
sad. That instead she'd been stuck with a clueless, grieving,
overwhelmed older sister who can't cook a proper meal to save

218

her life and who was more than useless answering questions about French or maths homework.

I talked for about 45 minutes non-stop, until my throat was dry and tight and I had run out of things to say. Autumn sat there, wordlessly (I hadn't given her much of a chance to say anything, to be fair), and when I'd finished, she looked absolutely horrified. For a minute, I was afraid she was going to start raging at me, or even jump up and slap me, but then she collapsed in on herself and started crying. It was awful to watch – I went over and took her in my arms and just held her. Finally, she calmed down and told me that her tears were just the enormous relief she was feeling because she'd been waiting so long to talk to me about this. She was distraught to hear that I'd felt this way for so long, and said she'd never blamed me, even in her darkest hours. 'It could just as easily have been Mum and Dad driving to one of my hockey matches,' she said. 'Remember that time Dad skidded on ice and bashed up the car? That was when he was rushing to my school nativity play. He was lucky he only got whiplash. What I'm saying is that these things – these terrible, tragic things – just bloody happen. There's no way to control them.'

Then she went on to say she had something to tell me, too: she'd wanted to apologise to me for a long time. She'd realised too late that she was being selfish in forcing me to give up my music and future. All these years, she's been guilt-ridden that I gave up my dreams to look after her just because she didn't want to go to Australia. For the longest time now, she's been trying not to burden me with her troubles, like the time she broke her ankle. That's why she didn't want me to visit her in hospital! She knew I was overworked and the last thing she wanted was to add to my burdens. She also said she felt guilty being so happy with Krish and that's why she was constantly trying to find me a boyfriend. Once that was finally out in the open, I made her promise to stop interfering in my love life. I think she meant it sincerely, but I'm not entirely sure she'll be able to. Time will tell.

She thanked me for sticking by her, even when she was in danger of becoming a juvenile delinquent. She said that looking back, she was mortified about some of the things she did (including things I never found out about, like driving a friend's car home from a party years before she got her licence) and wouldn't have blamed me if I'd given her up to a foster home.

Arnold, it was amazing to hear her side of things. Like, I never knew that the time she was brought home by the police for spray-painting a local supermarket wall, she'd been trying to stop the other kids. She was making such a racket that someone alerted the police. But of course, she didn't want to rat on her friends so she took the blame along with them. If only she'd told me! I'd been at my wits' end back then and totally convinced that I was failing her, and failing our parents for being such a rubbish substitute. And then we cried. We cried about our parents together for the first time and it was so liberating, I can't really put it into words. You see, we had never allowed ourselves to share in each other's grief. I suppose I wanted to shoulder the burden – seeing as I thought it was my fault anyway – and I failed to see that I was depriving Autumn of her chance to grieve.

We finally fell into bed at around three in the morning. On Sunday, we slept in late and then went to Chez Philippe for breakfast. It's this French-Caribbean cafe, where Autumn and Sandra used to meet up on Saturdays. I don't know if I've ever mentioned Sandra. She's my best friend Janey's mum, and she was there for us after our parents died. I really don't know how I would have got through Autumn's teenage years without her. She died last year, which upset Autumn terribly, as Sandra was like a mother to her, but she was too afraid to talk to me about it as she feared it might make me mourn our parents all over again. We toasted Sandra and cried again, until the waitress came over and politely suggested we pay up and leave.

I feel emotionally bruised, if that makes sense. But in a good way, like when you're sore all over after running a marathon.

This weekend made me realise that it's never too late to right the wrongs of the past, or at least that there's always a chance to move forward. I now feel so much more hopeful for the future. And I finally got Autumn to promise not to hassle me about my love life (or lack thereof)!

Thank you, thank you, thank you for forgiving me and writing to me again and not giving up on me and our friendship.

Love, Hope

FROM: Janey Williams
TO: Hope Sullivan
SUBJECT: Memorial

Dear Hope,

I've discussed it with Eric and we've decided not to wait any longer to hold Mum's memorial. Aika should be OK to travel now; she's finally sleeping better – a record six hours last night! – and I've booked a flight for us for March 19. I'll do as much of the preparation from here as I can, but maybe you and Autumn could sort out the bits I can't do online or on the phone? I'm so sorry to put this on you, because I know how crazy busy you both are, but this has been weighing on me for a while now, and I want to say my final goodbyes.

I never spoke to Mum about what she might like to happen after she dies except for the cremation part, which I now know was a stupid and cowardly oversight, but I knew her well enough to know she wouldn't have wanted to be buried. She was always afraid of dark enclosed spaces, so I wouldn't want to risk her coming back to haunt me if I had her put six feet under. That leaves me with the options to a) keep the urn, or b) scatter her ashes. Eric thinks I should keep them, but that seems a bit creepy, doesn't it? Keeping my dead Mum's cremains on the mantlepiece? I would live in a perpetual state of fear of knocking them over, or Aika getting her hands on them (she's got another couple of years of putting *everything* in her mouth . . .)

I've already written to Mum's friends; I don't suppose it'll be a big crowd, but I think we can make it a really meaningful day.

Love you lots,
Janey

FROM: Janey Williams
TO: Hope Sullivan
SUBJECT: Re: Memorial

Me again! I forgot the most important thing. I'm not sure if this is too big an ask, but would you consider playing a duet with me at the memorial service? We don't have to play anything difficult, or even a classical piece. It would mean the world to me if my very best friend helped me say farewell to Mum.

Hugs, Janey

2nd March

Dear Arnold,

I know I haven't given you a chance yet to respond to my last letter, but something has come up and I need some advice. Remember when I wrote to you about Janey's mum dying last year? Well, there's going to be a memorial service for her in two weeks' time; Janey's flying over especially and she's asked me and Autumn to help her plan the service. All that, of course, I don't mind in the least; in fact, I'm really happy to help. The reason I need some advice is that Janey's asked me to play a duet with her at the service. All this time, ever since Mum and Dad died, we haven't really spoken about my playing, or lack thereof. Over the years, Janey has asked me a few times if I was still playing, and I always avoided answering directly. If she knew, she would never let up and I just didn't need the added pressure. But now it's out there, and I have to answer her one way or the other. I don't know what to do. I'm completely rusty, for one thing, although I would hope that the fundamentals are still stored in my muscle memory somewhere. Also, my left fingertips are as soft as butter, so playing is likely to be painful to begin with.

God, these are just excuses, aren't they? The truth is that the thought of playing again frightens and excites me in equal measure. It's as though I've projected everything onto my violin – my hopes and dreams, but also my fear and my pain. *That's* why I've been 'shelving it for later': I'm frightened about what might or might not happen. If – when? – I ever play again, who's to know what I'll feel? But on the other hand, I know that this is really important to Janey, and I would hate to let her down. What do I do?

Love, Hope

6th March

Dear Hope,

I feel honoured – if that is the right word – that you've turned to me for advice. However, as much as it pains me, I'm afraid I cannot give you the answer. I appreciate your inner conflict – your understandable hesitancy as well as the responsibility you feel towards your friend. It would be the easiest thing for me to say: pick up your violin. It would be equally simple to say: explain this to Janey, she'll understand. But this is not something I can decide for you.

My dear Hope, I'm sorry, truly I am, because I would like nothing better than to give you all the answers to life's questions. But this, I'm afraid, is something you will have to decide for yourself. The only advice I can offer – inadequate as it may

be – is that you will only know what is on the other side of your fear if you pass through it. Just know that I believe in you.
    Good luck,
    Arnold

FROM: Hope Sullivan
TO: Janey Williams
SUBJECT: Re: Re: Memorial

Dear Janey,

I'll do it.

Love, Hope

CHAPTER 34

CASE NO.:   VP / 05 / 2901
INCIDENT: Attempted burglary
REPORTING OFFICER: Constable Patrick Marney
DATE OF REPORT: 18 March

At about 0650hrs on Monday, 18 March, Constable Vivian Patel and I were called out to 29 King's Road to the premises Harry's Harmonies after a 999 call from Ms Hope Sullivan. Upon our arrival, we discovered that the front plate glass window of the property had been smashed. The 999-caller, Ms Sullivan, was on the premises and appeared shaken but uninjured apart from a sprained wrist.

According to her witness statement, at approx. 0630hrs, Ms Sullivan was at the back of the premises with the front door locked when she heard the sound of breaking glass. She hurried to the front of the shop and discovered two males in black clothing on the verge of entering the premises, having smashed the front window to gain entry. Ms Sullivan states that the men were visibly surprised by her presence, so she took advantage of this and, grabbing a clarinet from a nearby shelf, she struck one of the perpetrators on the head. While his accomplice fled the scene, the man attempted to defend himself by lunging at Ms Sullivan. She fell and landed on her left hand, spraining her wrist, but managed to get back to her feet and continued to use the clarinet as a defence weapon. After landing several 'successful strikes', as Ms Sullivan put it, the man also fled the scene.

Despite a lack of other visible injuries, I radioed for an ambulance to ensure that Ms Sullivan was not more seriously hurt.

She was taken into hospital and treated for the wrist injury, but released shortly thereafter. The perpetrators did not manage to enter the premises due to the brave (though perhaps somewhat rash) actions of Ms Sullivan. As such, it is unlikely that fingerprints or DNA will have been left at the crime scene. According to Ms Sullivan, no items were stolen and the damage was limited to the smashed front window and the clarinet. Ms Sullivan provided a comprehensive description of the two male perpetrators, which I attach as an appendix.

OMG, Hope, I just heard. Are you
OK? I'm on my way. Ax

Dear Janey,

It was so lovely to see you. I hope your flight back was OK. Please don't worry about the rug; I don't think I'll bother having it professionally cleaned, though. It's old and tatty, anyway, and I've been meaning to buy a new one for ages. I guess Aika did me a favour by peeing on it. But OMG, hasn't she grown? She'll be walking and talking before you know it, and if she's anything like you, there'll be no stopping her.

I hope the memorial service was everything you wanted. I was only expecting a handful of people, but your mum was obviously really popular. The church hall was bursting at the seams! I don't know where Autumn got that choir from, but they were great, weren't they? And the dancing afterwards – I was sore all over the next morning. I think your mum would've really liked it – well, maybe not the joints that started circulating at 2 in the morning. Although, I'm pretty sure I saw them coming out of the handbag of that old lady who knew your mum from church. Ha, I can almost hear your mum 'tut-tutting' at the idea of sitting in a pew with Alice (or whatever her name was) stoned out of her head!

Your piece was beautiful, Janey, and I'm so sorry I couldn't play. My wrist is much better now, just the occasional twinge when I lift something heavy. It was a pretty scary experience, but the police have made two arrests (apparently, they were responsible for a whole spate of burglaries in the area) and I've arranged for a panic button to be installed. So, no need to worry about me!

I'm still waiting on a decision regarding the insurance claim, though. The paperwork is insane; I'm sure the insurance company does it on purpose to try and grind you down until you just drop the claim in frustration. At one point, I found myself thinking, 'What the hell, it's only the cost of a dented clarinet and a plate glass window,' but when I told Denise, she said she'd contact the insurers herself. She was absolutely fuming – I feel sorry for whoever answers her call!

Thanks for making the time to come to see me in the shop, and I'm so glad you like it. I've put so many hours and every ounce of spare energy into that place, it's gratifying for it all to have finally come together. When you're back for good, I'm expecting you to tell all your fellow musicians all about it! Seriously though, I'm genuinely proud of the shop. It's my own personal achievement, and I don't have many of those.

Oh, and I'm really pleased you got to meet Maisie! She's not usually that shy; she can talk the hind legs off a donkey when she feels like it, but I think it was the thought of meeting a real-life professional musician that made her so tongue-tied. It's a shame she didn't want to play for you, but I'm sure we'll all be hearing from her in the not-too-distant future. I really have to see about arranging some professional tuition for her, though. If you have any ideas on that front, let me know.

Right, lovely, I'll leave it there. Enjoy the rest of your time in Tokyo – once you're back, I won't be letting you leave again in a hurry!

Love, Hope

Dear Arnold,

I'll get straight to the point: I didn't play violin at Sandra's memorial service. After many sleepless nights spent soul-searching, I'd finally decided I owed it to Janey, knowing how much it meant to her. But two days before the memorial there was a break-in at the shop and I got hurt fending off the burglars. Nothing serious, a sprained wrist, but bad enough to prevent me from holding a violin. Janey tried to hide her disappointment, said that the main thing was that I was okay, but I could tell she was upset.

The truth is, the moment I stumbled and landed on my arm, I felt this huge sense of relief. I knew, even before the pain set in properly, that I wouldn't be able to play. It sounds cowardly and selfish, I know, but even after promising Janey I would, I had no idea if I could actually have done it. The only reason I was at the shop so early in the morning was because I hadn't been able to sleep all night, worrying about the duet, terrified I'd freeze up in front of the congregation. So when I fell onto my left arm, I thought . . . I don't know, I thought it might be a sign. A sign that maybe I'm just not ready yet to pass through the fear. Who knows, perhaps I should start coming to terms with the idea that I might never be ready.

Love, Hope

CHAPTER 35

8th April

Dear Arnold,

How are you? I haven't heard anything from you in a little while. I hope everything is OK?
Love, Hope

22nd April

Dear Arnold,

It's been quite a while since you last wrote and I'm getting a bit worried about you. Can you let me know you're OK?
Love, Hope

FROM: Hope Sullivan
TO: Sunny Fields Assisted Living Community
SUBJECT: Arnold Quince

To whom it may concern:

My name is Hope Sullivan and I am a friend of one of your residents, Arnold Quince. I've been writing to Arnold regularly for many months now, but he hasn't replied to any of my last three letters. I'm getting a bit concerned that he might be unwell. Would you please let me know if he's all right?

Kind regards, Hope Sullivan

Dear Ms Sullivan,

Thank you for your email. Unfortunately, we are not able to help you with your enquiry as to the wellbeing of our resident Arnold Quince. It is the policy of our facility not to disclose personal information of this kind.

Sincerely, Manager

Sunny Fields Assisted Living Community

Hi Autumn, have you by any chance heard anything from Arnold? He's not writing back to me and I'm getting seriously worried about him. I don't know who else to ask

Hey, this isn't really professional of me, but I don't feel right not telling you. Arnold's been in the hospital for 2 weeks and we can't track down his son. Do you know where he lives? We need to let him know, as next of kin. X

OMG is he OK? I hadn't heard from him for ages and was getting worried. Also, Arnold has a son?!! I had no idea. Do you know his name?

It's Joseph. Do you think you can track him down? Soon? It's not looking good. I'm really not allowed to give you any more details. Sorry.

You are messaging
Joseph Quince

Hi. Apologies if I'm writing to the wrong person, but are you by any chance the son of Arnold Quince?

No. Never heard of him

Hi @JQuince37. Apologies if I'm writing to the
wrong person, but are you by any chance the son
of Arnold Quince?

@hopesullivan No. And if you'd bothered to
check my profile, you'd see I'm not anyone's son
because I'm a woman.

Any luck finding Arnold's son? Ax

No. Still on it

You are messaging
Joe Quince
Hi there. Apologies if I'm writing to the wrong
person, but are you by any chance the son
of Arnold Quince? It's really important.
Hello. My father is called Arnold. Is this some sort of
scam? You're not a Nigerian prince or anything are you?
Hi. Thanks for getting back to me. No, I'm in the
UK and I'm not royalty of any kind. If you'd rather,
you can email me at harrysharmonies@uk.net (you
can google Harry's Harmonies if you like). It's really
important I talk to you. Best wishes, Hope Sullivan

FROM: Joe Quince
TO: Harry's Harmonies
SUBJECT: Facebook

Hello,

What do you want to talk to me about? Is my dad OK?

Regards,
Joe Quince

Harry's Harmonies
Joe Quince
Re: Facebook

Hi Joe,

Thanks for the speedy response. I'm a friend of your father's. I'm really sorry to have to tell you this, but Arnold isn't well. He's in ICU at St Michael's Hospital on Farnham Road. His doctor asked me to contact you as his next of kin and I've been trying to track you down for ages.

If it's OK, would you let me know how he's doing? I'm not a relative, so they're not allowed to give me any information regarding his condition, but we've been friends for a while now and I'd really like to know he's all right. My mobile number is below.

Thanks, and all best,
Hope

> Thanks for letting me know. I'm on my way
> to the hospital and will be in touch. Joe

Thanks!
On second thoughts, I'll come in later
this afternoon. See you there. Hope

CHAPTER 36

Hi Joe, so sorry I missed you. I was stuck in
traffic and when I got to the hospital, the
nurse told me that visits to ICU are family-
only. I'd be so grateful if you'd let me know
how your dad is doing, and please let me
know if there's anything you need. Hope

No worries, Hope. Dad's stable, thank God,
but still needs intensive care. They told me he
had a heart attack and they're keeping him in
an artificial coma until his vitals improve. I'll
be back in to see him first thing tomorrow.

Thanks for letting me know! And please give
him my best, even if he can't hear you.

Hey there, just wanted to let you know
I've told the nurses you're Dad's niece, so
you shouldn't have any problems getting
in to see him. Hope that's OK! Joe

Thank you so much! I can't make it till
late afternoon. Will you be there?

FROM: Joe Quince
TO: Harry's Harmonies
SUBJECT: Marmalade

Dear Hope,

I thought I'd write an email, seeing as we keep missing each other at the hospital, and I find text messaging quite limiting when you're trying to communicate anything beyond the basics. Dad's doing OK under the circumstances. The doctors induced an artificial coma to give his body a better chance of recovery, but it's heart-wrenching to see him like that. The hospital staff have been great though; they're happy to answer all my questions and they said I'm free to visit whenever I like.

May I ask how you know my dad? He and I lost touch a while ago – long story – so it's comforting to know he has people looking out for him. Unfortunately, I'm pretty tied up work-wise, so I can only manage an hour in the mornings.

I see your email address is Harry's Harmonies. That's the music shop on King's Road, right? Do you work there? I have a vague recollection of my mother buying me a recorder in that shop many years ago, back in the day when my parents thought I might have some musical talent. (It turned out I have none whatsoever – I was soon relegated to playing the triangle in the school orchestra . . .) I had no idea the shop was still going! So many indie retailers are struggling these days, and it's nice to hear that Harry's hasn't been bought up by some chain or turned into a Starbucks.

Listen, before I go, I've got a bit of a problem and I was wondering if there's any way you could help out. I'm truly sorry to be asking you this, but there really isn't anyone else I can think of. I don't know if you know, but Dad's got a dog, Marmalade? Sunny Fields contacted me to say they were happy to look after him for a couple of days, but that I'd need to come and get him by the end of the week. I'd take him in a heartbeat, it's just that my current work situation makes looking after a pet impossible. And I'd hate to take Marmalade in and then keep him locked up in the house all day. I contacted the local animal shelter, but they'd only be able to keep him with a view to rehoming him, and the last thing I want is for Dad to wake up to find out he's lost another dog. So, if there's any way you might help, or know

of anyone who wouldn't mind giving Marmalade a temporary
home, that would be great. Again, apologies for asking, and no
worries if you can't help.

Thanks for making the effort to contact me, Hope, I really
appreciate it.

All best,
Joe

FROM: Hope Sullivan
TO: Joe Quince
SUBJECT: Re: Marmalade

Dear Joe,

Thanks for your email. I know what you mean about text
messages! I'm far too verbose for that sort of thing and much
prefer old-school communication; in fact, that's sort of how
your dad and I met. My sister (she's a doctor at St Michael's)
put us in touch the year before last and we've been writing to
each other ever since. Actually, we'd never met in person until I
visited him in hospital (and thanks again for telling them I was
his niece!). I say 'met in person', but it was of course a one-
sided meeting. Like you said, it's heart-breaking to see him
wired up to those machines. I sat with him for two hours the
other night, just studying his face, wondering what he looks
like when he smiles, asking myself what his voice sounds like.

Regarding Marmalade: I'm really sorry, but I have a cat at
home who does not take kindly to dogs. She's a bit of a diva
and I would pity any animal who encroached on her territory!
But I agree, it would be awful for Arnold to lose Marmalade.
There is someone I could ask, though. I can't make any prom-
ises, but I'll let you know as soon as possible.

I don't mean to be pushy, but if you like, we can take turns
visiting your dad, just to make sure there's someone by his side

every day? I'm free most evenings, so it's no problem whatsoever for me to go in and sit with him. I like to think it might
help his recovery to have his hand held and to hear a human
voice.

How funny that you've been to Harry's Harmonies! It actually
isn't Harry's any more, though; Harry and his wife Ingrid
retired last year and I took over the shop. I've redecorated the
place extensively, so you probably wouldn't recognise it on the
inside, but I still sell recorders :)

Do please let me know if there's anything else I can do to help,
and I'll get back to you about Marmalade. Fingers crossed that
your dad gets better very soon.

Love, Hope

Glad to hear Joe's been in to visit Arnold
                    Yes. Well done for tracking him down, Hope
How could I not have known he has a son? Makes
me wonder why Arnold never said anything.
                 No idea why Arnold didn't mention him.
Joe doesn't sound like a total creep,
but maybe I'm missing something
              I don't think so. He seems like a normal guy.
            Polite, not bad looking, actually, wink wink . . .
What are you insinuating, sis?

                         Nothing

Surely Joe's old enough to be my
dad. *Our* dad, come to that
              Ewww. And no, Joe's just a couple
                of years older than you
Oh. I would've thought Arnold's
son would be older
             Wasn't wearing a ring, either
Enough! What did you promise me?
        'I promise I will not interfere in Hope's love life'

Bingo. Listen, I've got a favour to ask

> Sure, what is it?

Arnold has a dog, Marmalade, and Joe's got work
commitments and can't take care of him, and I've
got Yuuko, who doesn't take to dogs, and . . .

> . . . and would I possibly come to the rescue?

Yeah

> I'd love to! Just get Joe to call me,
> we'll arrange a drop off

Thanks, sis

> Ur welcome. See you on Friday for pizza?

It's a date :)

FROM: Joe Quince
TO: Hope Sullivan
SUBJECT: Dad

Dear Hope,

Thanks for your offer of taking turns to sit with Dad.
Unfortunately, my job keeps me tied up most evenings, so it's
comforting to know that he'll have company when I'm not there.
It would be nice to meet you in person at some point, though!

I felt Dad moving his fingers this morning. Maybe it was just a
reflex, but I'm hoping this means he's on the mend. His vitals
are OK but the doctors say they want to keep him under until
they're sure he's stable enough. I'm really worried about him,
though. He looks so frail. It's amazing, really, how you never
view your parents as anything other than strong, and what a
shock it is to see them when they're vulnerable. Dad's always
been quite tall, so in my recollection, he was always this strong
but gentle giant. And now, to see him like this . . . well, it's
sobering, I guess.

Oh, and I dropped off Marmalade at your sister's yesterday.
The two of them hit it off immediately; Autumn had already

been out and bought a bed and dog food and more chew toys than one dog could possibly chew through in a lifetime. I definitely think Marmalade is in good hands, though I'm not entirely sure she'll give him up without a fight!

Best wishes, Joe

PS. Shouldn't your shop be called Hope's Harmonies?

CHAPTER 37

FROM: Hope Sullivan
TO: Julie Welsh
SUBJECT: Maisie

Hi Julie!

If you have a moment, could you pop by the shop for a quick chat? Maisie's been progressing really well on the violin and I'd love her to take her Grade 1 exam. She's more than ready for it, but she needs a parent to sign the application forms.

Best, Hope

FROM: Hope Sullivan
TO: Joe Quince
SUBJECT: Re: Dad

Dear Joe,

I spent an hour last night staring at Arnold's fingers, willing them to move, but nothing, sadly. He's got a bit more colour to his cheeks now though, wouldn't you say? You know, in all these months writing to him (with a short break in between, but that's another story), I feel I've come to know him so well. I think we were really good for one another, Arnold and me. It's hard to explain, but I suppose we were going through similar challenges in our lives. It sounds silly, I know, because of the age difference and all that, but we were both, in a sense, holding ourselves back from fully living, and writing to each other gave us the feeling that we mattered. But now, the thought that I might never again come home from work to find one of his letters waiting for me makes me unbelievably sad. In fact, I still find myself checking the post, half-expecting to see an envelope with his big, looped handwriting on it.

All I can do is hope that he recovers soon, and try to keep myself as distracted as I can in the meantime. That, coincidentally, is quite easy to do, as work keeps me very busy. So, small mercies, I guess. Yesterday, for example, I spent hours on the phone to Frankfurt trying to clear up a misunderstanding about a stall we'd booked for the upcoming trade fair. And then, just as I'd managed to convince the guy that I wanted a stall with 100 square foot and not 100 square metres (the price difference runs into the thousands!), Maisie came in. She's a young girl from the neighbourhood who's serious about learning the violin, but her parents can't afford tuition so I've been helping her out. I used to play myself, years ago, and it's great to be able to put that to some use. Anyway, I've persuaded Maisie to have a go at taking her Grade 1 exam, and she's a bit nervous about it, so we spent two hours going over her piece. By the time I'd closed up the shop, I had to break every speed limit so I wouldn't miss visiting hours at the hospital.

It's funny you should mention the shop's name. I suppose as it's mine now, 'Hope's Harmonies' would be a more apt name, but the previous owners, Harry and Ingrid, built the shop from scratch and I promised Harry I would keep the name for as long as the shop was mine. A way of keeping his legacy alive, in a sense.

Anyway, enough about me and my work! Please keep me posted if you hear anything about your dad, and I promise to do the same.

Love, Hope

Dear Hope,

Thanks for your lovely email. It sounds like you and Dad were very close and I'm really glad he's had you in his life for the last couple of years. The nurse told me you brought flowers in for him yesterday. Thank you on his behalf! It's a shame they don't allow flowers on the ICU ward, but I guess the nurses' staffroom smells nice now. I don't know if you're aware of this, but lily-of-the-valley was my mother's favourite. She grew them on the allotment (she was very green-fingered) and we always had freshly cut flowers at home during the spring and summer. I'll let Dad know about the lilies-of-the-valley as soon as he wakes up.

Hope, I have a small confession to make. When Dad was taken to hospital, he had a bundle of letters among his things. The nurse gave them to me yesterday. I thought they might be important, so I had a look through them. They were your letters to him. I realise it probably wasn't my place to read them, but once I began, I found it impossible to stop. I was so touched to see how much you care for him. I've thought long and hard about whether to mention it at all, seeing how awkward this is, but reading through your correspondence has shown me how much I have neglected Dad. He didn't mention me once, did he? I shouldn't be surprised, I suppose, but it's upsetting all the same. I don't blame him though, not at all. I won't go into it here, but there was some unpleasantness – things I'm not proud of – after my mum died five years ago. And now that Dad's so ill, the thought of him dying before I get the chance to reconcile with him makes me sad beyond belief.

Sorry for dumping this on you, Hope. We barely know each other, so why would you want to hear about my troubles? I suppose I felt the need to offer some explanation. Apologies

241

again for reading the letters – I hope I haven't creeped you out. It would be great to stay in touch, if only for Dad's sake, but I understand if you'd rather not.

All best,
Joe

FROM: Hope Sullivan
TO: Joe Quince
SUBJECT: Re: Confession

Dear Joe,

I'm very sorry to hear things are so difficult between you and Arnold. I admit it did feel a bit weird at first to hear you've read my letters to your dad – I can't for the life of me remember most of what I wrote – but on reflection, I'm glad you were honest. And I'm also really moved that Arnold carries my letters with him. Our friendship means a lot to me, even though we've never met in person, and it's touching to think he feels the same way.

If truth be told, I *have* been wondering why he never mentioned you. I do remember asking him about his family, but he would never answer directly, so I kind of assumed there might be something going on. It must have been hard on you to lose your mum. As you'll undoubtedly have read in the letters, my parents died in a car crash when I was eighteen, and I still miss them every day. There are so many things I wish I'd told them, or asked them about. I know for a fact that my life would have taken a completely different direction if they'd lived. Not that I'm unhappy or anything. I suppose it just takes some time to realise that the path isn't always straight.

But hey, I'm sure you don't need advice from me! I think the important thing is that you're there for Arnold now, when it counts.

Love, Hope

Dear Maisie,

 Congratulations on passing your exam! I *knew* you'd nail those arpeggios! Grade 2, here we come . . .

 Love, Hope

FROM: Joe Quince
TO: Hope Sullivan
SUBJECT: Re: Re: Confession

Dear Hope,

Thanks for being so understanding. I feel I owe it to you now to tell you the whole story, though please reserve judgement until you've read it all. I haven't told anyone before and I can only hope I get the words down properly.

Like I mentioned in my last letter, Dad and I had a falling out when Mum died. She'd had a massive stroke and ended up in intensive care on a ventilator. Dad was devastated; I don't think I've ever known a couple as happily married as they were. They were married for almost twenty years before I came along, the proverbial late baby. Apparently, they'd tried and tried to conceive, but without success. They'd more or less given up. I think this can be a make-or-break situation for many childless couples, but thankfully, it only served to strengthen their relationship. So anyway, Mum was nearly 40 when she fell pregnant and at first assumed she'd hit the menopause early. As the story goes, they were both delighted beyond belief when they found out she was pregnant. For as long as I can remember, we were that mythical thing, the 'happy family'. That's not to say I was a spoiled child (at least not from where I was standing, haha); Mum was actually quite strict. I was the only kid at school who had fresh fruit and veg in his lunchbox and she'd only let me eat sweets once a week. She always went to great pains with her cooking; Dad was the baker in the family, but Mum regularly dished up the most fantastic meals.

I was familiar with artichokes and avocados before I could even spell the words. I guess that's where my appreciation for good food came from.

But then she had the stroke and Dad lost his partner and best friend overnight. I was gutted, too. Here was my mum – a vibrant 65-year-old woman, far too young to die – lying there with a tube down her throat. I couldn't believe she wouldn't recover. Even after months of her showing no improvement, I demanded second, third, fourth opinions from different doctors, but they all said the same thing: The chances of her recovering were close to zero. But you see, Hope, I clung to the 'close to' part of that statement. For me, it meant that recovery was very *unlikely*, but not *impossible*. I spent hours and hours online, trying to figure out if there was anything – experimental drugs, treatments, therapies etc. – that might help her. I found nothing, of course, yet I couldn't give up. Who knew if there wouldn't be a new drug on the market in a month's time? I tried to talk to Dad about it, but all he could see was Mum's suffering. I know now that his decision to keep her on the machines was for me, because he could tell I wasn't ready to say goodbye and he didn't want to hurt me.

But then one morning I came in, and the room Mum had been lying in was empty. The bed was stripped, the machines switched off and silent. For a surreal moment, I thought she must have woken up during the night and that they'd moved her to a different ward. I felt this incredible sensation of joy, but then I turned around and saw Dad standing there, his eyes red and swollen, and I knew what had happened. Dad had finally taken the decision to allow the doctors to switch off her life support. The elation I had felt seconds earlier turned into the darkest despair I'd ever felt. I hadn't had the chance to say goodbye. In an instant, that despair turned into anger – anger at Dad for depriving me of a final moment with my mother. We had a huge argument; that is, I turned on Dad and said some very cruel and nasty things. I let out every petty resentment I'd ever felt; stupid, trivial things. It all just exploded out of me.

I finally told him I never wanted to see him again. I'm not proud of that. My anger was so encompassing, so acute, that I failed to see how broken Dad was at that moment. Over the years, he has tried to reach out to me, but each time, I felt my anger at him reignite. I guess I've been using this anger to push away all the grief at my mum's death all these years. I hope this doesn't sound like I'm excusing my behaviour, because it was inexcusable. I just thought it was important to explain.

I'm so sorry to hear about your parents. And that you were so young when it happened – on the cusp of adulthood. It must have been very difficult for you, but it sounds like you've managed brilliantly. I can't imagine going through all that early grown-up stuff without my parents having my back. There was more than one occasion when they jumped in to settle an over-draft, or offered advice on careers or on taking out my first mortgage. I guess I took it for granted, and to be honest, your story makes me feel even more of an arrogant, ignorant fool for letting five years go by without telling my father how much I love him. I feel so bad for putting off making amends.

I hope I haven't bored you with all this, but thanks for being there. It really helps.

All very best,
Joe

FROM: Hope Sullivan
TO: Joe Quince
SUBJECT: Thanks

Dear Joe,

Thank you for confiding in me. I know it can't have been easy. I know from my own experience how difficult it can be to face up to things that happened in the past. Your dad never wrote about you, it's true, but in several of his letters to me he alluded to mistakes he's made, things he'd said or done, things he wished had never happened. He didn't go into any detail, but I can only assume he was referring to what happened between the two of you. I understand why you did what you did, and I'm sure Arnold does too.

I know a lot about guilt and self-blame, believe me. But I'm happy to pass on the advice your dad gave me, which is not to carry the pain forward. Once, he wrote that if he had his time back, he would do some things very differently, but that it had become near impossible to put certain things right again. Well, Joe, it's never impossible. You can't fix the past, but you can make sure the future isn't broken. I really hope this helps, and if you ever wanted to talk about it, I'm happy to listen.

Love, Hope

Hi Janey,

I felt like writing you a good old-fashioned letter for a change. I've missed putting pen to paper since Arnold got sick, so you'll have to stand in for him.

Thanks for the latest pics of Aika. I know you say she looks like Eric, but I can definitely see the resemblance to you. That smile, come on! Cute, but devilish. God knows what your life will be like when she hits puberty.

I'm counting down the days until you're back. Seriously, I have created a special Janey's Return Countdown Calendar, which I cross off every morning. Only 27 days to go!

Please don't worry about finding another orchestra to play in. Personally, I think it's outrageous that your old one isn't legally obliged to take you back after your maternity leave, but I guess it's still a man's world, right?

Speaking of men, you know I told you about Arnold's son, Joe? Well, we've been emailing and texting back and forth for a

246

couple of weeks now, and he seems lovely. We haven't managed to meet IRL yet, because ~~bad luck keeps intervening and maybe I should take the hint~~ we have different work schedules, but I think I'd really like to meet him in person. Well, part of me does. The other part thinks he might be a secret serial killer who just knows how to put on a charming facade. Because if he's as nice as he sounds, why doesn't he have a girlfriend? Or a wife? Oh shit, he probably does. But how would I find out? I can't just ask him. Or can I? And why am I even thinking about this when Arnold is lying in a coma?!

I'm telling you this in the strictest confidence, Janey Williams! If Autumn ever found out, she wouldn't let me hear the last of it. in fact, she'd probably contrive some sort of 'accidental' meeting between me and Joe, which with my luck would catch me on my absolutely worst hair day ever. So shush!

Give Aika lots of smushy kisses from me, and big hugs to Eric as well,

Love, Hope

CHAPTER 38

FROM: Hope Sullivan
TO: Denise Carlson
SUBJECT: Monthly review

Dear Denise,

I've attached this month's numbers. As you can see, the business seems to be going from strength to strength. This was the best month yet, and we are on course to exceed our quarterly target yet again.

I'm also writing to let you know that the luthier in Aberdeen is on board! This is great news, as it'll bring in lots of high-end business from international artists. Most luthiers sell directly to their customers, certainly at this level, but this one doesn't appear to have – how to put it? – the best people skills, so he's happy to outsource the sales, as it were. I'd love to go through the contract with you before I sign, make sure everything is as it should be. Do you have time to meet this week?

Best wishes, Hope

FROM: Denise Carlson
TO: Hope Sullivan
SUBJECT: Re: Monthly review

Dear Hope,

Thanks for sending the monthly review. Great numbers! I'd also like to express my appreciation for all your hard work.

When Eric first suggested investing in the shop, I admit I wasn't entirely convinced, but I thought, nothing ventured, nothing gained. Now, I am extremely glad I took the chance! I can see the hours you have been putting into the shop, and in light of the strong sales performance, I have a suggestion to make. What would you say about hiring a sales assistant? We're in a great financial position, and you can't possibly continue working these crazy hours before you burn out. Perhaps a part-time assistant, to give you some time to focus on yourself? Well, we can discuss this in detail when we meet. Just think on it.

Oh, one more thing: I've been thinking about whether it would be a good time to rename the shop. From a marketing perspective, it can be a bit of a risk to change the name of an ongoing business, brand loyalty and all that, but on balance, I don't think 'Harry's Harmonies' quite cuts it. It has some old-fashioned, quirky appeal, I suppose, but with all the changes we've implemented, I think the shop needs a fresh new name, too. I'm not the most creative person, but I was thinking something along the lines of 'No Strings Attached' or 'Don't Fret'. What do you think? (Be honest with me, Hope. I can take it.)

I'd be happy to look over the contract. Do let me know if Thursday evening suits. I can book us a table either at Marnie's or this new place everyone's raving about, The JQ. Which do you prefer? My treat.

Best regards, Denise

PS. What did the banana say to the vibrator?

FROM: Harry Clark
TO: Hope Sullivan
SUBJECT: Your shop

Dear Hope,

It was a delight to see you. And the shop – well, it brought tears to Ingrid's eyes to see how wonderful everything looks now! Makes me a little embarrassed that we didn't go to more effort when we were the owners. Seriously though, well done, Hope. You thoroughly deserve all the positives that are bound to come your way in the future.

You needn't have felt awkward about bringing up the name of the shop. Please change it, by all means! The shop is yours and should reflect that. I'd be grateful if you could let us have the old sign for posterity's sake, though. Just give me a quick call when the time comes and I'll pop by to collect it. For now, though, don't be a stranger!

Very best wishes,
Harry

FROM: Hope Sullivan
TO: Denise Carlson
SUBJECT: Thursday

Dear Denise,

Thanks for your email. Funnily enough, someone else mentioned the name of the shop just the other day, which prompted me to speak to Harry about it, and he's on board! I'm afraid I don't much like your suggestions, though. (You did tell me to be honest!) I'm not a big fan of puns in shop names, so perhaps something simple would be best. How about Simply Music?

I know I've been slogging away in the shop, but that wouldn't matter a jot if I didn't have you working your magic behind the scenes. Speaking of slogging away, I could definitely do with a bit of a break and I will certainly consider your suggestion of hiring an assistant. Did I ever tell you that's how I started here? It was ten long years ago, my very first full-time job. Back then, I would never have thought that somewhere down the line, I would be the one hiring my own assistant. But I guess life's funny like that, right?

Thursday evening sounds great. I've been visiting an old friend in hospital every evening for the past couple of weeks, so it will make a nice change to be wined and dined :) I've never been to The JQ before. Don't you have to be some sort of celebrity to get a reservation there?

Love, Hope

PS. I have no idea what the banana said to the vibrator

FROM: Denise Carlson
TO: Hope Sullivan
SUBJECT: Re: Thursday

The JQ it is.

Denise

PS. 'Why are you shaking? She's going to *eat* me.'

> Hi there! I've got a rare evening off on
> Thursday, so I'll be heading in to see Dad.
> Would be great to see you there! Joe

Hi Joe, I'm so sorry, but Thursday is the one day I won't be able to make it. How annoying! Hope x

FROM: Janey Williams
TO: Hope Sullivan
SUBJECT: Hope and Joe, sitting in a tree . . .

Hope Sullivan, you crafty thing! You've finally found someone you're interested in! It makes me wonder what else you've been up to since you posted your letter, which, incidentally, took TWO WHOLE WEEKS to get here. I'm still blaming the Royal Mail; the Japanese postal service is uber-efficient, so it can't be them. From now on, I want regular updates by email!

Right, I'm not sure whether you were asking for my advice, but you're getting it anyway: yes, you must definitely ask him out and I will accept no ifs or buts! It's the 21st century, so it is OK not to wait for him to make the first move. (Christ on a bike, Hope, I shouldn't really have to be telling you this.) If he's taken, he'll let you know, and if he's not interested, ditto. You said he works late hours (I'm wondering what kind of job he could possibly have – he's not a drug dealer, is he?), so maybe you could suggest a Saturday brunch or something?

My sweetest, oldest friend, please never put yourself down. You are lovely, attractive and successful, and any man you meet should thank his lucky stars for even a hint of interest from you.

Love, Janey

PS. I've been counting down the days, too. It's been an eye-opening experience living here, but I'll be glad to be home again

FROM: Hope Sullivan
TO: Janey Williams
SUBJECT: Update as per your request

Dear Janey,

Seeing as you show NO APPRECIATION WHATSOEVER for the effort I put into sending you a hand-written letter, I will henceforth only ever communicate with you digitally. And here is the update as per your request: I have not been out with Joe. FYI, I haven't been waiting for him to make the first move, I just wasn't sure it was entirely appropriate to ask out the son of my friend who is currently lying in hospital in a coma. The doctors say Arnold is stable, which they take as an encouraging sign at this point, but it's hard to think positively when I see him lying there looking so frail. Anyway, Joe contacted me the other day to say he has an evening off and was planning to go in to visit Arnold and asked if I would be there too. My first thought was, 'Yay, finally' (although I'm still a little anxious he might be a creep because why else would he be single?) and then a split-second later I remembered that I'd already agreed to meet up with Denise that night. So I had to tell Joe I wouldn't be able to make it, and I haven't heard anything back from him yet. Maybe he thinks I'm trying to avoid him.

Uff, Janey, something tells me this isn't meant to be. Maybe I should have another stab at online dating. There must be *someone* out there who isn't crazy/creepy/secretly-married-to-some-one-else! You and Eric don't know how lucky you are . . .

Love, Hope

PS. I can think of lots of people who work in the evenings and who are not drug dealers, e.g. musicians

FROM: Hope Sullivan
TO: Janey Williams
SUBJECT: Re: Update as per your request

Dear Hope,

1. Not everyone who is single is automatically a creep – *you're* single and you're not a creep
2. I know you think Eric and I have such a wonderful relation-ship, but our sex life post-Aika is, shall we say, less-than-optimal (this is a convo for a different email altogether)
3. 'Not meant to be'??? Come on, Hope. You're starting to sound like your nan
4. Great news about your shop! I'm really proud of you and I take back everything bad I've ever said (or thought) about Denise. Do you think she's up for a girls' night out when I'm back – with you, me and Autumn? I think I'm in the mood for strong drinks and dirty jokes (see Item no. 2).
5. Are list emails really annoying or what?

Right, now get out there and make a move on Joe. You know it's what Arnold would want you to do, right? And let me know *all* the details!

Love, Janey

FROM: Hope Sullivan
TO: Julie Welsh
SUBJECT: Retail assistant

Dear Julie,

I hope you are well. As you know, Maisie's playing is coming on nicely; she's an incredibly talented and focused student and a real credit to you. It'll be a few months until she's ready to take her next exam, but if she keeps practising as enthusiastically as she has until now, she's bound to ace it. It's been a real pleasure teaching her, but at some point, she'll need a proper tutor.

The reason I'm writing is that I'm looking for someone to help me in the shop. I do hope I'm not being too forward here, but I'd love to offer you the job. It's a part-time position, approx. 20 hours a week, and we can most definitely work around your family commitments. Maisie told me that you used to work at Beacon's Books before it closed down, so you're not a stranger to retail. And as Maisie spends most of her time after school at the shop anyway, you wouldn't have to worry about where she is and what she's up to.

Like I said, I hope I'm not being too forward, but if this is something you might be interested in, please let me know and we can talk in more detail.

With best wishes, Hope

SIMPLY MUSIC
Contract of employment

This contract is made between:

Hope Sullivan of 'Simply Music' (hereinafter: Employer)
and
Julie Welsh (hereinafter: Employee).

As a Sales Assistant, it is the duty of the Employee to perform all essential job functions and duties as outlined in the Appendix. The Employee's normal working hours will be 20 hours per week. A probationary period of one month is agreed. The Employer agrees to pay the Employee an annual salary of £8,000, payable in twelve monthly instalments.

Signed   Signed
Hope Sullivan   *Julie Welsh*
Employer   Employee

LOGOGRAPHIC SIGN DESIGN
Great Sign. Great Times.

Storefront Sign Simply Music	
Aluminium logo and lettering	£600
plus installation	£150
Total	£750 (incl. VAT)

CHAPTER 39

Hope, are you free right now? The hospital called and Dad's woken up! He's asking for you.

Fantastic news! I'm on my way. See you there?

I'm setting off as soon as I can get away from work, but it would be great if you could get there asap

Arnold's awake, Autumn! I'm in tears here!

FROM: Hope Sullivan
TO: Joe Quince
SUBJECT: Revolving doors

Dear Joe,

Missed you *again*! It honestly feels like we're stuck in a set of revolving doors! I stayed for as long as I could, but I was expecting a delivery at the shop at 12.30, so I had to leave. But how wonderful to see Arnold awake! He had no idea who I was, of course, which led to a bit of confusion at first. But as soon as I explained, he reached over and gave me the biggest bear hug ever. Quite strong for someone who's been in a coma for weeks. And he devoured the chocolates I brought him in next to no time! I'm so glad he seems to be on the road to recovery.

He said he was glad that someone had been watching over him, so I thought it was only fair to let him know you'd been in to see him every day, too. I hope I wasn't out of line doing so, but I didn't want to take all the credit. Initially he seemed a bit shocked and not a little apprehensive, but I assured him that you came in peace and were looking forward to talking to him. Once he'd recovered from that he asked what I thought of you and I had to admit we'd never actually met in person, which he seemed to find quite amusing. I told him we'd been emailing back and forth, which Arnold thought was quite sweet, though he said he hoped that didn't mean I would stop writing to him altogether. I reassured him that I would continue to write to him until he got sick and tired of hearing from me! By the way, I didn't mention that you'd read my letters to him; perhaps this is something best left to you?

Anyway, Joe, I think it's about time we forced the issue, or we might be stuck in these revolving doors for ages :) Would you like to have lunch at mine on Saturday? I live quite close to the hospital (only 10 minutes away) and we could go and see Arnold together afterwards. If you're busy, or if you have other commitments, no worries. I'm sure we'll meet at some point.

Love, Hope

FROM: Joe Quince
TO: Hope Sullivan
SUBJECT: Re: Revolving doors

Dear Hope,

I got to the hospital just after half twelve, so I must have missed you by mere minutes. Revolving doors indeed!

I'm going to go out on an unmanly (!) limb here and say that it was quite an emotional visit. Dad was still on a high from your visit; he said you'd told him that you and I have been in touch (thanks for the nice things you said about me, I'm pleased to say I was able to return the favour . . .). He didn't tell me you'd

brought him chocolates, the sly old devil! I gave him a box of
Cadbury Roses and he wolfed them down as though he hadn't
eaten in weeks. Didn't offer me a single one! But I can't tell
you how happy I am that he's finally awake. It's like this enormous weight has been lifted off me and I can go to sleep at
night without dreading a call from the hospital telling me he's
passed. Dad and I have a lot of talking to do but he's still fairly
weak so that can wait, but I'm so grateful that I've been given
this second chance. Thanks again for being there for Dad, I
really appreciate it, and I know he does, too. He thinks the
world of you, by the way!

Thanks for the invitation! It really is about time we met in
person. I don't have any commitments apart from my crazy
working hours, so I'd be happy to meet for lunch. Please don't
go to any trouble though; I'm happy with anything edible.

Looking forward to seeing you on Saturday!

All best, Joe

Hello dear

Hope? Are you there? Why aren't you answering
my message? I can see you're online.

Hope???

Sorry Nan, I was busy looking something up

Oh, there you are. Well, how are you?

Haven't heard from you in a while.

All's well here. How are you and Grandpa?

Not speaking.

Why? What happened?

He's started writing poetry.

And?

Grandpa and poetry, Hope! The man who claimed Sylvia
Plath wasn't a real poet because her poems didn't rhyme.
And now he sits there at the bay window all day, gazing

out at the callistemon shrub in the garden and sighing
        loudly and occasionally scribbling something down.
Yeah, that does sound odd. What's
that all about, do you reckon?
                I'll tell you what that's all about. Helena Harris.
Who?
        Helena Harris. She's the Aqua Zumba instructor and I'm
                sure she's got her eye on Grandpa. And vice versa.
Really, Nan?
            It's all winks and smiles and 'Ooh, look at those
                hips go, Frank!'. And now he's started writing
                these wretched poems. Hang on, I'll just see if
                I can find one of them and read it to you –
Nan, I'm a bit busy right now
        I thought you were just messing about on the computer?
No. Yes. I mean, I was looking up some recipes.
                Whatever for? You know as well as I do that
                    the women in this family can't cook
Ha! Well, that's exactly the reason I have
to look up some recipes. I've got
someone coming round for lunch on Saturday
                        Ooooh, tell me more!
Just someone I met
                        Male? Female?
            Not-quite-sure-where-they-are-on-the-spectrum?
Nan!
                        Sorry. Do go on.
It's a guy I met. He's the son of a friend
                        And you like him?
I do
                        What's his name?
Joe. Joe Quince
                        How old is he?
Don't know exactly. Early thirties? I actually have no idea
                    Are you doing this on purpose?
What?

For goodness' sake, Hope! This is the first time
you've ever mentioned being interested in a fella,
and you're making me squeeze the information
out of you like you have something to hide.

Sorry, Nan. It's just, we . . . we haven't
actually met. In person

Well that sounds very odd. How do you
know you like him if you've never met?

We've been emailing and texting for a
couple of weeks. He sounds really nice
and I'd like to meet him. Besides, Autumn's met
him and I'm sure she'd tell me if she thought
he was an axe murderer or something

Let's hope he isn't!

So anyway, I've invited him for lunch and
I need to find something simple to
cook

I have an idea.

About what?

Hang on, give me ten minutes.

Nan?

FROM: Wilma McDonald
TO: Hope Sullivan
SUBJECT: Food

Dear Hope,

Sorry – that took a lot longer than 10 minutes. I rang Madame
Zargo to ask what the best kind of food would be to serve to
someone you might be, shall we say, *interested* in. I was expecting to hear about aphrodisiacs, you know, oysters, figs and so
on, but instead she gave me a load of old claptrap about love
potions. I indulged her for a bit (she doesn't take kindly to
being interrupted), but when she got to the bit about charging
rose quartz crystals in the light of the full moon and stirring

pomegranate juice clockwise with your left hand, I politely suggested it sounded like she was making it up as she went along. 'Oh no,' she said, 'but you have to *believe*. This is, after all, about causing change to occur in conformity to will.' (Whatever that means.) She went on, at length, about the power of speaking things into existence and the power of manifestation. (She's really starting to lose it, Hope. And I know for a fact that her real name isn't Madame Zargo. It's Betty Johnson.)

She ended by saying that you would also have to have a 'reversal' on hand, just in case you changed your mind somewhere along the line, unless you want to end up with a stalker. 'Of course Hope doesn't want a bloody stalker!' I told her. She then had the audacity to say that it didn't surprise her in the slightest that I was being snappy, because the moon's north node is in Taurus and that's a sure way to put a Sagittarius in a bad mood. So I told her to stick her rose quartzes where the sun don't shine. Long story short, Madame Zargo – aka Betty Johnson – and I have parted ways.

Anyway, I'm not a quitter, as you know, so I swallowed my pride and went to ask Grandpa for suggestions. The thought of a Sullivan woman cooking a meal made him laugh so much he forgot we weren't speaking. After I'd told him to put a sock in it, he suggested a simple pasta dish followed by a chocolate mousse. I've attached the recipe. Grandpa swears it's absolutely foolproof (he forgets the time I set the kitchen curtains on fire boiling an egg) and that it would have any man 'eating out of your hand' (let me apologise on his behalf for the god-awful pun).

Darling Hope, do with this what you will, but perhaps you should get a takeaway just to be on the safe side?

Lots of love and good luck,
Nan

PS. It might be best to skip the garlic

Hope Sullivan
Wilma McDonald
Re: Food

Thanks, Nan! I appreciate your faith in my culinary abilities, haha. *Pasta alla Norma* sounds easy enough though. And it's not cheating if I use Angel Delight to make the chocolate mousse, right? I'll let you know how it goes.

Love, Hope

Autumn! Help!!! Any idea how
to unburn tomato sauce?

> Don't tell me you're trying to cook?!
> Hahahahahahaha

Joe, SOOOOO SORRY to do this to you at
the last minute, but something came up and
I'll have to cancel lunch. I promise to come
to the hospital, though. I'll be there at 3.

CHAPTER 40

FROM: Hope Sullivan
TO: Janey Williams
SUBJECT: Update!!!

Dear Janey,

It finally happened!!! I met Joe! And for your information, *I* made the first move and invited *him* out. Although, then *he* asked *me* out, so I don't know if I can take all the credit. But first things first: we'd missed each other *again* at the hospital, so I took the bull by the horns and wrote him an email yesterday saying I'd really like to meet. Joe wrote back saying he'd love to, and for some insane reason I suggested we have lunch at mine. The hospital isn't far, and my idea was that we have a quick bite at my flat and then go and visit Arnold together. Needless to say, me cooking = disaster. I somehow managed to set fire to the tomato sauce and set off the smoke alarm and the sprinklers. So I had to cancel lunch and grab a very quick shower, though I swear I was still reeking of smoke when I got to the hospital.

Joe was already there, standing just outside Arnold's room with a big box of chocolates under his arm. I recognised him immediately – he has the same kind eyes as Arnold, although his hair is still dark and full. He's tall, like his dad, and he has this cute habit of touching his earlobe when he's embarrassed, but more on that later. I don't mind admitting I was more than a little smitten! I made this lame excuse about a small fire starting at my neighbour's flat to explain the odd smell I was carrying around me like a bad aura, but I don't think he was really listening, because he just gave me this lovely smile and kept touching his earlobe. We went in and Arnold was delighted to see us together for the first time. We sat and chatted for a while, mostly about Arnold and his plans for when he leaves hospital. He said he'd been thinking long and hard about it, and decided it was time to start playing piano again, as a duet partner with his fellow resident, Frank. (Not the 'Turkish March' though, that was something he would always keep for Marion.) Joe and I sat and listened, both, I think, pleased that Arnold was so full of life again. After about an hour, the nurse came in and said it was time to go, but that she'd love to see us again as regular visits were doing Arnold no end of good.

Anyway, I didn't want to appear too forward (i.e. desperate) and ask Joe out *again*, so we said our goodbyes and left. I'd just got home when he sent me a text, saying how nice it was to have finally met etc., and that he'd managed to get some time off work the following night and would I like to have dinner with him!!! He suggested The JQ, this really fancy restaurant that opened a couple of months ago. I'd just been there a few nights earlier with Denise to talk over some business stuff. (The food is fantastic, by the way. We'll definitely have to go there when you're back.)

I spent literally *hours* in front of my wardrobe, deciding what to wear. I mean, when's the last time I went on a date? And was this even a date, in the proper sense, or just a friendly get-together between two people who have a mutual acquaintance. Right? Right. You can imagine the state I managed to get myself in as I tried on one outfit after the other – skinny jeans, Marlene-Dietrich-style slacks, a low-cut chiffon top, a floral hippie blouse – basically, my entire wardrobe. Eventually, when I realised it was seven thirty and I'd have to get going or I'd be later than late, I decided on a burgundy wraparound dress that's comfortable but stylish. For luck, I wore the silver treble clef earrings you got me all those years ago, remember?

The restaurant is at the end of Portland Road. It's fairly out of the way, up the hill and tucked behind the church, in a 17th-century building that used to be a cowshed or something, but is now a gorgeously cosy, low-ceilinged restaurant. It would be difficult to find if you didn't know it was there, but its reputation has spread so quickly that apparently, the place is always heaving. I'm sure I spotted one or two minor celebrities when Denise and I were there. That lady off *Newsnight*, what's her name?

So anyway, I was walking up the hill, cursing the fact that I'd chosen to wear heels instead of the flats I'm used to, wondering how Joe had managed to get a table at only a day's notice. I figured that Tuesdays must be a slow night or something. He was waiting for me outside the restaurant, looking lovely in a dark, casual suit with a collarless top. I said hi and stuck my hand out for him to shake while he leaned in for a kiss on the cheek, which was about as awkward as it sounds (cue lots of earlobe touching). We managed to make a joke of it, though, and he complimented me on my outfit (but not in a creepy way).

But Janey, you won't believe what happened next! Joe and I walked in and I noticed straight away that something was up. The maître d' obviously knew him, though they were very formal with each other, and the waiter took my coat with a knowing smile. For a moment, I thought I was on *You've Been Framed* or something. Then I figured Joe must be a regular customer, because the waiter seemed to know what Joe wanted before he'd even ordered. It took me ages to look through the menu and decide, because it all looked so delicious, but I finally went with the rack of lamb with Taggiasca olives and San Marzano tomatoes. Joe nodded and said that was an excellent choice. I'm sure you know where this is going, Janey, but I was still drawing a mental blank. The whole time, Joe was looking at me with a quizzically amused expression.

Eventually, I asked if he'd been here before, and he nodded. Then he broke into a huge grin and said, 'What do you think JQ stands for?' and finally, the penny dropped. *JQ – Joe Quince*. But it was so incredible, I was sure he was having me on. 'OK, if you don't believe me,' he said and got up and led me into the kitchen. To be perfectly honest, I was half-stunned he might be telling the truth and half-terrified he was some kind of madman who imagines himself to be someone he isn't. Like a delusional disorder when someone thinks they're Napoleon, or Jesus, you know? So I was tugging gently on his sleeve, telling him I didn't think this was such a good idea, when he opened the kitchen doors and everyone there stopped what they were doing and looked in our direction. You could have heard a pin drop, but a split-second later, they'd started up again, clanging pots and pans and shouting orders at each other. Joe walked over to this guy in a chef's hat, who was carefully decorating a rack of lamb with a sprig of thyme.

'This the lamb?' Joe said, pointing at the plate, and added, 'We have a special guest tonight. Make sure it's *à point*.'

'Oui, chef,' was the answer.

I must have been bright red when we sat back down. Joe's a chef! With his own restaurant! When the food came, I was so gobsmacked I'd completely lost my appetite and couldn't finish my meal, which is a real shame because the lamb was absolutely divine. (Do posh restaurants do doggie bags? I didn't want to embarrass myself by asking.) But once my heart rate had normalised and my face didn't feel like it was on fire any more, Joe and I started talking and didn't stop for hours. He told me that as a boy, he'd set his heart on becoming a pilot, but that he has red-green colour blindness. Then, when he was fifteen or so, he discovered the joy of cooking, of experimenting with foods and flavours, and decided to become a chef. This was partly inspired by Arnold's baking talent, and both his parents encouraged him to follow his dream. He trained in Italy and Vietnam, and has worked in kitchens all over the world. He told me that his work – the travelling, the crazy hours – made serious relationships difficult to maintain, but that recently he's started feeling a need to settle. So he finally opened his own restaurant two months ago, and he's aiming for a Michelin star next year.

I know this sounds like Joe talked the whole time, but in fact, I must have talked just as much. I told him about my childhood dream of becoming a world-famous violinist, about having to take care of Autumn after Mum and Dad died, about the bumpy ride with the shop, the failed cafe idea, the near-bank-ruptcy, my angel-in-disguise Denise, and of course, all about you. We talked for ages, and when all the other diners had left and the staff shut up shop, we retreated to the kitchen and ate the most gorgeous white chocolate mousse I've ever tasted. And we laughed so much! I've actually got sore stomach muscles.

Joe walked me home (I won't bore you with a description of the perfect inky sky with its pinpricks of stars, and the silver moonlight washing over us – but that was exactly what it was like!) and we fell into a deep, companionable silence. It was way past midnight by this time, and I should have been exhausted, having been on my feet all day, but I was *zinging*. So anyway, we got to my building and said goodbye, and this time it wasn't awkward at all. In fact, when Joe leaned in to kiss me, it felt like the only possible ending to the evening. Do you remember, way back, you sent me that Perfect Love Match thingy? Well, my perfect match is an INFJ, and that is Joe down to a T.

Love, Hope

Janey Williams
Hope Sullivan
Re: Update!!!

Babe! I've been saying it all along! I'm so happy for you and cannot *wait* to meet Joe.

Love, Janey x

FROM: Hope Sullivan
TO: Janey Williams
SUBJECT: Re: Re: Update!!!

Hi Janey,

It's late (or early, whichever way you want to look at it), but there's something I've been meaning to get off my chest for a while: I know I told you I was gutted about spraining my wrist before your mum's memorial service. That wasn't a lie, but the real truth is, I was more relieved than anything. You see, I haven't played the violin for ten years, since Mum and Dad died, and I wasn't sure I'd be able to do it. I know you've asked me about it occasionally, and I've never given you an honest answer. I've kept quiet about it for all these years because . . . because, oh, I don't know. A whole mix of feelings – shame, guilt, grief, fear. All the negative feelings, anyway. And when you asked me to play at your mum's memorial, I was suddenly facing this momentous decision. It took all my strength to agree to play, and then when the burglary happened and I hurt my wrist, I just felt this huge sense of relief. I didn't have to play, but I didn't have to chicken out, either. The decision had been made for me.

But lately, I've been getting this weird feeling that it wasn't a decision at all. More like . . . like a precursor, a harbinger, just before you get to the end of something. Do you know what I mean? Like when you've still got that final chapter of a story to

read, and without it, nothing that went before really makes
sense.

Sorry, I really have to get some sleep now, because I'm not
even making sense to *myself* any more. I love and miss you and
I'm beyond happy that you're coming home soon.

Love, Hope

FROM: Janey Williams
TO: Hope Sullivan
SUBJECT: Re: Re: Re: Update!!!

Hope! I'm sitting here in tears over your email. Do you
remember me telling you that music lives in your soul, always,
and that it will find you eventually? I think it's finally catching
up with you.

All my love, Janey

FROM: Joe Quince
TO: Hope Sullivan
SUBJECT: Dinner

Dear Hope,

I had a lovely time last night, and I hope you did too. Sorry
about dropping the surprise on you like that. It seemed a good
idea at the time, and it certainly wasn't my intention to put you
off your food!

I was awake for ages last night, going over everything we talked
about. Maybe it was the wine, but I can't remember the last
time I had such a long conversation that didn't feel like it was
dragging on. And I really can't remember the last time I
laughed so hard! (By the way, please believe me that I don't
usually spurt wine out of my nose on dates.) I'd completely

forgotten about the time I got detention at school for bringing my pet frog into class. But judging by what you used to get up to, I think we would have been good mates if we'd met as children :)

I know we talked for hours, but the funny thing is, I feel we've only just scratched the surface. What I'm trying to say is I'd love to see you again; if you don't fancy the restaurant, I'm happy to take you up on your offer of lunch?

I'm sitting at Dad's bedside as I type this. He's sleeping peacefully right now, and the doctors say that's a good thing. Before he nodded off, I told him that we'd been out for dinner (hope you don't mind?) and he was absolutely delighted that his 'two favourite people' had hit it off so well.

Thank you, Hope. I mean it. Without you, I would never have known about Dad being so ill and we might never have reconciled.

All best, Joe

PS. We do doggie bags at The JQ. If there's one thing my mum instilled in me growing up, it's that good food should never go to waste!

FROM: Hope Sullivan
TO: Joe Quince
SUBJECT: Re: Dinner

Dear Joe,

The shop is hectic right now, but I would love to see you again too! As for me cooking lunch, that is a very bad idea, I'm afraid. On an entirely unrelated note, I might have a small confession to make about my neighbour's fire . . .

Love, Hope

Hi Hope – great news! Dad's being released from hospital tomorrow. I'll be going to pick him up at around 10. Thought you might want to come, too :)

Dear Hope, this is Arnold Quince. I hope you are well and that this message reaches you. Joe insisted on me getting this smartphone (though I fear it's too smart for me!) so that if anything happens again, I can contact one of you. I look forward to your next letter. All the best, Arnold

Arnold! It's good to have your number & I'm always only a call away if you need me. I hope you settle in well at home and I'll come visit you soon! And don't worry about modern technology – I think smartphones are smarter than most of us :)

CHAPTER 41

Dear Hope,

Well, I'm finally back in my flat. It's funny really, I hadn't realised how much Sunny Fields feels like home until I walked – or rather hobbled – back through the door. The other residents had prepared a little party to celebrate my return, with a Welcome Home banner and tea and cakes, and Frank had even splashed out and bought me a bottle of rather nice 12-year-old Laphroaig. I'm not ashamed to say it brought a little tear to my eye. Autumn had dropped off Marmalade in the morning, so he was there to greet me, too. I'm not sure who was more excited, him or me!

I'm very much looking forward to your visit. Perhaps Frank and I will be able to treat you to a performance of one of our duets. Yes, I've decided that life is too short to deny myself the pleasure of playing. Lying in a hospital bed with nothing better to do than ruminate on how close I came to dying certainly took its toll! Without wanting to sound despondent (which I am not, believe me), I am acutely aware of how little time I have left, and I want to live every minute of it. Frank and I have been practising Pachelbel's 'Canon in D', a favourite among the ladies, though I can't promise you we'll have it polished enough to play for a proper musician such as yourself. But I'm sure we'll be able to play you a swing or a boogie-woogie (also popular with the ladies!).

When I'm not being tortured by the physical therapist – why must these people always have such icy cold hands?

– I'm being brought up to date about what the Four O'Clock Club has been up to in my absence. Frank now hosts an illicit poker game in his flat every Thursday afternoon, which you can only join if you know the code word ('all-in') and are prepared to gamble your custard creams and chocolate bourbons. I'm not a gambler, never have been, so I generally stick to playing Monopoly and Scrabble with Hugh in the common room (Marion probably would've loved the poker, though).

The biggest change is that I now have a regular visitor. Joe comes in to see me several times a week, and we spend a lot of time talking. It's been tough at times, I won't lie, but there are no longer any recriminations. No, we talk about our life with Marion, look at old photographs and go for walks with Marmalade. Joe even dug out an old 8mm film I'd made of Marion back in the 70s. I'd forgotten all about it. We were on holiday in the Scottish Highlands and I'd challenged Marion to swim in one of the lochs. There she is, in shaky black-and-white, plunging daringly into the freezing cold water of Loch Affric. Joe kindly left the film and projector with me, so perhaps I can show you when you come to visit.

Last week, Joe happened to be here at lunchtime, and when he saw what was being served – grey slabs of 'roast beef' (I put that in quotation marks, because it's anyone's guess what kind of meat it really is), reheated mashed potato and a very cold and very lumpy gravy – he demanded to speak to the manager of Sunny Fields. Long story short, the contract of our current caterer will not be renewed, and Joe has someone in mind who will be able to provide good-quality, tasty meals at a decent price. But never mind the food. Joe seems very taken with you, Hope! You're almost all he talks about. I'm so pleased the two of you have hit it off.

Oh, and the newspaper article on my baking exploits was published while I was in hospital. I've attached a copy. I've had to put the baking on hold, unfortunately, until the doctor gives me the all clear, because I'm still a little unsteady on my legs, but I have plenty of willing helpers from the Four O'Clock Club offering their services.

Like I said, I very much look forward to your visit, but I do hope this won't spell the end of our letter-writing. Two years ago, I wouldn't have thought it possible to develop such deep affection for another person this late in life, but writing to you has truly been one of the greatest joys. And if you'll allow me one melancholy thought, it's that I'm saddened you never got to meet Marion. I know the two of you would have become great friends.

All very best, and see you soon,
Arnold

BAKING FOR A BRIGHTER FUTURE

Retired schoolteacher Arnold Quince, 73 (pictured above with his dog, Marmalade), has raised £2000 for YOUNG MINDS, a charity that provides counselling and mental health support to children and young people.

Arnold, a resident at Sunny Fields Assisted Living Community, said, 'I've always loved baking, but after the death of my wife six years ago, I found my joy in baking had all but disappeared. But the kind words of a good friend lifted me out of my slump, and thanks to her invaluable support, I donned my apron and set about baking again. This time around I've become more adventurous in trying out new recipes and designs, which have found a positive reception from my customers. I'm overrun with orders at the moment, so anyone who would like to support YOUNG MINDS by purchasing one of my cakes, please be patient.'

Francine Mitchell, fundraising manager at YOUNG MINDS, said: 'We are blown away by Arnold's commitment and generosity, and having tasted his cakes ourselves, we can only recommend placing an order! He is a true inspiration, and we wouldn't be surprised to see him in next year's *GBBO*.'

Arnold says he hopes to continue baking and selling cakes for as long as he is able to whisk an egg.

To place an order with Arnold, please send an email to the address below. To donate to YOUNG MINDS, click <u>here</u>.

Hi from Frankfurt, Sis! My turn to send you a postcard for a change. The music fair is wild! I've made more contacts in two days than in the last two years. See you soon!

Love, Hope

29th May

Dear Arnold,

It's just after midnight now, and I'm totally exhausted and should really be catching up on my beauty sleep, but I'm still buzzing and thought I'd use the opportunity to write to you. I got your letter just as I was leaving for Frankfurt and brought it with me, but I've been so busy I've only now had time to read it. Thanks so much for the copy of the newspaper article! Looks like you're well on your way to becoming famous, Arnold! I shall have to get your autograph :)

As I write this, I'm sitting in a hotel in Frankfurt, looking out at the most amazing skyline. It's almost like being in New York! There are dozens of skyscrapers in my line of sight, each one twinkling with light. I've been sitting here imagining what kind of lives are being played out behind each lit window – dramas, tragedies, love stories; the whole gamut, I suppose. My room is on the 18th floor and not much bigger than a shoebox, but the window is floor-to-ceiling and I have the best view of the city. The moon tonight is a perfect crescent, hanging suspended in the blue-black sky, like something out of a children's storybook.

Tomorrow is the last day of the music fair, which has been hugely successful for us. I finally got to meet our Aberdeen luthier, Adair, who is the oddest little man (in a good way). He's only about 5' 2", has a shock of black hair that looks like it rarely sees a comb (with matching eyebrows), and very long fidgety fingers. He is besotted with his instruments, his 'babies', and we'd only just been introduced before he shared with me his grave concerns about the increased use of purflings made of plastic rather than pearwood or abalone, and that using an electric drill to cut f-holes into the belly of a violoncello was 'wrong, wrong, wrong'. It was a good 20 minutes before I could get a word in edgewise. Adair knows more about musical instruments than anybody I've ever met, but you can see why he's not the best person to deal with customers directly.

I don't know if Joe mentioned it, but he's flying out here tomorrow afternoon to take me to dinner! We're going to Lafleur, a 2-Michelin-star restaurant, and according to Joe, he's 'scouting out the competition', though I like to think he's coming here because he misses me :)

So, I'll be home on Saturday afternoon, with a whole 48 hours to rest and recuperate before I have to be back in the shop. It was such a great idea to hire an assistant. Julie is a rock – she's not only reliable, but she's also very smart and not afraid to take the initiative. If our order books stay as full as they are now, I might even be able to offer her a full-time position. Maisie has finally got a professional music teacher; actually, I managed to track down my former violin instructor at the academy, Miss Garland, who retired a couple of years ago. She still teaches a few students privately, though she's very selective. But she saw Maisie's potential after only a few minutes of playing (I mean, I wasn't surprised in the slightest; the girl has a bright future ahead of her) and took her on immediately.

Oh, and did you hear that Autumn got a dog? Apparently, she was so enamoured with Marmalade that giving him back nearly broke her heart. She and Krish went out the next day and got themselves a puppy. He's a Golden Retriever and they've named him Apollo. I have to admit, even a Cat Lady like myself thinks he's the cutest thing ever. (Don't tell Yuuko!)

But best of all, Janey is coming back next week, two days before my birthday!!! I have missed her so much, Arnold. Janey knows me better than anyone in the world, and it's been tough not having her close by. We've been best friends for twenty years, and it's incredible to think how we've ended up where we are now. I still can't quite get my head around Janey being a mum, but then again, I'm sure she struggles to picture me weighing up the pros and cons of inventory software in my spare time. And I know Janey is going to love Joe – she's a foodie, so how could she not?! I can't wait to introduce them to each other. Ha, listen to me! If you'd told me a year ago that I would be mentally planning a double date with Janey and Eric, I would have laughed in your face! So, all in all, things are looking pretty good. But – and I'm only sharing this with you, Arnold, because I know you won't judge me for it – I have the feeling that something is still missing, something very small but significant . . .

Well, there are almost no twinkling lights left on in the buildings opposite, so I think I'll call it a day as well. Take care of yourself, and see you soon.

Love, Hope

FROM: Hope Sullivan
TO: Wilma McDonald
SUBJECT: Secret life?!!

Dear Nan,

You never cease to amaze me! Since when have you been on Instagram? And how the hell did you get 20,000 followers? Don't tell me you're leading a secret life as a social media influencer! I'm lucky I stumbled across your post, actually, as I don't usually look at Instagram – all those beautiful people sharing beautiful pictures of their beautiful lives. It's quite sickening, really. I don't mean your posts, of course. You and Grandpa look really impressive doing that Zumba thing, although the image of Grandpa's neon Lycra shorts has burned itself unpleasantly onto my retina.

I think it's adorable that you and Grandpa have renewed your wedding vows (I guess that's the last we'll be hearing of Helena Harris, haha), but it would have been nice to be invited at least. A second wedding on the beach! And where exactly are you? That doesn't look like Bondi Beach, it's far too empty. But you look beautiful, Nan, you really do. I especially like the flowers in your hair and the way your dress catches the breeze. If ever I decide to get married (and you'll be pleased to hear that while still a very distant possibility, it *is* a possibility), that's how I want to look.

Give Grandpa a huge sloppy kiss from me, and I'll be following you on Instagram to keep up with all your exploits. So KEEP IT CLEAN!!!

Love,
Hope

CHAPTER 42

To my Best Friend Forever – Happy 29th Birthday!
  Love, Janey (& Eric & Aika)
    P.S. Autumn and I have the party all planned for
    Saturday, so all you have to do is turn up

You're on the fast track to 30 now!
  All my love, Autumn x

Have a very Happy Birthday, Hope!
  Best wishes, Arnold

A little bird told me it's your birthday! Have a great one –
dinner at mine?
  Joe x

Greetings from Fiji! We're busy second-honeymooning, but
we wanted to drop you a quick line to say Many Happy
Returns of the Day!
  Lots of love, Nan & Grandpa

FROM: Ainsworth & Gardener Solicitors
TO: Hope Sullivan
SUBJECT: Address

Dear Hope,

I trust all is well with you. I'm writing to enquire if you are still living at the same address as the one noted in our records, as I have a letter I have been charged with forwarding to you. It's nothing to be worried about!

Kind regards,
Thomas Ainsworth
Solicitor at Law

FROM: Hope Sullivan
TO: Ainsworth & Gardener Solicitors
SUBJECT: Re: Address

Dear Thomas,

My address hasn't changed. Do you mind telling me who the letter is from?

Regards,
Hope

Darling Baby,

You're already a couple of weeks old and we're still fiercely contesting your name – Dad wants to go for Mary, which I find hopelessly boring, and I'd rather have something unusual, Ophelia or Portia, which Dad finds pretentious. (Actually, I think he's afraid you might be bullied at school.) So until we have found something we're both happy with, you will remain 'Baby Sullivan' for the time being. Having said that, by the time you get this letter you will (hopefully!) have a name that suits you and that you are happy with.

Happy 29th Birthday, my darling!!!

Now, you might find it strange to be receiving a birthday letter written when you were only two weeks old, but memories are so easily lost and Dad and I thought it would be nice to surprise you with how we were feeling so soon after you came into our lives. We chose your 29th birthday, because that is how old Dad and I are now! It is inconceivable to me right now that I will be 58 when you read this. An old woman, argh! (Note to self: apply moisturiser regularly, avoid too much sun, drink copious amounts of water).

Joking aside, my darling, I hope your life up to now has been everything you've wished for. And even if you've hit some bumps along the way, or if things don't seem perfect, remember that you still have most of your life ahead of you. Anything and everything is possible with a little hope.

And we have so much hope for you, Baby Sullivan! Life is wonderful, but it does have its ups and downs, and you might have to be strong to get through them. But hey, I can tell just from the way you grip my little finger with your curled hand that you are strong! And I'm sure you will only get stronger along the way. I look at your perfect little face and my heart feels so full of love I'm afraid it will explode. Goodness me, I can tell I'm getting a little sentimental now, but you can blame that on lack of sleep and hormones. (You will know what I'm talking about if you ever have a baby yourself. Or perhaps you already are a mother!)

Your lips are the colour of crushed strawberries and you always purse them a split-second before you erupt into the loudest scream I've ever heard. I wouldn't say you're a fussy baby, but you do like to make yourself heard! Funnily enough though, all it takes to quieten you down is a few bars of Dvořák (from the Hovis TV ad!), which is odd, because Dad and I are more into David Bowie and Prince than Vivaldi and Mozart. I think we're going to have to invest in some classical CDs . . .

You're asleep beside me right now. You look so innocent when you're sleeping, although there is definitely a mischievous glint in your eye when you're awake. I hope I don't get too many grey hairs during your teenage years! You will know by now that I'm not the strictest parent that ever lived, but these are the rules I intend to instil in you and that I hope you have lived your life by:

Be happy.

Be kind.

Be strong.

Never lose hope.

Right, I'll leave it here before I start blubbing. (Also, I'm getting a little confused about whether I'm writing to you as a baby or you as a 29-year-old.) My darling, have yourself a wonderful birthday, surrounded hopefully by all those who love you.

Love, Mum xxx

PS. In case you're wondering why this letter is coming from Dad's law firm, Dad is going to make me hand it over to him so I don't slip up and give it to you sooner!

PPS. Is it just me, or does the concept of hope run through this letter? Hmm, maybe I've stumbled onto something . . . Hope Sullivan, how does that sound?

CHAPTER 43

Dear Arnold,

Do you remember, in one of your first letters to me, you talked about the magic of letter-writing? You said that letters arrive from the past, and that by the time you receive one, anything could have happened. Well, something *has* happened. Or rather, something has fallen into place, something that was there all along but needed the right circumstances to emerge. It's like one of those Chinese puzzles where everything has to line up *just so* to be solved. My relationship with Autumn, my best friend coming home, falling in love (yes, I'll shout it from the rooftops: I'm in love with your son!), the shop being a success. Each part is equally important; if even one of them were missing, there would be no solution to the puzzle.

So . . . I have a surprise for you. As you can see from the attachment, I'm about to discover what happens on the other side of fear. You said it would call me when I was least expecting it, and you were right. My biggest, heartfelt thanks, Arnold. I know I just said that all parts of this puzzle are equally important, but that's not entirely true. Without you, I never would have had the courage to take this step.

Love, Hope

Dear Ms Sullivan,

I hereby acknowledge your order for the following:
Violin 4/4
Ebony and rosewood fingerboard
Maple bridge
Spruce soundboard

Please allow approx. 10 weeks from order to receipt of the finished instrument.

Yours sincerely,
Adair Crannach

EPILOGUE

Six months later

In the far corner, a forgotten strip of bunting hangs limply from the ceiling, a remnant from some wedding celebration or a Boy Scout party. The hall seats just over a hundred and is surprisingly full. Autumn and Krish volunteered to do the advertising for the concert and rose to the challenge admirably; Krish came up with the hashtag *#OneNightWithTchaikovsky* and plastered it all over social media. Of course, the other performers have invited their friends and family, too, but that still doesn't account for the sheer number of people sitting there now, murmuring quietly in polite anticipation of the music.

It's warm in the hall; someone cranked up the radiators a few hours ago to take the damp February chill out of the air. But now, with all the bodies in the room releasing their heat, it's getting a little hard to breathe. Or maybe that's just her nerves. From where she stands in the wings, hidden from the audience by the dusty velvet curtain that has seen better days, Hope spots Janey and Eric, sitting in the front row. She takes a deep breath. The air streams into her lungs and the knot of anxiety in the pit of her stomach loosens a little. Janey has reserved the two seats beside her by covering them with her coat. Autumn and Krish should be here any minute.

Behind her, Hope hears the whine and buzz of the other performers tuning their instruments. They are all outstanding musicians; not professional players, but as close as it gets. With Joe's encouragement, Hope responded to a call for audition for a 'Night with Tchaikovsky' two months ago and surprised herself by playing so well that she was chosen to open the set. So here she now stands, with a thumping heart and a rising excitement that threatens to bubble over, ready to walk out onto the little stage. It's not the Royal Albert Hall, but it's a start.

Denise is also in the audience, in the third row, furiously tapping away at her phone. She wanted to make a big thing of the concert, tie it in with Simply Music to drive sales, but Hope was able to talk her out of it. There's enough expectation resting on her as it is. It's a shame Maisie couldn't make it, but she's currently attending a workshop for gifted young musicians. She and Hope have been each other's most fervent cheerleaders over the past few months, and Joe has promised to record the concert for her. Maisie has been her cheerleader, it's true, but Joe has been her rock. Thanks to his cooking, Hope is no longer all elbows and knees; according to Nan, who never fails to comment on her Facebook posts, she's 'got a bit of meat on her bones at last'.

A loud cranking noise startles her. The curtain is being raised and the audience falls into darkness. Hope takes one more deep breath and steps out onto the stage, blinking in the stream of light coming from above. Applause. Now, all she can see is a shadowy mass in front of her. As her eyes slowly adjust to the light, her gaze sweeps across the audience. There's Joe, beaming at her, and beside him, dressed like a real gentleman in a formal suit and tie, is Arnold. There was a heated discussion with the nurses at Sunny Fields – Arnold is still at risk of infection due to his immunosuppressants – but he was adamant that if coming to Hope's concert was the last worthwhile thing he did in his life, then so be it. The pride in his eyes makes her want to cry, but she manages a smile.

There's a muttering now from the back as a couple of latecomers make their way down the hall. It's Autumn and Krish; Autumn mouths an apology and Hope can't resist a half-smile. Trust her little sister to turn up at the very last minute.

Autumn gets out her phone and discreetly holds it up. Nan and Grandpa made her promise to live-stream Hope's performance to their computer so they can be with her in spirit, if not in person. Hope's heart flutters fast and light in her chest and she has to blink back a tear. It means everything to her that her closest friends and family are there, wishing her well.

The applause dies down. Hope's mouth is unexpectedly dry and she has to swallow before addressing the audience, introducing herself and Beth, her piano accompaniment. She lifts the violin to her shoulder, a frisson of excitement running through her as the warm wood makes contact with her bare skin. The dress she's wearing now, off the shoulder, emerald green, is the result of a frenzied, hilarious afternoon's shopping with Autumn, Janey and Denise.

Janey and Autumn came round again this afternoon to help her get ready. Not that she needed help, but she knew that this was their way of showing their support. They fussed over her like a bride, putting her hair up, down, in curls, straightened, until Hope shooed them out of the room and did her own hairstyle, a sleek, simple ponytail that shows off her slim neck and her silver clef earrings. Her friends mean well, but Hope knows, deep down, that they only have the barest grasp of what it has cost her to get this far. And that's fine, really it is. This is her journey, her challenge.

The air in the hall is suddenly silent. No coughs, whispers or shuffling in seats. Hope raises the bow to the strings in one fluid, graceful movement, feels a slight twinge as she tenses her left wrist, but ignores it. Just a ghost of a memory. The pianist plays the opening bars. Hope closes her eyes in anticipation of her entrance just after the hemiola. She may have the piano to accompany her, but she is alone up here on stage. This is the essence of music – musicians as solitary parts of a collective whole. Each is responsible for their own sound, yet each means nothing without the interaction and connection with the other. She is about to do what she has put off for the last ten years, a decade during which she has cried a lifetime's worth of tears;

has fostered and deepened a friendship that is special beyond belief; has made a new, special friend in the most unlikely of places; and has loved, lost, and loved again.

It hasn't been an easy ride – over the past few months, since her violin arrived from Adair, she has had to play through grief and tears, headaches, through cracked and bloody fingertips. But she didn't give up, not this time, and now her left finger-tips are hard and strong. This piece, Canzonetta: Andante 2nd movement from Concerto in D, Op. 35, she owes to her parents. It's the piece she tried, and failed, to play at their funeral, but now she is ready for it. The melody is a mournful cry – having lost his mother when he was young, Tchaikovsky knew a thing or two about grief himself. The Canzonetta, in the distant and unexpected key of G minor, expresses layers and layers of feeling that Hope connects with only too well. The piece is gentle, lyrical and haunting, taking every listener on an inescapable emotional journey.

Hope leans into the music, her left hand sliding up and down the fingerboard, her bow stroking back and forth across the strings. Earlier, during practice, she was nervous about messing up the trills, but now she plays them as though she's never done anything else in her life. She wants to be heard. Her wrist suddenly seizes up painfully and she misplaces a finger on the board. It's a minor, fleeting error, no one will have noticed, but she feels her lungs tighten. She closes her eyes and breathes through the fear.

If she wants to get anywhere close to the skill she possessed as a teenager, she has a whole number of mountains ahead of her to climb. And she knows, realistically, she might never succeed. But right now, the music gives her wings. Her bow slides across the strings, teasing out the harmonies, clean and clear. She knows she is doing justice to Adair's violin. It is a beautiful sound, and it is coming from her. This is what she was born to do. She melts into the music. Whatever comes in the future, will come.

For now, though, there is magic – and hope.

HOPE'S PLAYLIST FOR MAISIE

1. Tchaikovsky – *Violin Concerto in D Major* – Maxim Vengerov
2. Brahms – *Violin Concerto in D Major* – David Oistrakh
3. Mendelssohn – *Violin Concerto in E Minor* – Anne-Sophie Mutter
4. Shostakovich – *Violin Concerto No. 1 in A Minor* – Leonid Kogan
5. Elgar – *Violin Concerto in B Minor* – Itzhak Perlman
6. Bruch – *Violin Concerto in G Minor* – Hilary Hahn
7. Beethoven – *Violin Concerto in D Major* – Jascha Heifetz
8. Sibelius – *Violin Concerto in D Minor* – Janine Jansen
9. Saint-Saëns – *Violin Concerto No. 3 in B Minor* – Julia Fischer
10. J. S. Bach – *Violin Concerto No. 2 in E Major* – Henryk Szeryng
11. Prokofiev – *Violin Concerto No. 1 in D Major* – Sarah Chang
12. Paganini – *Violin Concerto No. 1 in D Major* – Yehudi Menuhin
13. Mozart – *Violin Concerto No. 5 in A Major* – Isaac Stern
14. Bartók – *Violin Concerto No. 2* – Anne-Sophie Mutter
15. Dvořák – *Violin Concerto in A Minor* – Josef Suk

ACKNOWLEDGEMENTS

At the start of 2020, I had plans to finish a book I'd started and edit the draft of another. Well . . . we all know what happened then. The COVID pandemic wreaked havoc on my imagination, my creativity and left me with barely enough mental energy to get my kids through the basics of homeschooling. Anxious, terrible times for us all.

Then, a few months in, I had the great fortune to be offered the opportunity to write a book that has hope, friendship and happiness at its heart. I immersed myself in the writing and didn't come up for air until the first draft was finished. Writing *Love, Hope* was – literally – an escape from the anxiety and uncertainty we were all living through. I don't know how I would have got through this year without it, and I genuinely hope the book conveys to my readers some of the joy I felt while writing it.

HUGE thanks to Thorne Ryan at Hodder, without whom this book would not exist. I hope I have done justice to your vision, Thorne! And many thanks to her grandparents Joan and Derrick Baker, without whom Marion and Arnold would not have been half as colourful.

Many thanks also to my agent Jenny Brown, for connecting the dots. I cannot imagine a kinder, more dedicated and brilliant agent in my corner. My writing career would not be where it is without her.

Thanks – as always – to all those who have shown the patience, kindness and encouragement I rely on so heavily: my husband Christian and my children Jake, Fay, Amy and June. Love you more/most/mostest.